THE
DRUGGED
CORNET

THE DRUGGED CORNET

And Other Mystery Stories

chosen by SUSAN DICKINSON

illustrated by Robert Micklewright

E. P. DUTTON & CO., INC.   NEW YORK

First published in the U.S.A. 1973 by E. P. Dutton & Co.

LIBRARY OF CONGRESS CATALOGING IN PUBLICATION DATA

Dickinson, Susan, comp.
The drugged cornet and other mystery stories.

First published in 1972 under title:
The case of the vanishing spinster.

CONTENTS: McLean, A. C.   The case of the vanishing
spinster.—Bell, J. J.   The message on the sundial.—
Sayers, D. L.   The inspiration of Mr. Budd.   [etc.]

1. Detective and mystery stories.
[1. Detective stories. 2. Mystery stories]
I. Micklewright, Robert, illus.   II. Title.
PZ5.D563Dr   823'.0872   [Fic]   73-77452   ISBN 0-525-28928-3

Printed in the U.S.A.
First Edition

Contents

Acknowledgments

The Editor and Publishers are grateful to the following for permission to reprint copyright material in this anthology.

A. M. Heath & Co Ltd for *The Case of the Vanishing Spinster* by Allan Campbell McLean, © Allan Campbell McLean 1972; for *Portrait of Henry* by Elisabeth Beresford, © Elisabeth Beresford 1970; for *What Sort of Person is this Amanda Jones Anyway?* by Joan Aiken, © Joan Aiken 1972.

David Higham Associates and Harper and Row, Publishers, Inc for *The Inspiration of Mr Budd* by Dorothy L. Sayers from *In the Teeth of the Evidence* published in Great Britain by Victor Gollancz Ltd, © 1940 by Dorothy Leigh Sayers Flemming. Copyright renewed, © 1967 by Anthony Flemming.

Miss D. E. Collins and Cassell & Co Ltd and Dodd Mead & Company Inc. for *The Invisible Man* from *The Innocence of Father Brown* by G. K. Chesterton, © Miss D. E. Collins.

The Estate of the late Ernest Bramah for *Who Killed Charlie Winpole?* by Ernest Bramah.

The Trustees of the Estate of Sir Arthur Conan Doyle and John Murray (Publishers) Ltd for *The Speckled Band* from *The Adventures of Sherlock Holmes* by Sir Arthur Conan Doyle.

Curtis Brown Ltd for *The Impossible Theft* by Julian Symons, © Julian Symons. All rights reserved.

Hughes Massie Ltd for *The Cupid Mirror* by Ngaio Marsh, © Ngaio Marsh Ltd 1972.

The author for *The Drugged Cornet* by John Verney, © John Verney 1959.

Every effort has been made to trace the ownership of copyright material in this book, but in the event of any question arising as to the use of any material, the publishers will be pleased to make the necessary correction in future editions of the book.

Foreword

What can be better relaxation than a good detective story? The slow unravelling of the threads culminating in the final denouement takes a lot of beating. The short detective story takes a different approach. Here the author has to set his scene, his crime and his characters speedily. And the truth too must be discovered quickly.

The stories in this collection are very varied. Some are completely modern, others are established classics featuring established personalities such as Father Brown and Sherlock Holmes – for what anthology would be complete without Holmes and Watson? Many of them may seem dated to our ears: Mr Budd dreaming of a threepenny tip, the references to the "last" war, meaning the 1914 – 18 war, but these touches merely add flavour to the stories and detract in no way from the quality of the detection.

I make no claim that these are necessarily the best of all short detective stories. Their right to a place in this book is that they will be enjoyed by young people, though many of them were by no means written for the young. The avid reader of detection will have read some of them before. Again I make no excuses. They are good stories, worthy of re-appearance and my thanks are due to the authors or their representatives for their permission to reprint them.

SUSAN DICKINSON

THE
DRUGGED
CORNET

The Case of
The Vanishing Spinster

ALLAN CAMPBELL McLEAN

Mrs Cartwright was waiting for them, holding the door open; a large, red-faced woman, swathed in a white nylon overall. They squeezed past her into the gloomy hall.

"She's upset is Miss Eunice, at me having to get the police," Mrs Cartwright said, letting the door swing shut, looking from Detective-Inspector Burt to Detective-Sergeant Holroyde, thinking they did not look like policemen at all, the older one thin and brainy looking, the dead spit of the professor chap in the new telly serial; the young fellow too young altogether, *Top of the Pops* more his line. "It gave me a turn, I can tell you, Miss Gertrude vanishing. I didn't know what to say."

She had plenty to say on the telephone, Inspector Burt thought. "If we could see Miss Eunice Lane," he suggested.

Mrs Cartwright sniffed, and led the way through a frosted glass door to the low-ceilinged tea-room. It was crowded with small, glass-topped tables, only one of them occupied. A little old lady, with short, iron-grey hair, sat with her back to the spreading fern that blocked the window. She was dabbing at her eyes with a tiny scrap of cambric.

"It's the police, dear," Mrs Cartwright murmured. "Don't you worry none, like I said. The police will find Miss Gertrude, see if they don't."

The old lady shook her head. "The police can't help," she said. "I know they can't."

"Well, Miss Lane," Inspector Burt began, "perhaps – ."

"Why was the table laid for one?" she burst out, her prominent blue eyes switching from Burt to Holroyde and back to

Burt again. "Why? That's Gertrude at her tricks, I know it is."

"If you could start at the beginning, Miss Lane," Burt said gently, "the very beginning."

Miss Eunice clasped her hands tightly. It was clear she was doing her best to master her agitation. "Gertrude left the house a little before me," she said. "I was just finishing things off in the garden – getting the scarecrow ready for the spring." She gave an apologetic little smile. "I like to have everything just so in the garden, well in advance."

"What time was it when your sister left the house?"

"About four, I think. We usually take tea at Mrs Cartwright's at four."

"Can you describe her?"

"Well, Gertrude resembles me, I suppose. She was wearing a similar coat to mine – and a hat, of course. Gertrude never goes a step outside the house without a hat. It was cream-coloured, with a floppy brim. Most unpractical. But then I don't like hats. Oh, and she wore spectacles – pince-nez. Not very fashionable nowadays, but only the young worry about fashions." She gave Holroyde her nervous, apologetic smile.

"Did you leave home soon after your sister?" Inspector Burt asked.

"About ten minutes later. I came straight down the lane to Mrs Cartwright's. You see, Gertrude hated hanging about. If I was busy in the garden, she always went on ahead and ordered tea."

"Tell me exactly what happened when you came into the room."

"Well, nothing *happened*." She faltered. "It . . . it was just that – well, Gertrude wasn't here. I sat down at our table, and then I saw that it was laid for one." She gestured helplessly at the single cup, saucer and plate before her. "You can see for yourself."

"What did you do?"

"I waited for a while, and then I summoned Mrs Cartwright. She said Gertrude had told her I was busy in the garden and would be along shortly, and she had served our usual tea." She glanced at the cake tray in the centre of the table. "She said Gertrude couldn't possibly have left or she would have heard her go. I . . . I don't know what to do. It seemed so silly calling the police, and yet – ."

"How old is your sister, Miss Lane?"

Miss Eunice rubbed the bridge of her nose. "Sixty-eight next month."

"Was she in good health?"

"Physically, yes."

"Mentally?"

The old lady bridled. "Really, Inspector, I don't see why you – ." She broke off, biting her lip.

"Has anything like this ever happened before?"

"You mean, Gertrude disappearing?"

"Yes."

Miss Eunice dabbed at her eyes. "About a month ago," she murmured, her voice so low both detectives leaned forward to catch the words. "Gertrude had a bad cold. She went to bed early – earlier than usual, that is – and asked me to take her a hot toddy. Her room was empty when I went up with it. I searched the house, but I couldn't find her. When I went back to her room, she was lying in bed, reading. She had drunk the toddy. I asked her where she had been. She laughed, and said, 'You would not believe me, if I told you.' When I persisted, she looked at me strangely, and said, 'The power of the spirit is boundless, if you have faith.' "

Sergeant Holroyde concentrated on his notebook, avoiding the inspector's eyes. Burt was silent. The old lady added, "I think Gertrude was trying to frighten me."

"Why should she do that, Miss Lane?"

"Do what, Inspector?"

"Frighten you."

"Oh, I believe it was the garden. Gertrude didn't like me working in the garden. She thought I should spend more time with her."

"Was that – er – episode last month the only time you noticed anything strange about her behaviour?"

"No. One day last week. It was a sunny day and we were sitting in the summer-house after luncheon. I looked up – and Gertrude had vanished. I couldn't understand it. The summer-house door has a terrible squeak, but I hadn't heard a sound. I thought perhaps I had nodded off to sleep for a moment, and Gertrude had gone indoors. But she wasn't in the house – or in the garden." Miss Eunice gulped, and stroked her nose nervously. "When I went back to the summer-house, my sister was sitting in her chair as if she had never moved. *She* said to *me*, 'I didn't hear you get up and go out, Eunice.' "

"What did you say, Miss Lane?"

The old lady hung her head. "Nothing. I was frightened."

"Did you mention this to anyone – about your sister vanishing?"

"Certainly not. It's not the sort of thing one talks about."

Inspector Burt nodded sympathetically. Miss Lane gave him an anxious look. "What can have happened to Gertrude, Inspector?" She rubbed at her nose. "Do you think you will find her?"

"We'll find her, Miss Lane," Burt said. "Now, I suggest you try to relax, and let us do the worrying. Sergeant Holroyde will see you home."

The old lady smiled uncertainly, and picked up her leather pouch bag. She fiddled with the thongs of the draw-string. "It's the vanishing thing I don't like," she said. "It's not natural."

Mrs Cartwright confirmed that she had served Miss Gertrude tea for two. The maiden ladies called every Monday, Wednesday and Friday, regular as clockwork. Had done for years. Only in the winter-time, though. They stayed at home when the tourist rush was on. Miss Gertrude nearly always came in first. It was the only way she could get Miss Eunice out of the garden. A great gardener, Miss Eunice.

"Was Miss Gertrude still in the room when you served the tea?" Burt asked.

" 'Course she was," Mrs Cartwright affirmed. "Sitting where you are, with her back to the door."

"Did you close the door when you went out?"

She nodded.

"And the kitchen door as well?"

"No, I always leave the kitchen door ajar so's I can see who's coming in when the bell rings. Not much doing in the tea-room this time of year, but there's the shop to see to."

Inspector Burt went to the door and looked out. The small hall narrowed into a passage that led into the kitchen. The kitchen door stood open; he could see the double-sink below the window, the corner of a scrubbed deal table. He went back to the tea-room.

"You couldn't see into the hall unless you were standing with your back to the sink," he said.

"That's right."

"So there was nothing to stop Miss Gertrude walking out quietly."

Mrs Cartwright shook her head. "Couldn't 'ave," she declared. "I'd have heard the doorbell. You try opening the door. That bell goes ting-a-ling-ling. Hear it a mile off. Used to get on Mr Cartwright's nerves something terrible."

"What if she had left the front door open when she came in?"

"Couldn't 'ave; it's on a spring."

"And you didn't hear a sound after you served the tea?"

"Not for a couple of minutes. Then the bell rang. I popped my head out the kitchen, and there was Miss Eunice coming in. A minute later she called me and asked where her sister was. I was flabbergasted. And when I saw there was a cup and saucer and plate missing – the table only set for one – well!"

"She couldn't have walked out without you hearing her," said Burt, half to himself, "and there's only the one window in this room – ."

"And it don't open from the bottom anyways," Mrs Cartwright said, "and the top half only comes down an inch or two." She pointed to the wooden blocks. "My son did that. Albert says you can't be too careful these days, there's burglars on the go all over the place."

Burt looked from the window to the table and down to the faded blue carpet. Something gleamed in the worn pile. It was a hat-pin. He bent down and slipped it into his pocket. Mrs Cartwright was watching him curiously. "There's lots of queer things happen there's no accounting for," she observed, "but I never heard the like of this."

"Nor me," Inspector Burt said.

"I've had a frightful night, Inspector," Miss Lane wailed. "Simply frightful."

Burt tucked the receiver into the crook of his shoulder, and lit a cigarette. He grimaced at Sergeant Holroyde.

"I've been hearing things," the old lady went on.

"What sort of things, Miss Lane?"

"Voices. I think it's Gertrude, playing tricks on me, hiding in the house and the garden. Will you come over, Inspector? Gertrude's too clever for me, but I'm sure you will be able to find her."

"Be over directly, Miss Lane," Burt said. He slammed down the receiver, and turned to Holroyde. "Hear that?" he said. "Miss Eunice. Thinks Miss Gertrude's playing hide and seek with her. Wants us to search the house."

"It's bad enough having one old maid disappear without the other going dotty," Sergeant Holroyde said.

"Dotty world, son," Burt said. "Older you are, dottier it gets."

The Misses Lane's house was no more than two hundred yards along the tree-lined lane from Mrs Cartwright's tea-room on the main road. It was built of Cotswold stone and the garden was sheltered by a high laurel hedge. Miss Eunice met them on the steps of the porch. "Gertrude's hiding here, Inspector," she cried. "I heard her calling – during the night – from the garden. I came down, put all the lights on, went out to the porch – and she stopped. When I went back to bed, she started calling again. It happened three times. In the end, I got dressed and sat up and waited for morning. You've got to find her, Inspector, for her own sake as well as mine. I know she's here, somewhere."

"Don't worry, Miss Lane," Burt said, "if your sister is here, we'll find her."

The two detectives searched the trim scullery, the dining-room, drawing-room, bathroom, lavatory and all three bedrooms. Sergeant Holroyde climbed through a trap into the roof and flashed his torch on the rafters. Miss Gertrude was not to be seen.

They returned to the porch.

"There's the summer-house and the jobbing shed," Miss Eunice ventured timidly. "If the sergeant wouldn't mind staying here, just in case Gertrude pops in out of the garden, we could – ."

Inspector Burt accompanied her to the hexagonal-shaped summer-house. A glance showed that it was empty, two cane chairs drawn up to a rustic table. But he pushed the door open, and peered inside.

Miss Eunice led the way down the garden. "Mind you stoop

under the rose arch, Inspector," she said. "I've been too busy
to cut back the rambler."

The neatly ordered kitchen garden lay beyond the rustic arch,
bisected by a stone-flagged path. There was a small wooden hut
about half-way down the path. The old lady stopped outside the
hut, and pointed to the scarecrow guarding a line of pea-sticks.
"Gertrude was always complaining about the magpies eating our
peas," she said, "but there's nothing like a scarecrow for keeping
them away. Don't you agree, Inspector?"

"I'm not much of a gardener," Burt confessed. "Fishing's
more in my line. Doesn't take so much bending."

He followed her into the hut.

One side was taken up with gardening implements, laid out
neatly in a row. There was an open bag of cement in the corner
behind the door, a heap of damp straw beside the bag. He scooped
up a handful of cement, and let it trickle slowly through his
fingers. The rest of the space in the hut was occupied by folding
garden furniture. There was no place for an old lady to hide, no
matter how small or agile she might be.

"Straw's damp," Burt remarked, as he stepped out of the hut.
"Roof leak?"

"Dear me, I suppose it must," Miss Eunice murmured. "I'll
have to get it attended to. Jobs never get done when there isn't
a man about the house."

"Don't know if my wife would agree with you, Miss Lane,"
Burt said.

He was pleased to see the old lady smile. She seemed more at
ease now that he had satisfied her that her sister was not lurking
about the house or garden.

They joined Sergeant Holroyde outside the porch. "Not a
sight or sound of anyone," he reported.

Miss Eunice sighed, but she was looking more cheerful. "It's
all so different in daylight," she said. "Last night I was sure I
heard Gertrude calling me. I suppose I was imagining things.
You know how it is when one can't sleep. But it was stupid of
me. I daresay poor Gertrude is miles away by now."

"It would help if we could have a recent photograph of your sister," Burt said. "We'll circulate it to all stations."

Miss Eunice produced a photograph taken outside the summer-house. Miss Gertrude was standing with one hand on the back of a rustic seat, her lips parted stiffly in a self-conscious smile. Even though the wide-brimmed hat shadowed her face, it was possible to see the resemblance to her sister. But she was frailer than Miss Eunice, and the shapeless woollen dress, and the way she seemed to droop over the seat, gave her a curiously lifeless appearance, like a marionette upon a string.

"It's the last photograph I took of Gertrude in the garden," the old lady said. "Do take care of it, Inspector."

Inspector Burt paced up and down his office. From time to time he picked up a photograph from his desk, glowered at it, and put it down again. Holroyde's dark eyes followed him around the room.

"How do you reckon she got out of the tea-shop?" the sergeant said at last. "She couldn't use the front door without the bell clanging, the window is blocked, and the only other way out is through the kitchen. And Mrs Cartwright never left the kitchen! And what became of the missing cup and saucer and plate? Why should they vanish?"

"Fancy trimmings," Burt said absently. "Bit of flummery to deflect the eye. Forget 'em."

Sergeant Holroyde picked up the photograph of Miss Gertrude. He examined it closely. "Beats me how she hasn't been seen," he said, "and her such a right old scarecrow."

Burt pursed his lips, and expelled his breath in a long, slow whistle. "You've got it, son," he said fervently.

"Got what?"

"Why Miss Gertrude hasn't been spotted."

"What I want to know is how she got out of the tea-shop," Holroyde said.

"*She never went in.*"

"What?"

"She never went in. She was dead – murdered."

"Murdered? Who by?"

"Her sister. Little Miss Eunice."

"You say Miss Gertrude never went into the tea-shop," Holroyde persisted. "What about the hat-pin you found? Miss Eunice never wears a hat."

"She did this time. She killed her sister, then went down to the tea-shop in one of Miss Gertrude's hats. And she was wearing her sister's pince-nez. I wondered why she kept rubbing the bridge of her nose; it must have been the unaccustomed pressure of the spectacles pinching her. She was very much like her sister. The hat shadowed her face, and she sat with her back to the door. I don't suppose Mrs Cartwright looked twice at her.

"As soon as the tea was served, she pulled off her hat and glasses and bundled them – and a cup, saucer and plate – into her bag. Then she tiptoed into the hall and opened the front door. The bell rang. Mrs Cartwright poked her head out of the kitchen and saw – ."

"Miss Eunice coming in," Holroyde added.

Burt nodded. "And she was all set to pump us full of that rubbish about her sister disappearing mysteriously. But she overdid it when she said the summer-house door squeaked. I tried it this morning. It doesn't."

"But why kill her sister?"

"She's dotty, of course," Burt said gravely. "Her sister must have seen that the garden had become an obsession, and tried to get her away from it."

Sergeant Holroyde shook his head. "It's not enough," he said. "A hat-pin and a door that doesn't squeak – it's not enough, chief."

"There's more," Burt said. "There was a heap of damp straw in the jobbing shed beside an open sack of cement. The cement was dry – running free – it hadn't set. Why not? Because the hut didn't leak – the hut was dry."

"I don't get it."

"If the hut didn't leak, the damp straw must have been brought in from outside. But I couldn't figure out what a heap of damp straw was doing in the shed. You told me."

"Me?"

"Yes, you. It was the stuffing out of the scarecrow. And the old girl couldn't rest until I had seen it. She thought she was so clever she could rub my nose in it."

"You are going too fast for me, chief," Holroyde said. "Even supposing Miss Eunice killed her sister, there's the little matter of a body. We searched the house, didn't we? And the garden? You are not telling me she's dug a great big hole and buried it?"

"No."

"Then where's the body?"

"Where do you think it would be?" Burt said. "Miss Gertrude hated gardening, didn't she?"

"What's that got to do with it?"

"Plenty," Inspector Burt said, getting up and reaching for his cap. "She's down the bottom of the garden keeping the birds off Miss Eunice's peas."

The Message on the Sundial

J. J. BELL

For a good many weeks the morning mail of Mr Philip Bolsover
Wingard had usually contained something unpleasant, but never
anything quite so unpleasant as the letter, with its enclosure,
now in his hand. And the letter was from his cousin, Philip
Merivale Wingard, the man to whom he owed more benefits,
and whom he hated more, than any man in the world. Certainly
the letter was rather a shocking one to have place in the morning
mail of a gentleman; but, oddly enough, it had never occurred to
Bolsover, as he was commonly called to distinguish him from
the other Philip, that he had long since forfeited his last rights
to the designation.

The letter was dated from the other Philip's riverside residence,
and ran as follows:

Cousin Bolsover,

I send you herewith an appeal just received from a
deeply injured woman, to whom you have apparently
given my name, instead of your own. This ends our
acquaintance. If you insist on a further reason, I would
merely mention your forgery of my name to a bill for
£500, which fact has also been brought to my notice this
morning. In the face of these two crimes it does not seem
worth while to remind you that for seven years I have
tried to believe in you and to help you in a material
way.

You will receive this in the morning, and it gives you
forty-eight hours to be out of this country. Within that
time there is a sailing for South Africa. My banker has

received instructions to pay you £500, one half of which you shall send to the writer of the enclosed. On that condition, and so long as you remain abroad, your forgery is my secret. This is your last chance.

Philip Merivale Wingard

Bolsover, enduring a sickness almost physical, re-read the letter. The enclosure did not trouble him, except in so far as it looked like costing him £250. But the discovery of his forgery shook him, for it was a shock against which he had been altogether unprepared. He had not dreamed of the moneylender showing the bill, which was not due for six weeks, to his cousin. What infernal luck!

Bolsover read the letter a third time, seeking some glimmer of hope, some crevice for escape. Hitherto he had regarded his cousin as a bit of a softy, a person to be gulled or persuaded; but every word of the letter seemed to indicate a heart grown hard, a mind become unyielding.

Go abroad? Why, that would simply be asking for it! The clouds of debt were truly threatening, but if he continued to walk warily at home they might gradually disperse, whereas the outcry that would surely follow his apparent flight would, like an explosion, bring down the deluge of ruin.

What a fool was Philip! It did not occur to Bolsover then that, during all those seven years, he had lived by fooling Philip. And the most maddening thought of all was that had Philip not come back from the Great War he, Bolsover, would be in Philip's place today! That, indeed, was the root of the hatred, planted in disappointment and nourished from the beginning on envy and greed, and lately also on chagrin and jealousy, since Philip had won the girl, as wealthy as himself, whom Bolsover had coveted for his own.

Bolsover's mouth was dry. He went over to the neglected breakfast-table, poured shakily a cup of the cooled coffee and drank it off. He took out and opened his cigarette-case. His fingers fumbled a cigarette, and he noticed their trembling. This would not do. He must get command of his nerves, of his wits.

Raging was of no use. He lighted the cigarette and sat down.

Somehow he must see Philip; somehow he must prevail on Philip to abate his terms – either that, or induce Philip to pay all his debts. But the total of his debts amounted to thousands, and some of them were owing to persons whom he would fain avoid naming to his straitlaced cousin. Still, he must make the appeal, in the one direction or the other. The situation was past being desperate.

He knew that his cousin was entertaining a house-party. On the mantelshelf was a dance invitation, received three weeks ago, for that very evening. He did not suppose that Philip would now expect to see him, as a guest; yet for a moment or two he dallied with the idea of presenting himself, as though nothing had happened. But there was the possibility, a big one, too, to judge from this damned letter, that Philip would simply have the servants throw him out!

He looked at his watch – 10.20 – and went over to the telephone. He ought to have phoned at the outset, he told himself. Philip might have gone out, on the river with his friends, for the day. The prospect of seven or eight hours of uncertainty appalled him.

But at the end of a couple of minutes he heard Philip's voice inquiring who was speaking.

"Philip," said Bolsover quickly, "bear with me for a few moments. I have your letter. I must obey it. But, as a last favour, let us have one more meeting. There are things – "

"No! I have nothing to say to you; I wish to hear nothing from you."

"There are things I can explain."

"No! Excuse me. My friends are waiting for me. Good – "

"Philip, let your invitation for tonight stand. Let me come, if only for an hour."

"What! Let you come among those girls, after that letter from that unhappy woman? A thousand times, no!"

"Well, let us meet somewhere, during the evening, outside the house. I shan't keep you long. Look here, Philip! I'll be at the sundial, at ten, and wait until you come. Don't refuse the last request I'll ever make of you."

There was a pause till Philip said coldly:

"Very well. But, I warn you, it can make not the slightest difference."

"Thank you, Philip. Ten, or a little after?" Bolsover retained the receiver awhile.

But there was no further word from his cousin.

He went back to his chair and sat there, glowering at space. Undeniably there had been a new firmness in his cousin's voice. While he did not doubt that Philip would keep the tryst, he could no longer hope that anything would come of the interview. That being so, what was left for him?

To a man like Bolsover the disgrace was secondary; the paramount dread was a life without money for personal indulgence. He had been cornered before, but never so tightly, it seemed, as now. For the first time in his unworthy career he thought of death as the way of escape, knowing all the while that were he in the very toils of despair, he could never bring himself to take the decided step in death's direction. But he toyed gloomily with the thought, till his imagination began to perceive its other side.

What if Philip were out of the world?

At first the idea was vague and misty, but gradually it became clear, and all at once his mind recoiled, as a man recoils from the brink of a precipice – recoiled, yet only to approach again, cautiously, to survey the depths, searching furtively the steep, lest haply it should provide some safe and secret downward path. And peering into his own idea, Bolsover seemed to see at the bottom of it a pleasant place where freedom was, where fear was not. For while Bolsover had no illusions of inheriting a penny in hard cash from his cousin, he knew that a small landed estate, unencumbered, was bound on his cousin's death to come to him: and on that estate he could surely raise the wherewithal to retrieve his wretched fortunes. The greatest optimist in the world is the most abandoned gambler.

A maid came in to remove the breakfast things.

"Ain't you well this morning, Mr Wingard?" she inquired. Bolsover, resident in the private hotel for a good many months, had been generous enough in his gratuities to the servants.

"Feeling the heat," he answered, wiping his brow. "Dreadfully sultry, isn't it?"

"It *is* 'ot for May. Guess we're going to 'ave a thunderstorm soon. Shall I fetch some fresh coffee, or would you like a cup of tea?"

"Thanks, but I have got to go out now."

Perhaps he was thankful for the interruption.

The bank with which his cousin dealt was in the Strand. Feeling weak, he took a taxi thither. He was known at the bank, his cousin's instructions had been duly received, and the money was handed over to him, without delay. He rather overdid his amusement, as he realised afterwards, at his shaky signature on the receipt. "Looks as if I had been having a late night," he remarked, passing the paper back to the grave cashier.

As the door swung behind him, he called himself a fool and wiped his face.

He lunched leisurely at an unusually early hour. He preceded the meal with a couple of cocktails, accompanied it with a pint of champagne, and followed it with a liqueur. He felt much better, though annoyed by an unwonted tendency to perspire. On his leaving the restaurant, the tendency became more pronounced, so much so that he feared it must be noticeable, and once more he took a taxi, telling the man to go Kensington way. A little later, he was sitting in a shady part of Kensington Gardens. He had wanted to get away from people.

For a while he felt comfortable in body, and almost easy in mind. He was now quite hopeful that Philip would see the unreasonableness of the terms of that letter, which had obviously been written in haste. After all, his debts amounted to no more than £6,000 – well, say, £7,000 – a sum that would scarcely trouble his cousin to disburse, especially as it would not be required all at once. No doubt, Philip would kick, to begin with, and deliver a pretty stiff lecture, but in the end he would capitulate. Oh, yes, it had been a black morning, but there would be another story to tell by midnight. Bolsover smoked a cigarette or two, surrendered himself to a pleasant drowsiness, and fell into a doze.

He awoke heavy of limb – hot in the head and parched, and with a great spiritual depression upon him. He must have a drink. He looked at his watch. Only 4.30. His hotel, however, was not far distant, and thither he went on foot.

The hall porter presented an expressed letter which had come at midday. The writing was familiar, and Bolsover was not glad to see it. In his room he helped himself to brandy before opening the letter – a curt warning that a fairly large sum must be paid by noon on the morrow. It acted as a powerful irritant and brought on the silent frenzy against things and persons which had shaken him in the morning.

He took another drink, and presently his fiery wrath at fortune gave place to the old smouldering hate against his cousin, who now seemed to block the road to salvation. He unlocked and opened a drawer, and for a long while sat glowering at the things it contained, a revolver, which he had purchased years ago on the eve of a trip abroad, and a package of cartridges, never opened.

He saw himself at the sundial in Philip's garden, the loaded weapon in his pocket. He saw Philip coming in the darkness, from the house with its lights and music. And then he began to realise that the house was not so very far away, and imagined how the report of the revolver would shatter the night. He must think of another way, he concluded, shutting the drawer, and turning to the bottle once more.

It was near to seven o'clock when he went out. He ought to have been drunk, but apparently he was quite sober when he entered the cutler's shop in the Paddington district. He was going abroad on a game-hunting expedition, he explained, and wanted something in the way of a sheath-knife. This was supplied, and with the parcel he returned to the hotel.

After dinner he dressed, not carelessly. The brandy bottle tempted, and he put off the craving with a dose much diluted. He took the train to a riverside station, then a cab for the last two miles of the journey. At five minutes before ten he was in his cousin's grounds.

The ancient sundial stood in the centre of a rose garden, which was separated from the house by a broad walk, a lawn and a path, and walled round by high, thick hedges. Beyond the bottom of the rose garden was a narrow stretch of turf, and then the river.

The night was very dark; the atmosphere heavy, breathless. It seemed to Bolsover, waiting by the dial, that the storm might burst at any moment, and his anxiety was intense lest the deluge should descend and prevent the coming of Philip. Though the knife, loosened in the sheath, lay ready in a pocket of his cloak, he kept telling himself that he would never use it, save as a threat; that he had bought it only to strengthen his courage and purpose. The effects of the alcohol apart, the man was not quite sane. A brain storm was as imminent as the storm of nature.

Peering, listening, he stood by the dial, seeing above the hedge the glow from the open windows, hearing dimly the chatter and laughter of the guests. He had arrived in the garden to the sound of music, but soon it had ceased, and now the pause between the dances seemed very long. He argued that Philip, who doubtless desired secrecy as much as himself, would leave the house only when a dance was in progress, and, fingering the knife's haft, he cursed the idle musicians and the guests resting on the verandah, or strolling on the lawn.

The minutes passed, and at last the music started again. And when Bolsover, savage with exasperation, was telling himself that another dance was nearly over, he became aware of a sound of footfalls on gravel, and a dark figure, with a glimmer of white, appeared in the gap.

Philip Merivale Wingard came quickly down to the dial and halted opposite his cousin.

"So you are here, in spite of my warning," he said.

"Philip, I came to ask – "

"Ask nothing. Did you get the money from the bank?"

"Thank you, yes."

"Have you sent half of it to the woman?"

"Yes," Bolsover lied. "Let me explain – "

"No!" the other interrupted. "I am going to tell you why I am here. I have decided to let you have a further five hundred, which will give you a start, wherever you may settle abroad. It shall go to you as soon as I receive your address there. But I must have your signature to a promise, that for five years you will not attempt to return to this country, without my permission. Will you sign?"

No man is so infamous that he cannot feel insulted. Bolsover felt insulted, and once more the silent frenzy shook him.

"Come," said Philip, laying a single sheet of notepaper on the smooth table of granite. "Here is a simple promise written out by myself – I need not say that all between us is private – and here is a pen. I'll hold a match while you sign. Come, man, unless you wish us to be discovered!"

Bolsover, his right hand in his pocket, moved round till he was against his cousin's left arm.

"Take the pen," said Philip.

"One moment," Bolsover returned in a thick voice.

He took a step backwards, threw up his arm, and drove the knife down between Philip's shoulders. In that moment he experienced a sort of sickness of astonishment at the ease with which the blade penetrated; in the next moment he stepped back, withdrawing the knife and holding it away from him.

Philip squirmed, made a choking noise, and fell across the broad dial, one hand clutching at the far edge. The paper, dislodged, fluttered to the feet of Bolsover, who picked it up, pocketed it, and retreated up the path, backwards, yet with eyes averted from his handiwork. And having reached a distance of seven yards, he turned right round and stood with hunched shoulders, waiting for the ghastly labouring sound to cease. Had he not killed Philip after all? For a little while he knew not what he did – prayed, maybe – and then the end came, a gasping, choking noise, a slithering sound, a soft thud. He turned slowly about. There was a heap, slightly moving on the path under the dial, and then – there was a heap that was very still.

Bolsover remembered his own safety. Running softly on the grass verge, he came to the gap in the lower hedge, passed through, crossed the strip of turf, and halted at the river's edge. From the river came no sound at all. The most enthusiastic of boating people had sensed the coming storm. Gingerly Bolsover fitted the knife into its sheath, and slung it far out into the darkness. He tore the paper into tiny bits, and scattered them on the black water. Slowly they drifted away.

By a roundabout route he reached the main walk leading to the house, and deliberately went forward to the door. The servant in attendance, who knew him as his master's cousin, received him as a late arriving guest; if he noticed his pallor, he was not interested.

And the pallor was not so extreme. Bolsover was playing a part now, and so intent thereon that in a measure he forgot why he was playing it.

Before long he was among the guests, greeting those whom he knew, explaining that he had just arrived and was looking for the host, his cousin. A curate, a particular friend of Philip's, whom Bolsover had always rather disliked, remarked that he thought he had seen Philip go out by the french window of the library, about ten minutes earlier.

"You appear to be feeling the heat, Mr Wingard," he added. "You look quite haggard."

"Yes, I want a drink," Bolsover answered somewhat roughly, and was going to get it, when a girl, who with her partner had strayed to the rose garden, ran into the hall, screaming that Mr Wingard was lying by the sundial, dead – murdered!

It had come sooner than Bolsover could have wished, and for the moment he was staggered – but appropriately so. He was the first to recover his wits, and, as was his natural duty, proceeded to take charge, ordering a servant to phone for doctor and police, and requesting several of the men guests to accompany him to the scene, with the elements of first aid, lest life should still be there.

"We shall want lights!" cried Mr Minn, the curate, whose company Bolsover had not requested. "I'll get my torch from my overcoat."

Several torches were procured, and the party hurried down to the rose garden. The young man, whose partner had brought the alarm to the house, met them with a word of warning to prepare for a dreadful sight.

"He was alive, and no more, when we found him, but he's gone now," the young man added. "I'm glad you've come. I've used all my matches."

"Did he speak?" asked the curate, as the others gathered round the dial.

"Oh, no; didn't even attempt it, poor chap. I fancied, though, that he tried to make signs."

"How so?"

"Towards the dial above him. And then he collapsed – in my arms. Heavens, I'm all bloody – everything is bloody!"

"Go up to the house and take some whisky," said the curate kindly. "But stay a moment! Did you look at the dial? Was there anything unusual about it?"

"Blood – and a fountain pen."

"A pen!"

"Lying against the pointer."

"Did you remove it?"

"Didn't touch it. It's a gold pen with a green stone in the top."

"His own," said Mr Minn. "What on earth – ? Well, don't wait, Mr Marshall. I think you will find the library window open, so you can slip in and ring for a servant to fetch your overcoat to cover the – the stains. This is terrible!" The curate gave way to emotion. "Poor Philip! My good friend and the best of men!"

Presently he joined the group. Bolsover was speaking.

"I wish we could take him to the house, but dare we do so before the doctor – and the police – have seen him?"

"I'm afraid we must wait," said a guest.

"I felt a spot of rain just now," said another. "We can't let him lie here if the storm breaks. What do you say, Mr Minn?"

The curate did not seem to hear. He was playing the shuddering light of his torch on the dial.

"Gentlemen," he said unsteadily, "please give me your attention for a moment."

There was a catching of breaths at the sight of the dark pool and rivulets on the smooth grey stone, followed by faint exclamations as the beam caught and lingered on the gold pen.

"His own pen, gentlemen – and with it he has written something on the dial, for there is one line of ink not quite dry – and the nib of the pen has given way."

The beam moved towards the right, and stopped.

Here was no blood; only some writing – of a sort. The guests leaned forward, peering – all save Bolsover, who shrank back, open-mouthed, the sweat of terror on his skin. Had the dying man left a message?

"Figures!" softly exclaimed a guest.

"Yes," said Mr Minn, producing a pencil, following with the point of it the wavering, broken lines and curves. "A one – a three – a nought – a six – an eight – another nought – and something that might have been a four, had the nib not broken, or had the hand not failed. One, three, nought, six, eight, nought – "

A big drop of rain splashed on his hand, and he started as though it had been blood.

"If the storm breaks now, this message, which may be a clue, will be lost!" he cried. "Will one of you run to the house and fetch something waterproof to cover the dial? Hurry, please!"

A guest ran off. Another drop fell, and another, on the dial.

Mr Minn handed the torch to his neighbour, saying:

"Kindly, all of you, direct your lights on the figures." He whipped out a little notebook. "In case of accidents, I shall make a copy as exactly as possible."

There was a silence while he drew, rather than wrote down, the figures.

Bolsover's panic had passed. There was nothing in those large ill-formed figures that could in any way draw attention to himself. He cleared his throat, and said:

"Mr Minn, do these figures convey anything at all to you, as a friend of poor Philip's?"

"Nothing, Mr Wingard." Mr Minn shook his head. "But whatever their meaning, they must surely represent almost the last thought – if not the very last thought – of our cruelly murdered friend – and an urgent message. Whether or not they may provide the police with a clue – "

There was a blinding glare, a stunning crash, a throbbing silence in the blackness, and the clouds turned, as it seemed, to water.

The inquest was over, the jury returning an open verdict, the only verdict in keeping with the evidence, as every person in court had agreed. The fact that Philip must have had an enemy made a mystery in itself. The figures written on the dial were a mystery also; a search through Philip's papers revealed nothing with which they could be connected. Mr Minn was, however, congratulated by the coroner on the presence of mind which he had shown in recording them.

Bolsover won the sympathy of all by his quiet, frank answers to the coroner's questions, by his tribute to the high character and generosity of his late cousin, and by his sad, pale, stricken appearance. Yes, there was a small estate to come to him, but other expectations he had none, the gifts of his cousin in the past having been almost princely.

On the fatal night, he explained, being detained in town, he had arrived at his cousin's house, shortly after ten. His inquiries for his cousin brought from Mr Minn the reply that his cousin had gone out, and immediately thereafter came the shocking news. It was possible that the crime in the rose garden was committed while he was walking up the avenue; but if so, it must have been done silently. At this point he had asked for a glass of water, and the coroner had expressed himself satisfied.

On the morrow, he attended the funeral, as chief mourner, looking a wreck of a man. But with the turning away from the grave, the worst was over. He was safe! Only one duty remained – his presence at the reading of the will.

It was not a large gathering, and Bolsover was the person least interested. The will had been made five years ago. Bolsover, his heavy lids almost closing his eyes, listened indifferently till –

"And to my cousin and friend, Philip Bolsover Wingard, the sum of fifty thousand pounds, free of legacy duty."

He nearly fainted. It was Mr Minn, the curate, who brought him a drink.

Lunch had been provided for the mourners, but Bolsover begged to be excused. He was feeling far from well, he said, and wished to consult his doctor in town, without delay.

"I think you are wise, Mr Wingard," said Mr Minn, kindly. "You are looking ill, and no wonder. But before you go, I would beg for just a few minutes' talk. Let us go to the rose garden, where we shall not be disturbed."

"Very well," assented Bolsover. He had hoped never again to enter the rose garden, but did not see how he could reasonably refuse to do so now. Anyway, it would be the final torment.

In silence they crossed the lawn, and passed through the gap in the hedge. In silence, also, since Bolsover had not the speech for protest, they came to the sundial.

Mr Minn bared his head, and said:

"As God Almighty's rain has washed away all the signs of this tragedy, so is His infinite mercy able to wash away the sin that caused it. Amen."

He replaced his hat and looked very gently and gravely at Bolsover.

"Mr Wingard, I wish to show you something. I wish to show you Philip's last thought before he died." So saying he took out his notebook and a scarlet chalk pencil.

"The figures!" muttered Bolsover, wondering.

"Yes," replied Mr Minn, and proceeded to copy them carefully from the page to the stone, thus:

130680n

"It is strange," said Mr Minn, adding a touch to the "3", "that the truth did not strike us at once. It did not come to me till early this morning. And yet, once we make allowance for the penmanship of a man dying quickly and in pain, struggling to write in the dark, the thing becomes as plain as day."

"Not to me," said Bolsover thickly; "but, as you know, I am worn out and – "

"Only a minute more," said Mr Minn gently. "I want just to tell you that those marks were not figures at all."

"Then I'm blind."

"We were all blind, but now we see clearly. Observe that '1' and that '3'; note how they are rather close together. But bring them quite together and we have a 'B'." Mr Minn drew a sprawling "B" on the dial. "Then the nought becomes an 'O', and what we took for a six is really an 'L' – see, I put them down after the 'B' – and what might well pass for an eight must now be accepted as an 'S' – so! Then we have another 'O', and, next, the greater part of a 'V' – and there the nib broke, or the hand failed. But surely – surely enough is there, Mr Wingard, to show you your cousin's last thought, or message."

On the dial, written in scarlet by Mr Minn, appeared these two lines:

$$13\,0\,6\,8\,0\,\upsilon$$

$$Bolsov\,(er)$$

Over the face of Bolsover, gazing dumbly thereon, came a greyish shadow.

Mr Minn, watching narrowly, raised his left hand as with an effort, while his own countenance paled.

Followed what seemed a long silence. Then, all at once, Bolsover lifted up his face, a dreadful, hunted look in his eyes. His gaze sought the gap in the upper hedge, then fled round to the gap in the lower. In each gap stood a burly man, a stranger.

The curate wiped his eyes.

"My friend," he said softly, "I will pray for you."

The Inspiration of Mr Budd

DOROTHY L. SAYERS

£500 REWARD

The Evening Messenger, *ever anxious to further the ends of justice, has decided to offer the above reward to any person who shall give information leading to the arrest of the man, William Strickland, alias Bolton, who is wanted by the police in connection with the murder of the late Emma Strickland at* 59 *Acacia Crescent, Manchester.*

DESCRIPTION OF THE WANTED MAN

The following is the official description of William Strickland: Age 43*; height* 6 ft 1 *or* 2*; complexion rather dark; hair silver-grey and abundant, may dye same; full grey moustache and beard, may now be clean-shaven; eyes light grey; rather close-set; hawk nose; teeth strong and white, displays them somewhat prominently with laughing, left upper eye-tooth stopped with gold; left thumb-nail disfigured by a recent blow.*

Speaks in rather loud voice; quick, decisive manner. Good address.

May be dressed in a grey or dark blue lounge suit, with stand-up collar (*size* 15) *and soft felt hat.*

Absconded 5*th inst., and may have left, or will endeavour to leave, the country.*

Mr Budd read the description through carefully once again and sighed. It was in the highest degree unlikely that William Strickland should choose his small and unsuccessful saloon, out of all the barbers' shops in London, for a hair-cut or a shave, still less for "dyeing same"; even if he was in London, which Mr Budd saw no reason to suppose.

Three weeks had gone by since the murder, and the odds were a hundred to one that William Strickland had already left a country too eager with its offer of free hospitality. Nevertheless, Mr Budd committed the description, as well as he could, to memory. It was a chance – just as the Great Crossword Tournament had been a chance, just as the Ninth Rainbow Ballot had been a chance, and the Bunko Poster Ballot, and the Monster Treasure Hunt organised by the *Evening Clarion*. Any headline with money in it could attract Mr Budd's fascinated eye in these lean days, whether it offered a choice between fifty thousand pounds down and ten pounds a week for life, or merely a modest hundred or so.

It may seem strange, in an age of shingling and bingling, Mr Budd should look enviously at Complete Lists of Prizewinners. Had not the hairdresser across the way, who only last year had eked out his mean ninepences with the yet meaner profits on cheap cigarettes and comic papers, lately bought out the greengrocer next door, and engaged a staff of exquisitely coiffed assistants to adorn his new "Ladies' Hairdressing Department" with its purple and orange curtains, its two rows of gleaming marble basins, and an apparatus like a Victorian chandelier for permanent waving?

Had he not installed a large electric sign surrounded by a scarlet border that ran round and round perpetually, like a kitten chasing its own cometary tail? Was not his sandwich-man even now patrolling the pavement with a luminous announcement of Treatment and Prices? And was there not at this moment an endless stream of young ladies hastening into those heavily perfumed parlours in the desperate hope of somehow getting a shampoo and a wave "squeezed in" before closing-time?

If the reception clerk shook a regretful head, they did not think of crossing the road to Mr Budd's dimly-lighted window. They made an appointment for days ahead and waited patiently.

Day after day Mr Budd watched them flit in and out of the rival establishment, willing, praying even, in a vague, ill-directed manner, that some of them would come over to him; but they never did.

And yet Mr Budd knew himself to be the finer artist. He had seen shingles turned out from over the way that he would never have countenanced, let alone charged three shillings and sixpence for. Shingles with an ugly hard line at the nape, shingles which were a slander on the shape of a good head or brutally emphasised the weak points of an ugly one; hurried, conscienceless shingles, botched work, handed over on a crowded afternoon to a girl who had only served a three years' apprenticeship and to whom the final mysteries of "tapering" were a sealed book.

And then there was the "tinting" – his own pet subject, which he had studied *con amore* – if only those too-sprightly matrons would come to him! He would gently dissuade them from that dreadful mahogany dye that made them look like metallic robots – he would warn them against that widely advertised preparation which was so incalculable in its effects; he would use the cunning skill which long experience had matured in him – tint them with the infinitely delicate art which conceals itself.

Yet nobody came to Mr Budd but the navvies and the young loungers and the men who plied their trade beneath the naphtha-flares in Wilton Street.

And why could not Mr Budd also have burst out into marble and electricity and swum to fortune on the rising tide?

The reason is very distressing, and, as it fortunately has no bearing on the story, shall be told with merciful brevity.

Mr Budd had a young brother, Richard, whom he had promised his mother to look after. In happier days Mr Budd had owned a flourishing business in their native town of Northampton, and Richard had been a bank clerk. Richard had got into bad ways (poor Mr Budd blamed himself dreadfully for this). There had been a sad affair with a girl, and a horrid series of affairs with bookmakers, and then Richard had tried to mend bad with worse by taking money from the bank. You need to be very much more skilful than Richard to juggle successfully with bank ledgers.

The bank manager was a hard man of the old school: he prosecuted. Mr Budd paid the bank and the bookmakers, and saw the girl through her trouble while Richard was in prison, and paid their fares to Australia when he came out, and gave them something to start life on.

But it took all the profits of the hairdressing business, and he couldn't face all the people in Northampton any more, who had known him all his life. So he had run to vast London, the refuge of all who shrink from the eyes of their neighbours, and bought this little shop in Pimlico, which had done fairly well, until the new fashion which did so much for hairdressing businesses killed it for lack of capital.

That is why Mr Budd's eye was so painfully fascinated by headlines with money in them.

He put the newspaper down, and as he did so, caught sight of his own reflection in the glass and smiled, for he was not without a sense of humour. He did not look quite the man to catch a brutal murderer single-handed. He was well on in the middle forties – a trifle paunchy, with fluffy pale hair, getting a trifle thin on top (partly hereditary, partly worry, that was), five feet six at most, and soft-handed, as a hairdresser must be.

Even razor in hand, he would hardly be a match for William Strickland, height six feet one or two, who had so ferociously battered his old aunt to death, so butcherly hacked her limb from limb, so horribly disposed of her remains in the copper. Shaking his head dubiously, Mr Budd advanced to the door, to cast a forlorn eye at the busy establishment over the way, and nearly ran into a bulky customer who dived in rather precipitately.

"I beg your pardon, sir," murmured Mr Budd, fearful of alienating ninepence; "just stepping out for a breath of fresh air, sir. Shave, sir?"

The large man tore off his overcoat without waiting for Mr Budd's obsequious hands.

"Are you prepared to dye?" he demanded abruptly.

The question chimed in so alarmingly with Mr Budd's thoughts about murder that for a moment it quite threw him off his professional balance.

"I beg your pardon, sir," he stammered, and in the same moment decided that the man must be a preacher of some kind. He looked rather like it, with his odd, light eyes, his bush of fiery hair, and short, jutting chin-beard. Perhaps he even wanted a subscription. That would be hard, when Mr Budd had already set him down as ninepence, or, with tip, possibly even a shilling.

"Do you do dyeing?" said the man impatiently.

"Oh!" said Mr Budd, relieved, "yes, sir, certainly sir."

A stroke of luck, this. Dyeing meant quite a big sum – his mind soared to seven-and-sixpence.

"Good," said the man, sitting down and allowing Mr Budd to put an apron about his neck. (He was safely gathered in now – he could hardly dart away down the street with a couple of yards of white cotton flapping from his shoulders.)

"Fact is," said the man, "my young lady doesn't like red hair. She says it's conspicuous. The other young ladies in her firm make jokes about it. So, as she's a good bit younger than I am, you see, I like to oblige her, and I was thinking perhaps it would be changed into something quieter, what? Dark brown, now – that's the colour she has a fancy for. What do *you* say?"

It occurred to Mr Budd that the young ladies might consider this abrupt change of coat even funnier than the original colour, but in the interests of business he agreed that dark brown would be very becoming and a great deal less noticeable than red. Besides very likely there was no young lady. A woman, he knew, will say frankly that she wants different coloured hair for a change, or just to try, or because she fancies it would suit her, but if a man is going to do a silly thing he prefers, if possible, to shuffle the responsibility on to someone else.

"Very well, then," said the customer, "go ahead. And I'm afraid the beard will have to go. My young lady doesn't like beards."

"A great many young ladies don't, sir," said Mr Budd. "They're not so fashionable nowadays as they used to be. It's very fortunate that you can stand a clean shave very well, sir. You have just the chin for it."

"Do you think so?" said the man, examining himself a little anxiously. "I'm glad to hear it."

"Will you have the moustache off as well, sir?"

"Well, no – no, I think I'll stick to that as long as I'm allowed to, what?" He laughed loudly, and Mr Budd approvingly noted well-kept teeth and a gold stopping. The customer was obviously ready to spend money on his personal appearance.

In fancy, Mr Budd saw this well-off and gentlemanly customer advising all his friends to visit "his man" – "wonderful fellow– wonderful – round at the back of Victoria Station – you'd never find it by yourself – only a little place, but he knows what he's about – I'll write it down for you." It was imperative that there should be no fiasco. Hair-dyes were awkward things – there had been a case in the paper lately.

"I see you have been using a tint before, sir," said Mr Budd with respect. "Could you tell me – ?"

"Eh?" said the man. "Oh, yes – well, fact is, as I said, my fiancée's a good bit younger than I am. As I expect you can see, I began to go grey early – my father was just the same – all our family – so I had it touched up – streaky bits restored, you see. But she doesn't take to the colour, so I thought, if I have to dye it at all, why not a colour she *does* fancy while we're about it, what?"

It is a common jest among the unthinking that hairdressers are garrulous. This is their wisdom. The hairdresser hears many secrets and very many lies. In his discretion he occupies his unruly tongue with the weather and the political situation, lest, restless with inaction, it plunge unbridled into a mad career of inconvenient candour.

Lightly holding forth upon the caprices of the feminine mind, Mr Budd subjected his customer's locks to the scrutiny of trained eye and fingers. Never – never in the process of nature could hair of that texture and quality have been red. It was naturally black hair, prematurely turned, as some black hair will turn, to a silvery grey. However, that was none of his business. He elicited the information he really needed – the name of the dye formerly used, and noted that he would have to be careful. Some dyes do not mix kindly with other dyes.

Chatting pleasantly, Mr Budd lathered his customer, removed the offending beard, and executed a vigorous shampoo, pre-liminary to the dyeing process. As he wielded the roaring drier,

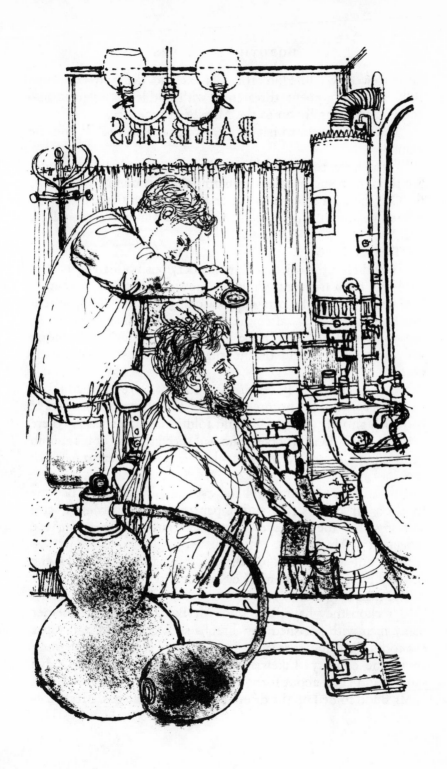

he reviewed Wimbledon, the Silk-tax and the Summer Time
Bill – at that moment threatened with sudden strangulation –
and passed naturally on to the Manchester murder.

"The police seem to have given it up as a bad job," said the
man.

"Perhaps the reward will liven things up a bit,' said Mr Budd,
the thought being naturally uppermost in his mind.

"Oh, there's a reward, is there? I hadn't seen that."

"It's in tonight's paper, sir. Maybe you'd like to have a look
at it."

"Thanks, I should."

Mr Budd left the drier to blow the fiery bush of hair at its own
wild will for a moment, while he fetched the *Evening Messenger*.
The stranger read the paragraph carefully and Mr Budd, watching him in the glass, after the disquieting manner of his craft,
saw him suddenly draw back his left hand, which was resting
carelessly on the arm of the chair, and thrust it under the
apron.

But not before Mr Budd had seen it. Not before he had taken
conscious note of the horny, misshapen thumb-nail. Many people
had such an ugly mark, Mr Budd told himself hurriedly – there
was his friend, Bert Webber, who had sliced the top of his thumb
right off in a motor-cycle chain – his nail looked very much like
that.

The man glanced up, and the eyes of his reflection became
fixed on Mr Budd's face with a penetrating scrutiny – a horrid
warning that the real eyes were steadfastly interrogating the
reflection of Mr Budd.

"Not but what," said Mr Budd, "the man is safe out of the
country by now, I reckon. They've put it off too late."

The man laughed.

"I reckon they have," he said. Mr Budd wondered whether
many men with smashed left thumbs showed a gold left upper
eye-tooth. Probably there were hundreds of people like that going
about the country. Likewise with silver-grey hair ("may dye
same") and aged about forty-three. Undoubtedly.

Mr Budd folded up the drier and turned off the gas. Mechanically he took up a comb and drew it through the hair that never, never in the process of nature had been that fiery red.

There came back to him, with an accuracy which quite unnerved him, the exact number and extent of the brutal wounds inflicted upon the Manchester victim – an elderly lady, rather stout, she had been. Glaring through the door, Mr Budd noticed that his rival over the way had closed. The streets were full of people. How easy it would be –

"Be as quick as you can, won't you?" said the man, a little impatiently, but pleasantly enough. "It's getting late. I'm afraid it will keep you over time."

"Not at all, sir," said Mr Budd. "It's of no consequence – not the least."

No – if he tried to bolt out of the door, his terrible customer would leap upon him, drag him back, throttle his cries, and then with one frightful blow like the one he had smashed in his aunt's skull with –

Yet surely Mr Budd was in a position of advantage. A decided man would do it. He would be out in the street before the customer could disentangle himself from the chair. Mr Budd began to edge round towards the door.

"What's the matter?" said the customer.

"Just stepping out to look at the time, sir," said Mr Budd, meekly pausing. (Yet he might have done it then, if he only had the courage to make the first swift step that would give the game away.)

"It's five-and-twenty past eight," said the man, "by tonight's broadcast. I'll pay extra for the overtime."

"Not on any account," said Mr Budd. Too late now, he couldn't make another effort. He vividly saw himself tripping on the threshold – falling – the terrible fist lifted to smash him into a pulp. Or perhaps, under the familiar white apron, the disfigured hand was actually clutching a pistol.

Mr Budd retreated to the back of the shop, collecting his materials. If only he had been quicker – more like a detective in a book – he would have observed that thumb-nail, that tooth, put two and two together, and run out to give the alarm while the man's head was wet and soapy and his face buried in the towel. Or he could have dabbed lather in his eyes – nobody could possibly commit a murder or even run away down the street with his eyes full of soap.

Even now – Mr Budd took down a bottle, shook his head and put it back on the shelf – even now, was it really too late? Why could he not take a bold course? He had only to open a razor, go quietly up behind the unsuspecting man and say in a firm, loud, convincing voice: "William Strickland, put up your hands. Your life is at my mercy. Stand up till I take your gun away. Now walk straight out to the nearest policeman." Surely, in his position, that was what Sherlock Holmes would do.

But as Mr Budd returned with a little trayful of requirements, it was borne in upon him that he was not of the stuff of which great manhunters are made. For he could not seriously see that attempt "coming off". Because if he held the razor to the man's throat and said: "Put up your hands," the man would probably merely catch him by the wrists and take the razor away. And greatly as Mr Budd feared his customer unarmed, he felt it would be a perfect crescendo of madness to put a razor into his hands.

Or, supposing he said, "Put up your hands," and the man just said, "I won't." What was he to do next? To cut his throat then and there would be murder, even if Mr Budd could possibly have brought himself to do such a thing. They could not remain there, fixed in one position, till the boy came to do out the shop in the morning.

Perhaps the policeman would notice the light on and the door unfastened and come in? Then he would say, "I congratulate you, Mr Budd, on having captured a very dangerous criminal." But supposing the policeman didn't happen to notice – and Mr Budd would have to stand all the time, and he would get exhausted and his attention would relax, and then –

After all, Mr Budd wasn't called upon to arrest the man himself. "Information leading to arrest" – those were the words. He would be able to tell them the wanted man had been there, that he would now have dark-brown hair and moustache and no beard. He might even shadow him when he left – he might . . .

It was at this moment that the great inspiration came to Mr Budd.

As he fetched a bottle from the glass-fronted case he remembered, with odd vividness, an old-fashioned wooden paperknife that had belonged to his mother. Between sprigs of blue forget-me-not, hand-painted, it bore the inscription "Knowledge is Power".

A strange freedom and confidence were vouchsafed to Mr Budd; his mind was alert; he removed the razors with an easy, natural movement, and made nonchalant conversation as he skilfully applied the dark-brown tint.

The streets were less crowded when Mr Budd let his customer out. He watched the tall figure cross Grosvenor Place and climb on to a 24 bus.

"But that was only his artfulness," said Mr Budd, as he put on his hat and coat and extinguished the lights carefully, "he'll take another at Victoria, like as not, and be making tracks from Charing Cross or Waterloo."

He closed the shop door, shook it, as was his wont, to make sure that the lock had caught properly, and in his turn made his way, by means of a 24, to the top of Whitehall.

The policeman was a little condescending at first when Mr Budd demanded to see "somebody very high up", but finding the little barber insist so earnestly that he had news of the Manchester murderer, and that there wasn't any time to lose, he consented to pass him through.

Mr Budd was interviewed first by an important-looking inspector in uniform, who listened very politely to his story and made him repeat very carefully about the gold tooth and the thumb-nail and the hair which had been black before it was grey or red and was now dark brown.

The inspector then touched a bell, and said, "Perkins, I think Sir Andrew would like to see this gentleman at once," and he was taken to another room, where sat a very shrewd, genial gentleman in mufti, who heard him with even greater attention, and called in another inspector to listen too, and to take down a very exact description of the – yes, surely the undoubted William Strickland as he now appeared.

"But there's one thing more," said Mr Budd – "and I'm sure to goodness," he added, "I hope, sir, it is the right man, because if it isn't it'll be the ruin of me – "

He crushed his soft hat into an agitated ball as he leant across the table, breathlessly uttering the story of his great professional betrayal.

"Tzee – z-z-z – tzee – tzee – z-z – tzee – z-z – "

"Dzoo – dz-dz-dz – dzoo – dz – dzoo – dzoo – dz – "

"Tzee – z – z."

The fingers of the wireless operator on the packet *Miranda* bound for Ostend moved swiftly as they jotted down the messages of the buzzing wireless mosquito-swarms.

One of them made him laugh.

"The Old Man'd better have this, I suppose," he said.

The Old Man scratched his head when he read, and rang a little bell for the steward. The steward ran down to the little round office where the purser was counting out his money and checking it before he locked it away for the night. On receiving the Old Man's message, the purser put the money quickly into the safe, picked up the passenger list and departed aft. There was a short consultation, and the bell was rung again – this time to summon the head steward.

"Tzee – z-z – tzee – z-z-z – tzee – tzee – z – tzee."

All down the Channel, all over the North Sea, up to the Mersey Docks, out into the Atlantic soared the busy mosquito-swarms. In ship after ship the wireless operator sent his message to the captain, the captain sent for the purser, the purser sent for the head steward and the head steward called his staff about him. Huge liners, little packets, destroyers, sumptuous private yachts – every floating thing that carried aerials – every port in England, France, Holland, Germany, Denmark, Norway, every police centre that could interpret the mosquito message, heard, between laughter and excitement, the tale of Mr Budd's betrayal. Two Boy Scouts at Croydon, practising their Morse with a home-made valve set, decoded it laboriously into an exercise book.

"Cripes," said Jim to George, "what a joke! D'you think they'll get the beggar?"

The *Miranda* docked at Ostend at 7 a.m. A man burst hurriedly into the cabin where the wireless operator was just taking off his headphones.

"Here!" he cried; "this is to go. There's something up and the Old Man's sent over for the police. The consul's coming on board."

The wireless operator groaned, and switched on his valves.

"Tzee – z – tzee," a message to the English police.

"Man on board answering to description. Ticket booked name of Watson. Has locked himself in cabin and refuses to come out. Insists on having hairdresser sent out to him. Have communicated Ostend police. Await instructions."

The Old Man with sharp words and authoritative gestures cleared a way through the excited little knot of people gathered about First Class Cabin No. 36. Several passengers had got wind of "something up". Magnificently he herded them away to the gangway with their bags and suitcases. Sternly he bade the stewards and the boy, who stood gaping with his hands full of breakfast dishes, to stand away from the door. Terribly he commanded them to hold their tongues. Four or five sailors stood watchfully at his side. In the restored silence, the passenger in No. 36 could be heard pacing up and down the narrow cabin, moving things, clattering, splashing water.

Presently came steps overhead. Somebody arrived, with a message. The Old Man nodded. Six pairs of Belgian police boots came tiptoeing down the companion. The Old Man glanced at the official paper held out to him and nodded again.

"Ready?"

"Yes."

The Old Man knocked at the door of No. 36.

"Who is it?" cried a harsh, sharp voice.

"The barber is here, sir, that you sent for."

"Ah!" There was relief in the tone. "Send him in alone, if you please. I – I have had an accident."

"Yes, sir."

At the sound of the bolt being cautiously withdrawn, the Old Man stepped forward. The door opened a chink, and was slammed to again, but the Old Man's boot was firmly wedged against the jamb. The policemen surged forward. There was a yelp and a shot which smashed harmlessly through the window of the first-class saloon, and the passenger was brought out.

"Strike me pink!" shrieked the boy, "strike me pink if he ain't gone green in the night!"

Green!

Not for nothing had Mr Budd studied the intricate mutual reactions of chemical dyes. In the pride of his knowledge he had set a mark on his man, to mark him out from all the billions of this overpopulated world. Was there a port in all Christendom where a murderer might slip away, with every hair on him green as a parrot – green moustache, green eyebrows, and that thick, springing shock of hair, vivid, flaring midsummer green?

Mr Budd got his £500. The *Evening Messenger* published the full story of his great betrayal. He trembled, fearing this sinister fame. Surely no one would ever come to him again.

On the next morning an enormous blue limousine rolled up to his door, to the immense admiration of Wilton Street. A lady, magnificent in musquash and diamonds, swept into the saloon.

"You *are* Mr Budd, aren't you?" she cried. "The *great* Mr Budd? Isn't it *too* wonderful? And now, *dear* Mr Budd, you *must* do me a favour. You must dye my hair green, *at once. Now.* I want to be able to say I'm the *very first* to be done by *you.* I'm the Duchess of Winchester, and that awful Melcaster woman is chasing me down the street – the cat!"

If you want it done, I can give you the number of Mr Budd's parlour in Bond Street. But I understand it is a terribly expensive process.

The Invisible Man

A Father Brown story

G. K. CHESTERTON

In the cool blue twilight of two steep streets in Camden Town, the shop at the corner, a confectioner's, glowed like the butt of a cigar. One should rather say, perhaps, like the butt of a firework, for the light was of many colours and some complexity, broken up by many mirrors and dancing on many gilt and gaily-coloured cakes and sweetmeats. Against this one fiery glass were glued the noses of many gutter-snipes, for the chocolates were all wrapped in those red and gold and green metallic colours which are almost better than chocolate itself; and the huge white wedding-cake in the window was somehow at once remote and satisfying, just as if the whole North Pole were good to eat. Such rainbow provocations could naturally collect the youth of the neighbourhood up to the ages of ten or twelve. But this corner was also attractive to youth at a later stage; and a young man, not less than twenty-four, was staring into the same shop window. To him, also, the shop was of fiery charm, but this attraction was not wholly to be explained by chocolates; which, however, he was far from despising.

He was a tall, burly, red-haired young man, with a resolute face but a listless manner. He carried under his arm a flat, grey portfolio of black-and-white sketches which he had sold with more or less success to publishers ever since his uncle (who was an admiral) had disinherited him for Socialism, because of a lecture which he had delivered against that economic theory. His name was John Turnbull Angus.

Entering at last, he walked through the confectioner's shop

into the back room, which was a sort of pastry-cook restaurant, merely raising his hat to the young lady who was serving there. She was a dark, elegant, alert girl in black, with a high colour and very quick, dark eyes; and after the ordinary interval she followed him into the inner room to take his order.

His order was evidently a usual one. "I want, please," he said with precision, "one halfpenny bun and a small cup of black coffee." An instant before the girl could turn away he added, "Also, I want you to marry me."

The young lady of the shop stiffened suddenly, and said: "Those are jokes I don't allow."

The red-haired young man lifted grey eyes of an unexpected gravity.

"Really and truly," he said, "it's as serious – as serious as the halfpenny bun. It is expensive, like the bun; one pays for it. It is indigestible, like the bun. It hurts."

The dark young lady had never taken her dark eyes off him, but seemed to be studying him with almost tragic exactitude. At the end of her scrutiny she had something like the shadow of a smile, and she sat down in a chair.

"Don't you think," observed Angus, absently, "that it's rather cruel to eat these halfpenny buns? They might grow up into penny buns. I shall give up these brutal sports when we are married."

The dark young lady rose from her chair and walked to the window, evidently in a state of strong but not unsympathetic cogitation. When at last she swung round again with an air of resolution, she was bewildered to observe that the young man was carefully laying out on the table various objects from the shop-window. They included a pyramid of highly coloured sweets, several plates of sandwiches, and the two decanters containing that mysterious port and sherry which are peculiar to pastry-cooks. In the middle of this neat arrangement he had carefully let down the enormous load of white sugared cake which had been the huge ornament of the window.

"What on earth are you doing?" she asked.

"Duty, my dear Laura," he began.

"Oh, for the Lord's sake, stop a minute," she cried, "and don't talk to me in that way. I mean what is all that?"

"A ceremonial meal, Miss Hope."

"And what is *that*?" she asked impatiently, pointing to the mountain of sugar.

"The wedding-cake, Mrs Angus," he said.

The girl marched to that article, removed it with some clatter, and put it back in the shop-window; she then returned, and, putting her elegant elbows on the table, regarded the young man not unfavourably, but with considerable exasperation.

"You don't give me any time to think," she said.

"I'm not such a fool," he answered; "that's my Christian humility."

She was still looking at him; but she had grown considerably graver behind the smile.

"Mr Angus," she said steadily, "before there is a minute more of this nonsense I must tell you something about myself as shortly as I can."

"Delighted," replied Angus gravely. "You might tell me something about myself, too, while you are about it."

"Oh, do hold your tongue and listen," she said. "It's nothing that I'm ashamed of, and it isn't even anything that I'm specially sorry about. But what would you say if there were something that is no business of mine and yet is my nightmare?"

"In that case," said the man seriously, "I should suggest that you bring back the cake."

"Well, you must listen to the story first," said Laura, persistently. "To begin with, I must tell you that my father owned the inn called the 'Red Fish' at Ludbury, and I used to serve people in the bar."

"I have often wondered," he said, "why there was a kind of a Christian air about this one confectioner's shop."

"Ludbury is a sleepy, grassy little hole in the Eastern Counties, and the only kind of people who ever came to the 'Red Fish' were occasional commercial travellers, and for the rest, the most awful people you can see, only you've never seen them. I mean little, loungy men, who had just enough to live on, and had nothing to do but lean about in bar-rooms and bet on horses, in bad clothes that were just too good for them. Even these wretched young rotters were not very common at our house; but there were two of them that were a lot too common – common in every sort of way. They both lived on money of their own, and were wearisomely idle and over-dressed. But yet I was a bit sorry for them, because I half believe they slunk into our little empty bar because each of them had a slight deformity; the sort of thing that some yokels laugh at. It wasn't exactly a deformity either; it was more an oddity. One of them was a surprisingly small man, something like a dwarf, or at least like a jockey. He was not at all jockeyish to look at, though, he had a round black head and a well-trimmed black beard, bright eyes like a bird's; he jingled money in his pockets; he jangled a great gold watch chain; and he never turned up except dressed just too much like a gentleman to be one. He was no fool, though, though a futile idler; he was curiously clever at all kinds of things that couldn't be the slightest use; a sort of impromptu conjuring; making fifteen matches set fire to each other like a regular firework; or cutting a banana or some such thing into a dancing doll. His name was Isidore Smythe; and I can see him still, with his little dark face, just coming up to the counter, making a jumping kangaroo out of five cigars.

"The other fellow was more silent and more ordinary; but somehow he alarmed me much more than poor little Smythe. He was very tall and slight, and light-haired; his nose had a high bridge, and he might almost have been handsome in a spectral sort of way; but he had one of the most appalling squints I have ever seen or heard of. When he looked straight at you, you didn't know where you were yourself, let alone what he was looking at. I fancy this sort of disfigurement embittered the poor chap a little; for while Smythe was ready to show off his monkey tricks anywhere, James Welkin (that was the squinting man's name) never did anything except soak in our bar parlour, and go for great walks by himself in the flat, grey country all round. All the same, I think Smythe, too, was a little sensitive about being so small, though he carried it off more smartly. And so it was that I was really puzzled, as well as startled, and very sorry, when they both offered to marry me in the same week.

"Well, I did what I've since thought was perhaps a silly thing. But, after all, these freaks were my friends in a way; and I had a horror of their thinking I refused them for the real reason, which was that they were so impossibly ugly. So I made up some gas of another sort, about never meaning to marry anyone who hadn't carved his way in the world. I said it was a point of principle with me not to live on money that was just inherited like theirs. Two days after I had talked in this well-meaning sort of way, the whole trouble began. The first thing I heard was that both of them had gone off to seek their fortunes, as if they were in some silly fairy tale.

"Well, I've never seen either of them from that day to this. But I've had two letters from the little man called Smythe, and really they were rather exciting."

"Ever heard of the other man?" asked Angus.

"No, he never wrote," said the girl, after an instant's hesitation. Smythe's first letter was simply to say that he had started out walking with Welkin to London; but Welkin was such a good walker that the little man dropped out of it, and took a rest by the roadside. He happened to be picked up by some travelling show, and, partly because he was nearly a dwarf, and partly because he was really a clever little wretch, he got on quite well in the show business, and was soon sent up to the Aquarium, to do some tricks that I forgot. That was his first letter. His second was much more of a startler, and I only got it last week."

The man called Angus emptied his coffee-cup and regarded her with mild and patient eyes. Her own mouth took a slight twist of laughter as she resumed: "I suppose you've seen on the hoardings all about this 'Smythe's Silent Service'? Or you must be the only person that hasn't. Oh, I don't know much about it, it's some clockwork invention for doing all the housework by machinery. You know the sort of thing: 'Press a button – A Butler who Never Drinks'. 'Turn a handle – Ten Housemaids who Never Flirt'. You must have seen the advertisements. Well, whatever these machines are, they are making pots of money; and they are making it all for that little imp whom I knew down in Ludbury. I can't help feeling pleased the poor little chap has fallen on his feet; but the plain fact is, I'm in terror of his turning up any minute and telling me he's carved his way in the world – as he certainly has."

"And the other man?" repeated Angus with a sort of obstinate quietude.

Laura Hope got to her feet suddenly. "My friend," she said: "I think you are a witch. Yes, you are quite right. I have not seen a line of the other man's writing; and I have no more notion than the dead of what or where he is. But it is of him that I am frightened. It is he who is all about my path. It is he who has half driven me mad. Indeed, I think he has driven me mad; for I have felt him where he could not have been, and I have heard his voice when he could not have spoken."

"Well, my dear," said the young man, cheerfully, "if he were Satan himself, he is done for now you have told somebody. One goes mad all alone, old girl. But when was it you fancied you felt and heard our squinting friend?"

"I heard James Welkin laugh as plainly as I hear you speak," said the girl, steadily. "There was nobody there, for I stood just outside the shop at the corner, and could see down both streets at once. I had forgotten how he laughed, though his laugh was as odd as his squint. I had not thought of him for nearly a year. But it's a solemn truth that a few seconds later the first letter came from his rival."

"Did you ever make the spectre speak or squeak, or anything?" asked Angus, with some interest.

Laura suddenly shuddered, and then said with an unshaken voice: "Yes. Just when I had finished reading the second letter from Isidore Smythe announcing his success, just then, I heard Welkin say: 'He shan't have you though.' It was quite plain, as if he were in the room. It is awful; I think I must be mad."

"If you really were mad," said the young man, "you would think you must be sane. But certainly there seems to me to be something a little rum about this unseen gentleman. Two heads are better than one – I spare you allusions to any other organs –

and really, if you would allow me, as a sturdy, practical man, to bring back the wedding-cake out of the window – "

Even as he spoke, there was a sort of steely shriek in the street outside, and a small motor, driven at devilish speed, shot up to the door of the shop and stuck there. In the same flash of time a small man in a shiny top hat stood stamping in the outer room.

Angus, who had hitherto maintained hilarious ease from motives of mental hygiene, revealed the strain of his soul by striding abruptly out of the inner room and confronting the new-comer. A glance at him was quite sufficient to confirm the savage guesswork of a man in love. This very dapper but dwarfish figure, with the spike of black beard carried insolently forward, the clever unrestful eyes, the neat but very nervous fingers, could be none other than the man just described to him: Isidore Smythe, who made dolls out of banana skins and match-boxes: Isidore Smythe, who made millions out of undrinking butlers and unflirting housemaids of metal. For a moment the two men, instinctively understanding each other's air of possession, looked at each other with that curious cold generosity which is the soul of rivalry.

Mr Smythe, however, made no allusion to the ultimate ground of their antagonism, but said simply and explosively: "Has Miss Hope seen that thing on the window?"

"On the window?" repeated the staring Angus.

"There's no time to explain other things," said the small millionaire shortly. "There's some tomfoolery going on here that has to be investigated."

He pointed his polished walking-stick at the window, recently depleted by the bridal preparations of Mr Angus; and that gentle-man was astonished to see along the front of the glass a long strip of paper pasted, which had certainly not been on the window when he had looked through it some time before. Following the energetic Smythe outside into the street, he found that some yard and a half of stamp paper had been carefully gummed along the glass outside, and on this was written in straggly characters: "If you marry Smythe, he will die."

"Laura," said Angus, putting his red head into the shop, "you're not mad."

"It's the writing of that fellow Welkin," said Smythe gruffly. "I haven't seen him for years, but he's always bothering me. Five times in the last fortnight he's had threatening letters left at my flat, and I can't even find out who leaves them, let alone if it is Welkin himself. The porter of the flats swears that no suspicious characters have been seen, and here he has pasted up a sort of dado on a public shop window, while the people in the shop – "

"Quite so," said Angus modestly, "while the people in the shop were having tea. Well, sir, I can assure you I appreciate your common sense in dealing so directly with the matter. We can talk about other things afterwards. The fellow cannot be very far off yet, for I swear there was no paper there when I went last to the window, ten or fifteen minutes ago. On the other hand, he's too far off to be chased, as we don't even know the direction. If you'll take my advice, Mr Smythe, you'll put this at once in the hands of some energetic inquiry man, private rather than public. I know an extremely clever fellow, who has set up in business five minutes from here in your car. His name's Flambeau, and though his youth was a bit stormy, he's a strictly honest man now, and his brains are worth money. He lives in Lucknow Mansions, Hampstead."

"That is odd," said the little man, arching his black eyebrows. "I live myself in Himalaya Mansions round the corner. Perhaps you might care to come with me; I can go to my rooms and sort out these queer Welkin documents, while you run round and get your friend the detective."

"You are very good," said Angus politely. "Well, the sooner we act the better."

Both men, with a queer kind of impromptu fairness, took the same sort of formal farewell of the lady, and both jumped into the brisk little car. As Smythe took the wheel and turned the great corner of the street, Angus was amused to see a gigantesque poster of "Smythe's Silent Service", with a picture of a huge headless iron doll, carrying a saucepan with the legend, "A Cook Who is Never Cross."

"I use them in my own flat," said the little black-bearded man, laughing, "partly for advertisement, and partly for real convenience. Honestly, and all above board, those big clockwork dolls of mine do bring you coals or claret or a time-table quicker than any live servants I've ever known, if you know which knob to press. But I'll never deny, between ourselves, that such servants have their disadvantages too."

"Indeed?" said Angus; "is there something they can't do?"

"Yes," replied Smythe coolly; "they can't tell me who left those threatening letters at my flat."

The man's motor was small and swift like himself; in fact, like his domestic service, it was of his own invention. If he was an advertising quack, he was one who believed in his own wares. The sense of something tiny and flying was accentuated as they swept up long white curves of road in the dead but open daylight of evening. Soon the white curves came sharper and dizzier; they were upon ascending spirals, as they say in the modern religions. For, indeed, they were cresting a corner of London which is almost as precipitous as Edinburgh, if not quite so picturesque. Terrace rose above terrace, and the special tower of flats they sought, rose above them all to almost Egyptian height, gilt by the level sunset. The change, as they turned the corner and entered the crescent known as Himalaya Mansions, was as abrupt as the opening of a window; for they found that pile of flats sitting above London as above a green sea of slate. Opposite to the mansions, on the other side of the gravel crescent, was a bushy enclosure more like a steep hedge or dyke than a garden, and some way below that ran a strip of artificial water, a sort of canal, like the moat of that embowered fortress. As the car swept round the crescent it passed, at one corner, the stray stall of a man selling chestnuts; and right away at the other end of the curve, Angus could see a dim blue policeman walking slowly. These were the only human shapes in that high suburban solitude; but he had an irrational sense that they expressed the speechless poetry of London. He felt as if they were figures in a story.

The little car shot up to the right house like a bullet, and shot out its owner like a bomb shell. He was immediately inquiring of a tall commissionaire in shining braid, and a short porter in shirt sleeves, whether anybody or anything had been seeking his apartments. He was assured that nobody and nothing had passed these officials since his last inquiries; whereupon he and the slightly bewildered Angus were shot up in the lift like a rocket, till they reached the top floor.

"Just come in for a minute," said the breathless Smythe. "I want to show you those Welkin letters. Then you might run round the corner and fetch your friend." He pressed a button concealed in the wall, and the door opened of itself.

It opened on a long, commodious ante-room, of which the only arresting features, ordinarily speaking, were the rows of tall half-human mechanical figures that stood up on both sides like tailors' dummies. Like tailors' dummies they were headless; and like tailors' dummies they had a handsome unnecessary humpiness in the shoulders, and a pigeon-breasted protuberance of chest; but barring this, they were not much more like a human figure than any automatic machine at a station that is about the human height. They had two great hooks like arms, for carrying trays; and they were painted pea-green, or vermilion, or black for convenience of distinction; in every other way they were only automatic machines and nobody would have looked twice at them. On this occasion, at least, nobody did. For between the two rows of these domestic dummies lay something more interesting than most of the mechanics of the world. It was a white, tattered scrap of paper scrawled with red ink; and the agile inventor had snatched it up almost as soon as the door flew open. He handed it to Angus without a word. The red ink on it actually was not dry, and the message ran: "If you have been to see her today, I shall kill you."

There was a short silence, and then Isidore Smythe said quietly: "Would you like a little whisky? I rather feel as if I should."

"Thank you; I should like a little Flambeau," said Angus, gloomily. "This business seems to me to be getting rather grave. I'm going round at once to fetch him."

"Right you are," said the other, with admirable cheerfulness. "Bring him round here as quick as you can."

But as Angus closed the front door behind him he saw Smythe push back a button, and one of the clockwork images glided from its place and slid along a groove in the floor carrying a tray with syphon and decanter. There did seem something a trifle weird about leaving the little man alone among those dead servants, who were coming to life as the door closed.

Six steps down from Smythe's landing the man in shirt sleeves was doing something with a pail. Angus stopped to extract a promise, fortified with a prospective bribe, that he would remain in that place until the return with the detective, and would keep count of any kind of stranger coming up those stairs. Dashing down to the front hall he then laid similar charges of vigilance on the commissionaire at the front door, from whom he learned the simplifying circumstance that there was no back door. Not content with this, he captured the floating policeman and induced him to stand opposite the entrance and watch it; and finally paused an instant for a pennyworth of chestnuts, and an inquiry as to the probable length of the merchant's stay in the neighbourhood.

The chestnut seller, turning up the collar of his coat, told him he should probably be moving shortly, as he thought it was going to snow. Indeed, the evening was growing grey and bitter, but Angus, with all his eloquence, proceeded to nail the chestnut man to his post.

"Keep yourself warm on your own chestnuts," he said earnestly. "Eat up your whole stock; I'll make it worth your while. I'll give you a sovereign if you'll wait here till I come back, and then tell me whether any man, woman, or child has gone into that house where the commissionaire is standing."

He then walked away smartly, with a last look at the besieged tower.

"I've made a ring round that room, anyhow," he said. "They can't all four of them be Mr Welkin's accomplices."

Lucknow Mansions were, so to speak, on a lower platform of that hill of houses, of which Himalaya Mansions might be called the peak. Mr Flambeau's semi-official flat was on the ground floor, and presented in every way a marked contrast to the American machinery and cold hotel-like luxury of the flat of the Silent Service. Flambeau, who was a friend of Angus, received him in a rococo artistic den behind his office, of which the ornaments were sabres, harquebuses, Eastern curiosities, flasks of Italian wine, savage cooking-pots, a plumy Persian cat, and a small dusty-looking Roman Catholic priest, who looked particularly out of place.

"This is my friend, Father Brown," said Flambeau. "I've often wanted you to meet him. Splendid weather, this; a little cold for Southerners like me."

"Yes, I think it will keep clear," said Angus, sitting down on a violet-striped Eastern ottoman.

"No," said the priest quietly; "it has begun to snow."

And indeed, as he spoke, the first few flakes, foreseen by the man of chestnuts, began to drift across the darkening window-pane.

"Well," said Angus heavily. "I'm afraid I've come on business, and rather jumpy business at that. The fact is, Flambeau, within a stone's throw of your house is a fellow who badly wants your help; he's perpetually being haunted and threatened by an invisible enemy – a scoundrel whom nobody has even seen." As Angus proceeded to tell the whole tale of Smythe and Welkin beginning with Laura's story, and going on with his own, the supernatural laugh at the corner of two empty streets, the strange distinct words spoken in an empty room, Flambeau grew more and more vividly concerned, and the little priest seemed to be left out of it, like a piece of furniture. When it came to the scribbled stamp-paper pasted on the window, Flambeau rose, seeming to fill the room with his huge shoulders.

"If you don't mind," he said, "I think you had better tell me the rest on the nearest road to this man's house. It strikes me somehow, that there is no time to be lost."

"Delighted," said Angus, rising also, "though he's safe enough for the present, for I've set four men to watch the only hole to his burrow."

They turned out into the street, the small priest trundling after them with the docility of a small dog. He merely said, in a cheerful way, like one making conversation: "How quick the snow gets thick on the ground."

As they threaded the steep side streets already powdered with silver, Angus finished his story; and by the time they reached the crescent with the towering flats, he had leisure to turn his attention to the four sentinels. The chestnut seller, both before and after receiving a sovereign, swore stubbornly that he had watched the door and seen no visitor enter. The policeman was even more emphatic. He said he had experience of crooks of all kinds, in top hats and in rags; he wasn't so green as to expect suspicious characters to look suspicious; he looked out for anybody, and, so help him, there had been nobody. And when all three men gathered round the gilded commissionaire, who still stood smiling astride of the porch, the verdict was more final still.

"I've got a right to ask any man, duke or dustman, what he wants in these flats," said the genial and gold-laced giant, "and

I'll swear there's been nobody to ask since this gentleman went away."

The unimportant Father Brown, who stood back, looking modestly at the pavement, here ventured to say meekly: "Has nobody been up and down stairs, then, since the snow began to fall? It began while we were all round at Flambeau's."

"Nobody's been in here, sir, you can take it from me," said the official, with beaming authority.

"Then I wonder what that is?" said the priest, and stared at the ground blankly like a fish.

The others all looked down also; and Flambeau used a fierce exclamation and a French gesture. For it was unquestionably true that down the middle of the entrance guarded by the man in gold lace, actually between the arrogant, stretched legs of that colossus, ran a stringy pattern of grey footprints stamped upon the white snow.

"God!" cried Angus involuntarily; "the Invisible Man!"

Without another word he turned and dashed up the stairs, with Flambeau following; but Father Brown still stood looking about him in the snow-clad street as if he had lost interest in his query.

Flambeau was plainly in a mood to break down the door with his big shoulder; but the Scotsman, with more reason, if less intuition, fumbled about on the frame of the door till he found the invisible button; and the door swung slowly open.

It showed substantially the same serried interior; the hall had grown darker, though it was still struck here and there with the last crimson shafts of sunset, and one or two of the headless machines had been moved from their places for this or that purpose, and stood here and there about the twilit place. The green and red of their coats were all darkened in the dusk, and their likeness to human shapes slightly increased by their very shapelessness. But in the middle of them all, exactly where the paper with the red ink had lain, there lay something that looked very like red ink spilled out of its bottle. But it was not red ink.

With a French combination of reason and violence Flambeau simply said "Murder!" and, plunging into the flat, had explored every corner and cupboard of it in five minutes. But if he expected to find a corpse he found none. Isidore Smythe simply was not in the place, either dead or alive. After the most tearing search the two men met each other in the outer hall with streaming faces and staring eyes. "My friend," said Flambeau, talking French in his excitement, "not only is your murderer invisible, but he makes invisible also the murdered man."

Angus looked round at the dim room full of dummies, and in some Celtic corner of his Scotch soul a shudder started. One of the life-size dolls stood immediately overshadowing the blood-stain, summoned, perhaps, by the slain man an instant before he fell. One of the high-shouldered hooks that served the thing for arms, was a little lifted and Angus had suddenly the horrid fancy that poor Smythe's own iron child had struck him down. Matter had rebelled, and these machines had killed their master. But even so, what had they done with him?

"Eaten him?" said the nightmare at his ear; and he sickened for an instant at the idea of rent, human remains absorbed and crushed into all that acephalous clockwork.

He recovered his mental health by an emphatic effort, and said to Flambeau: "Well, there it is. The poor fellow has evaporated like a cloud and left a red streak on the floor. The tale does not belong to this world."

"There is only one thing to be done," said Flambeau, "whether it belongs to this world or the other, I must go down and talk to my friend."

They descended, passing the man with the pail, who again asseverated that he had let no intruder pass, down to the commissionaire and the hovering chestnut man, who rightly reasserted their own watchfulness. But when Angus looked round for his fourth confirmation he could not see it, and called out with some nervousness: "Where is the policeman?"

"I beg your pardon," said Father Brown; "that is my fault. I just sent him down the road to investigate something – that I just thought worth investigating."

"Well, we want him back pretty soon," said Angus abruptly, "for the wretched man upstairs has not only been murdered, but wiped out."

"How?" asked the priest.

"Father," said Flambeau, after a pause, "upon my soul I believe it is more in your department than mine. No friend or foe has entered the house, but Smythe is gone, as if stolen by the fairies. If that is not supernatural, I – "

As he spoke they were all checked by an unusual sight; the big blue policeman came round the corner of the crescent running. He came straight up to Brown.

"You're right, sir," he panted, "they've just found poor Mr Smythe's body in the canal down below."

Angus put his hand wildly to his head. "Did he run down and drown himself?" he asked.

"He never came down, I'll swear," said the constable, "and he wasn't drowned either, for he died of a great stab over the heart."

"And yet you saw no one enter?" said Flambeau in a grave voice.

"Let us walk down the road a little," said the priest.

As they reached the other end of the crescent he observed abruptly: "Stupid of me! I forgot to ask the policeman something. I wonder if they found a light brown sack."

"Why a light brown sack?" asked Angus, astonished.

"Because if it was any other coloured sack, the case must begin over again," said Father Brown; "but if it was a light brown sack, why, the case is finished."

"I am pleased to hear it," said Angus with hearty irony. "It hasn't begun, so far as I am concerned."

"You must tell us all about it," said Flambeau, with a strange heavy simplicity, like a child.

Unconsciously they were walking with quickening steps down the long sweep of road on the other side of the high crescent, Father Brown leading briskly, though in silence. At last he said with an almost touching vagueness: "Well, I'm afraid you'll think it so prosy. We always begin at the abstract end of things, and you can't begin this story anywhere else.

"Have you ever noticed this – that people never answer what you say? They answer what you mean – or what they think you mean. Suppose one lady says to another in a country house,

'Is anybody staying with you?' the lady doesn't answer 'Yes; the butler, the three footmen, the parlour-maid, and so on,' though the parlour-maid may be in the room, or the butler behind her chair. She says: 'There is *nobody* staying with us,' meaning nobody of the sort you mean. But suppose a doctor inquiring into an epidemic asks, 'Who is staying in the house?' then the lady will remember the butler, the parlour-maid, and the rest. All language is used like that; you never get a question answered literally, even when you get it answered truly. When those four quite honest men said that no man had gone into the Mansions, they did not really mean that *no man* had gone into them. They meant no man whom they could suspect of being your man. A man did go into the house, and did come out of it, but they never noticed him."

"An invisible man?" inquired Angus, raising his red eyebrows.

"A mentally invisible man," said Father Brown.

A minute or two after he resumed in the same unassuming voice, like a man thinking his way. "Of course, you can't think of such a man, until you do think of him. That's where his cleverness comes in. But I came to think of him through two or three little things in the tale Mr Angus told us. First, there was the fact that this Welkin went for long walks. And then there was the vast lot of stamp paper on the window. And then, most of all there were the two things the young lady said – things that couldn't be true. Don't get annoyed," he added hastily, noting a sudden movement of the Scotsman's head; "she thought they were true all right, but they couldn't be true. A person *can't* be quite alone in a street a second before she receives a letter. She can't be quite alone in a street when she starts reading a letter just received. There must be somebody pretty near her; he must be mentally invisible."

"Why must there be somebody near her?" asked Angus.

"Because," said Father Brown: "barring carrier pigeons, somebody must have brought her the letter."

"Do you really mean to say," asked Flambeau, with energy, "that Welkin carried his rival's letters to his lady?"

"Yes," said the priest. "Welkin carried his rival's letters to his lady. You see, he had to."

"Oh, I can't stand much more of this," exploded Flambeau. "Who is this fellow? What does he look like? What is the usual get-up of a mentally invisible man?"

"He is dressed rather handsomely in red, blue and gold," replied the priest promptly with decision, "and in this striking, and even showy costume he entered Himalaya Mansions under eight human eyes; he killed Smythe in cold blood, and came down into the street again carrying the dead body in his arms – "

"Reverend sir," cried Angus, standing still, "are you raving mad, or am I?"

"You are not mad," said Brown, "only a little unobservant. You have not noticed such a man as this, for example."

He took three quick strides forward, and put his hand on the shoulder of an ordinary passing postman who had bustled by them unnoticed under the shade of the trees.

"Nobody ever notices postmen, somehow," he said thoughtfully; "yet they have passions like other men, and even carry large bags where a small corpse can be stowed quite easily."

The postman, instead of turning naturally, had ducked and tumbled against the garden fence. He was a lean fair-bearded man of very ordinary appearance, but as he turned an alarmed face over his shoulder, all three men were fixed with an almost fiendish squint.

Flambeau went back to his sabres, purple rugs and Persian cat, having many things to attend to. John Turnbull Angus went back to the lady at the shop, with whom that imprudent young man contrives to be extremely comfortable. But Father Brown walked those snow-covered hills under the stars for many hours with a murderer, and what they said to each other will never be known.

Who Killed Charlie Winpole?

ERNEST BRAMAH

Some time during November of a recent year newspaper readers who are in the habit of being attracted by curious items of quite negligible importance might have followed the account of the tragedy of a St Abbots schoolboy which appeared in the Press under the headings, "Fatal Dish of Mushrooms", "Are Toadstools Distinguishable" or other similarly alluring titles.

The facts relating to the death of Charlie Winpole were simple and straightforward and the jury sworn to the business of investigating the cause had no hesitation in bringing in a verdict in accordance with the medical evidence. The witnesses who had anything really material to contribute were only two in number – Mrs Dupreen and Robert Wilberforce Slark, M.D. A couple of hours would easily have disposed of every detail of an inquiry that was generally admitted to have been a pure formality, had not the contention of an interested person delayed the inevitable conclusion by forcing the necessity of an adjournment.

Irene Dupreen testified that she was the widow of a physician and lived at Hazlehurst, Chesset Avenue, St Abbots, with her brother. The deceased was their nephew, an only child and an orphan, and was aged twelve. He was a Ward of Chancery and the Court had appointed her as guardian, with an adequate provision for the expenses of his keep and education. That allowance would, of course, cease with her nephew's death.

Coming to the particulars of the case, Mrs Dupreen explained that for a few days the boy had been suffering from a rather severe cold. She had not thought it necessary to call in a doctor, recognising it as a mild form of influenza. She kept him from school and restricted him to his bedroom. On the previous Wednesday, the day before his death, he was quite convalescent, with a good pulse and a normal temperature, but as the weather was cold she decided still to keep him in bed as a measure of precaution. He had a fair appetite, but did not care for the lunch they had, and so she asked him, before going out in the afternoon, if there was anything that he would especially fancy for his dinner. He had thereupon expressed a wish for some mushrooms, of which he was always very fond.

"I laughed and pulled his ear," continued the witness, much affected at her recollection, "and asked him if that was his idea of a suitable dish for an invalid. But I didn't think that it really mattered in the least then, so I went to several shops about them. They all said that mushrooms were over, but finally I found a few at Lackington's, the greengrocer in Park Road. I bought only half-a-pound; no one but Charlie among us cared for them and I thought that they were already very dry and rather dear."

The connection between the mushrooms and the unfortunate boy's death seemed inevitable. When Mrs Dupreen went upstairs after dinner she found Charlie apparently asleep and breathing soundly. She quietly removed the tray and without disturbing him turned out the light and closed the door. In the middle of the night she was suddenly and startlingly awakened by something. For a moment she remained confused, listening. Then a curious sound coming from the direction of the boy's bedroom drew her there. On opening the door she was horrified to see her nephew lying on the floor in a convulsed attitude. His eyes were open and widely dilated; one hand clutched some bed-clothes which he had dragged down with him, and the other still grasped the empty water-bottle that had been by his side. She called loudly for help and her brother and then the servant appeared. She sent the latter to a medicine cabinet for mustard leaves and told her brother to get in the nearest available doctor. She had already lifted Charlie on to the bed again. Before the doctor arrived, which was in about half an hour, the boy was dead.

In answer to a question the witness stated that she had not seen her nephew between the time she removed the tray and when she found him ill. The only other person who had seen him within a few hours of his death had been her brother, Philip Loudham, who had taken up Charlie's dinner. When he came down again he had made the remark: "The youngster seems lively enough now."

Dr Slark was the next witness. His evidence was to the effect that about three-fifteen on the Thursday morning he was hurriedly called to Hazlehurst by a gentleman whom he now knew to be Mr Philip Loudham. He understood that the case was one of convulsions and went provided for that contingency, but on his arrival he found the patient already dead. From his own examination and from what he was told he had no hesitation in diagnosing the case as one of agaric poisoning. He saw no reason to suspect any of the food except the mushrooms, and all the symptoms pointed to bhurine, the deadly principle of *Amanita Bhuroides*, or the Black Cap, as it was popularly called, from its fancied resemblance to the head-dress assumed by a judge in passing death sentence, coupled with its sinister and well-merited reputation. It was always fatal.

Continuing his evidence, Dr Slark explained that only after maturity did the Black Cap develop its distinctive appearance. Up to that stage it had many of the characteristics of *Agaricus campestris*, or common mushroom. It was true that the gills were paler than one would expect to find, and there were other slight differences of a technical kind, but all might easily be overlooked in the superficial glance of the gatherer. The whole subject of edible and noxious fungi was a difficult one and at present very imperfectly understood. He, personally, very much doubted if true mushrooms were ever responsible for the cases of poisoning which one occasionally saw attributed to them. Under scientific examination he was satisfied that all would resolve themselves into poisoning by one or other of the many noxious fungi that could easily be mistaken for the edible varieties. It was possible to prepare an artificial bed, plant it with proper spawn and be rewarded by a crop of mushroom-like growth of undoubted

virulence. On the other hand, the injurious constituents of many poisonous fungi passed off in the process of cooking. There was no handy way of discriminating between the good and the bad except by the absolute identification of species. The salt test and the silver-spoon test were all nonsense and the sooner they were forgotten the better. Apparent mushrooms that were found in woods or growing in the vicinity of trees or hedges should always be regarded with the utmost suspicion.

Dr Slark's evidence concluded the case so far as the sub-poenaed witnesses were concerned, but before addressing the jury the coroner announced that another person had expressed a desire to be heard. There was no reason why they should not accept any evidence that was tendered, and as the applicant's name had been mentioned in the case it was only right that he should have the opportunity of replying publicly.

Mr Lackington thereupon entered the witness-box and was sworn. He stated that he was a fruiterer and greengrocer, carrying on a business in Park Road, St Abbots. He remembered Mrs Dupreen coming to his shop two days before. The basket of mushrooms from which she was supplied consisted of a small lot of about six pounds, brought in by a farmer from a neighbouring village, with whom he had frequent dealings. All had been disposed of and in no other case had illness resulted. It was a serious matter to him as a tradesman to have his name associated with a case of this kind. That was why he had come forward. Not only with regard to mushrooms, but as a general result, people would become shy of dealing with him if it was stated that he had sold unwholesome goods.

The coroner, intervening at this point, remarked that he might as well say that he would direct the jury that, in the event of their finding the deceased to have died from the effects of the mushrooms or anything contained among them, that there was no evidence other than that the occurrence was one of pure mischance.

Mr Lackington expressed his thanks for the assurance, but said that a bad impression would still remain. He had been in business in St Abbots for twenty-seven years and during that time he had handled some tons of mushrooms without a single complaint before. He admitted, in answer to the interrogation, that he had not actually examined every mushroom in the half-pound sold to Mrs Dupreen, but he had weighed them, and he was confident that if a toadstool had been among them he would have detected it. Might it not be a cooking utensil that was the cause?

Dr Slark shook his head and was understood to say that he could not accept the suggestion.

Continuing, Mr Lackington then asked whether it was not possible that the deceased, doubtless an inquiring, adventurous boy and as mischievous as most of his kind, feeling quite well again and being confined to the house, had got up in his aunt's absence and taken something that would explain this sad affair? They had heard of a medicine cabinet. What about tablets of trional or veronal or something of that sort that might perhaps look like sweets? . . . It was all very well for Dr Slark to laugh, but this matter was a serious one for the witness.

Dr Slark apologised for smiling – he had not laughed – and gravely remarked that the matter was a serious one for all concerned in the inquiry. He admitted that the reference to trional and veronal had, for the moment, caused him to forget the surroundings. He would suggest that in the circumstances perhaps the coroner would think it desirable to order a more detailed examination of the body to be made.

After some further discussion the coroner, while remarking that in most cases an analysis was quite unnecessary, decided that in view of what had transpired it would be more satisfactory to have a complete autopsy made. The inquest was accordingly adjourned.

A week later most of those who had taken part in the first inquiry assembled again in the room of the St Abbots Town Hall which did duty for the Coroner's Court. Only one witness was heard and his evidence was brief and conclusive.

Dr Herbert Ingpenny, consulting pathologist to St Martin's Hospital, stated that he had made an examination of the contents of the stomach and viscera of the deceased. He found evidence of the presence of the poison bhurine in sufficient quantity to account for the boy's death, and the symptoms, as described by Dr Slark and Mrs Dupreen, in the course of the previous hearing were consistent with bhurine poisoning. Bhurine did not occur naturally except as a constituent of *Amanita Bhuroides*. One-fifth of a grain would be fatal to an adult; in other words a single fungus in the dish might poison three people. A child especially if experiencing the effects of a weakening illness, would be even more susceptible. No other harmful substance was present.

Dr Ingpenny concluded by saying that he endorsed his colleague's general remarks on the subject of mushrooms and other fungi, and the jury, after a plain direction from the corner, forthwith brought in a verdict in accordance with the medical evidence.

It was a foregone conclusion with anyone who knew the facts

or had followed the evidence. Yet five days later Philip Loudham was arrested suddenly and charged with the astounding crime of having murdered his nephew.

It is at this point that Max Carrados makes his first appearance in the Winpole tragedy.

A few days after the arrest, being in a particularly urbane frame of mind himself, and having several hours with no demands on them that could not be fitly transferred to his subordinates, Mr Carlyle looked round for some social entertainment, and with a benevolent condescension very opportunely remembered the existence of his niece living at Groat's Heath.

"Elsie will be delighted," he assured himself, on evolving this suggestion. "She is rather out of the world up there, I imagine. Now if I get across by four, put in a couple of hours . . ."

Mrs Bellmark was certainly pleased, but she appeared to be still more surprised at something, and behind that lay an effervescence of excitement that even to Mr Carlyle's complacent self-esteem seemed out of proportion to the occasion. The reason could not be long withheld.

"Did you meet anyone, Uncle Louis?" was almost her first inquiry.

"Did I meet anyone?" repeated Mr Carlyle with his usual precision. "Um, no, I cannot say that I met anyone particular. Of course – "

"I've had a visitor and he's coming back again for tea. Guess who it is? But you never will. Mr Carrados."

"Max Carrados!" exclaimed her uncle in astonishment. "You don't say so. Why, bless my soul, Elsie, I'd almost forgotten that you knew him. It seems years ago – what on earth is Max doing in Groat's Heath?"

"That is the extraordinary thing about it," replied Mrs Bellmark. "He said that he had come up here to look for mushrooms."

"Mushrooms?"

"Yes; that was what he said. He asked me if I knew of any

woods about here that he could go into and I told him of the one down Stonecut Lane."

"But don't you know, my dear child," exclaimed Mr Carlyle, "that mushrooms growing in woods or even near trees are always to be regarded with suspicion? They may look like mushrooms, but they are probably poisonous."

"I didn't know," admitted Mrs Bellmark; "but if they are, I imagine Mr Carrados will know."

"It scarcely sounds like it – going to a wood, you know. As it happens, I have been looking up the subject lately. But, in any case, you say that he is coming back here?"

"He asked me if he might call on his way home for a cup of tea, and of course I said, 'Of course.' "

"Of course," also said Mr Carlyle. "Motoring, I suppose?"

"Yes, a big grey car. He had Mr Parkinson with him."

Mr Carlyle was slightly puzzled, as he frequently was by his friend's proceedings, but it was not his custom to dwell on any topic that involved an admission of inadequacy. The subject of Carrados and his eccentric quest was therefore dismissed until the sound of a formidable motor car dominating the atmosphere of the quiet suburban road was almost immediately followed by the entrance of the blind amateur. With a knowing look towards his niece Carlyle had taken up a position at the farther end of the room, where he remained in almost breathless silence.

Carrados acknowledged the hostess's smiling greeting and then nodded familiarly in the direction of the playful guest.

"Well, Louis," he remarked, "we've caught each other."

Mrs Bellmark was perceptibly startled, but rippled musically at the failure of the conspiracy.

"Extraordinary," admitted Mr Carlyle, coming forward.

"Not so very," was the dry reply. "Your friendly little maid" – to Mrs Bellmark – "mentioned your visitor as she brought me in."

"Is it a fact, Max," demanded Mr Carlyle, "that you have been to – er – Stonecut Wood to get mushrooms?"

"Mrs Bellmark told you?"

"Yes. And did you succeed?"

"Parkinson found something that he assured me looked just like mushrooms."

Mr Carlyle bestowed a triumphant glance on his niece.

"I should very much like to see these so-called mushrooms. Do you know, it may be rather a good thing for you that I met you."

"It is always a good thing for me to meet you," replied Carrados. "You shall see them. They are in the car. Perhaps I shall be able to take you back to town?"

"If you are going very soon. No, no, Elsie" – in response to Mrs Bellmark's protesting "Oh!" – "I don't want to influence Max, but I really must tear myself away the moment after tea. I still have to clear up some work on a rather important case I am just completing. It is quite appropriate to the occasion, too. Do you happen to know all about the Winpole business, Max?"

"No," admitted Carrados, without any appreciable show of interest. "Do you, Louis?"

"Yes," responded Mr Carlyle with crisp assurance, "yes, I think that I may claim I do. In fact it was I who obtained the evidence that induced the authorities to take up the case against Loudham."

"Oh do tell us all about it," exclaimed Elsie. "I have only seen something in the *Indicator*."

Mr Carlyle shook his head, hemmed and looked wise, and then gave in.

"But not a word of this outside, Elsie," he stipulated. "Some of the evidence won't be given until next week and it might be serious – "

"Not a syllable," assented the lady. "How exciting! Go on."

"Well, you know, of course, that the coroner's jury – very rightly, according to the evidence before them – brought in a verdict of accidental death. In the circumstances it was a reflection on the business methods or the care or the knowledge or whatever one may decide of the man who sold the mushrooms, a greengrocer called Lackington. I have seen Lackington, and with a rather remarkable pertinacity in the face of the evidence he insists that he could not have made this fatal blunder – that in weighing so small a quantity as half-a-pound, at any rate, he would at once have spotted anything that wasn't quite all right."

"But the doctor said. Uncle Louis – "

"Yes, my dear Elsie, we know what the doctor said, but, rightly or wrongly, Lackington backs his experience and practical knowledge against theoretical generalities. In ordinary circumstances nothing more would have come of it, but it happens that Lackington has for a lodger a young man on the staff of the local paper, and for a neighbour a pharmaceutical chemist. These three men talking things over more than once – Lackington restive under the damage that had been done to his reputation, the journalist stimulating and keen for a newspaper sensation, the chemist contributing his quota of practical knowledge. At the end of a few days a fabric of circumstance had been woven which might be serious or innocent according to the further development of the suggestion and the manner in which it could be met. These were the chief points of the attack:

"Mrs Dupreen's allowance for the care and maintenance of Charlie Winpole ceased with his death, as she had told the jury. What she did not mention was that the deceased boy would have come into an inheritance of some fifteen thousand pounds at age and that this fortune now fell in equal shares to the lot of his two nearest relatives – Mrs Dupreen and her brother Philip.

"Mrs Dupreen was by no means in easy circumstances. Philip Loudham was equally poor and had no assured income. He had tried several forms of business and now, at about thirty-five, was spending his time chiefly in writing poems and painting water-colours, none of which brought him in any money so far as one could learn.

"Philip Loudham, it was admitted, took up the food round which the tragedy centred.

"Philip Loudham was shown to be in debt and urgently in need of money. There was supposed to be a lady in the case – I hope I need say no more, Elsie."

"Who is she?" asked Mrs Bellmark with poignant interest.

"We do not know yet. A married woman, it is rumoured, I

regret to say. It scarcely matters – certainly not to you, Elsie. To continue:

"Mrs Dupreen got back from her shopping in the afternoon on the day of her nephew's death at about three o'clock. In less than half an hour Loudham left the house and going to the station took a return ticket to Euston. He left by the 3.41 and was back in St Abbots at 5.43. That would give him barely an hour in town for whatever business he transacted. What was that business?

"The chemist next door supplied the information that although bhurine only occurs in nature in this one form, it can be isolated from the other constituents of the fungus and dealt with like any other liquid poison. But it was a very exceptional commodity, having no commercial uses and probably not half a dozen retail chemists in London had it on their shelves. He himself had never stocked it and never been asked for it.

"With this suggestive but by no means convincing evidence," continued Mr Carlyle, "the young journalist went to the editor of *The Morning Indicator*, to which he acted as St Abbots correspondent and asked him whether he cared to take up the inquiry as a 'scoop'. The local trio had carried it as far as they were able. The editor of the *Indicator* decided to look into it and asked me to go on with the case. This is how my connection with it arose."

"Oh, that's how newspapers get to know things?" commented Mrs Bellmark. "I often wondered."

"It is one way," assented her uncle.

"An American development," contributed Carrados. "It is a little overdone there."

"It must be awful," said the hostess. "And the police methods! In the plays that come from the States – " The entrance of the friendly handmaiden, bringing tea, was responsible for this platitudinous wave. The conversation, in deference to Mr Carlyle's scruples, marked time until the door closed on her departure.

"My first business," continued the inquiry agent, after making himself useful at the table, "was naturally to discover among the chemists in London whether a sale of bhurine coincided with

Philip Loudham's hasty visit. If this line failed, the very founda-
tion of the edifice of hypothetical guilt gave way; if it succeeded
... Well, it did succeed. In a street off Caistor Square, Tottenham
Court Road – Trenion Street – we found a man called Lightcraft
who at once remembered making such a sale. As bhurine is a
specified poison the transaction would have to be entered, and
Lightcraft's book contained this unassailable piece of evidence.
On Wednesday, the sixth of this month, a man signing his name
as 'J. D. Williams', and giving '25 Chalcott Place' as his address,
purchased four drachms of bhurine. Lightcraft fixed the time as
about half-past four. I went to 25 Chalcott Place and found it to
be a small boarding-house. No one of the name of Williams was
known there."

If Mr Carlyle's tone of finality went for anything, Philip
Loudham was as good as pinioned. Mrs Bellmark supplied the
expected note of admiration.

"Just fancy!" was the form it took.

"Under the Act the purchaser must be known to the chemist?"
suggested Carrados.

"Yes," agreed Mr Carlyle; "and there our friend Lightcraft may
have let himself in for a little trouble. But, as he says – and we
must admit that there is something in it – who is to define what
'known to' actually means? A hundred people are known to
him as regular or occasional customers and he has never heard
their names; a score of names and addresses represent to him
regular or occasional customers whom he has never seen. This
'J. D. Williams' came in with an easy air and appeared at all
events to know Lightcraft. The face seemed not unfamiliar and
Lightcraft was perhaps a little too facile in assuming that he *did*
know him. Well, well, Max, I can understand the circumstances.
Competition is keen – especially against the private chemist
– and one may give offence and lose a customer. We must all
live.'

"Except Charlie Winpole," occurred to Max Carrados, but he
left the retort unspoken. "Did you happen to come across any
inquiry for bhurine at other shops?" he asked instead.

"No," replied Carlyle, "no, I did not. It would have been an indication then, of course, but after finding the actual place the others would have no significance. Why do you ask?"

"Oh, nothing. Only don't you think that he was rather lucky in getting it first shot if our St Abbots authority was right?"

"Yes, yes; perhaps he was. But this is of no interest to us now. The great thing is that a peculiarly sinister and deliberate murder is brought home to its perpetrator. When you consider the circumstances, upon my soul, I don't know that I have ever unmasked a more ingenious and cold-blooded ruffian."

"Then he has confessed, Uncle?"

"Confessed, my dear Elsie," said Mr Carlyle with a tolerant smile, "no, he has not confessed – men of that type never do. On the contrary, he asserted his outraged innocence with a considerable show of indignation. What else was he to do? Then he was asked to account for his movements between 4.15 and 5 o'clock on that afternoon. Egad, the fellow was so cocksure of the safety of his plans that he hadn't even taken the trouble to think that out. First he denied that he had been away from St Abbots at all. Then he remembered. He had run down to town in the afternoon for a few things. – What things? – Well, chiefly stationery. – Where had he bought it? – At a shop in Oxford Street; he did not know the name. – Would he be able to point it out? – He thought so. – Could he identify the attendant? – No, he could not remember him in the least. – Had he the bill? – No, he never kept small bills. – How much was the amount? – About three or four shillings. – And the return fare to Euston was three-and-eightpence. Was it not rather an extravagant journey? – He could only say that he did so. – Three or four shillings' worth of stationery would be a moderate parcel. Did he have it sent ? – No, he took it with him. – Three or four shillings' worth of stationery in his pocket? – No, it was in a parcel. – Too large to go in his pocket? – Yes. – Two independent witnesses would testify that he carried no parcel. They were townsmen of St Abbots who had travelled down in the same carriage with him. Did he still persist that he had been engaged in buying stationery? Then he declined to say anything further – about the best thing he could do."

"And Lightcraft identifies him?"

"Um, well, not quite so positively as we might wish. You say, a fortnight has elapsed. The man who bought the poison wore a moustache – put on, of course – but Lightcraft will say that there is a resemblance and the type of the two men the same."

"I foresee that Mr Lightcraft's accommodating memory for faces will come in for rather severe handling in cross-examination," said Carrados, as though he rather enjoyed the prospect.

"It will balance Mr Philip Loudham's unfortunate forgetfulness for localities, Max," rejoined Mr Carlyle, delivering the thrust with his own inimitable aplomb.

Carrados rose with smiling acquiescence to the shrewdness of the riposte.

"I will be quite generous, Mrs Bellmark," he observed. "I will take him away now, with the memory of that lingering in your ears – all my crushing retorts unspoken."

"Five-thirty, egad!" exclaimed Mr Carlyle, displaying his imposing gold watch. "We must – or, at all events, I must. You can think of them in the car, Max."

"I do hope you won't come to blows," murmured the lady. Then she added: "When will the real trial come on, Uncle Louis?"

"The Sessions? Oh, early in January."

"I must remember to look out for it." Possibly she had some faint idea of Uncle Louis taking a leading part in the proceedings. At any rate Mr Carlyle looked pleased, but when adieux had been taken and the door was closed Mrs Bellmark was left wondering what the enigma of Max Carrados's departing smile had been.

It was when they were in the car that Mr Carlyle suddenly remembered the suspected mushrooms and demanded to be shown them. A very moderate collection was produced for his inspection. He turned them over sceptically.

"The gills are too pale for true mushrooms, Max," he declared sapiently. "Don't take any risk. Let me pitch them out of the window?"

"No." Carrados's hand quietly arrested the threatened action.

"No; I have a use for them, Louis, but it is not culinary. You are quite right; they are rank poison. I only want to study them for . . . a case I am interested in."

"A case! You don't mean to say that there is another mushroom poisoner going?"

"No; it is the same."

"But – but you said – "

"That I did not know all about it? Quite true. Nor do I yet. But I know rather more than I did then."

"Do you mean that Scotland Yard – "

"No, Louis." Mr Carrados appeared to find something rather amusing in the situation. "I am for the other side."

"The other side! And you let me babble out the whole case for the prosecution! Well, really, Max!"

"But you are out of it now? The Public Prosecutor has taken it up?"

"True, true. But, for all that, I feel devilishly had."

"Then I will give you the whole case for the defence and so we shall be quits. In fact I am relying on you to help me with it.'

"With the defence? I – after supplying the evidence that the Public Prosecutor is acting on?"

"Why not? You don't want to hang Philip Loudham – especially if he happens to be innocent – do you?"

"I don't want to hang anyone," protested Mr Carlyle. "At least – not as a private individual."

"Quite so. Well suppose you and I between ourselves find out the actual facts of the case and decide what is to be done. The more usual course is for the prosecution to exaggerate all that tells against the accused and to contradict everything in his favour; for the defence to advance fictitious evidence of innocence and to lie roundly on everything that endangers his client; while on both sides witnesses are piled up to bemuse the jury into accepting the desired version. That does not always make for impartiality or for justice . . . Now you and I are two reasonable men, Louis – "

"I hope so," admitted Mr Carlyle. "I think so."

"You can give away the case for the prosecution and I will

expose the weakness of the defence, so, between us, we may arrive at the truth."

"It strikes me as a deuced irregular proceeding. But I am curious to hear the defence all the same."

"You are welcome to all of it that there yet is. An alibi, of course."

"Ah!" commented Mr Carlyle with expression.

"So recently as yesterday a lady came hurriedly, and with a certain amount of secrecy, to see me. She came on the strength of the introduction afforded by a mutual acquaintanceship with Fromow, the Greek professor. When we were alone she asked me – besought me, in fact – to advise her what to do. A few hours before, Mrs Dupreen had rushed across London to her with the tale of young Loudham's arrest. Then out came the whole story. This woman – well, her name is Guestling, Louis – lives a little way down in Surrey and is married. Her husband, according to her own account – and I have certainly heard a hint about it elsewhere – leads her a studiedly outrageous existence; an admired silken-mannered gentleman in society, a tolerable pole-cat at home, one infers. About a year ago Mrs Guestling made the acquaintance of Loudham, who was staying in that neighbourhood painting his pretty, unsaleable country lanes and golden sunsets. The inevitable, or, to accept the lady's protestations, half the inevitable, followed. Guestling, who adds an insatiable jealousy to his other domestic virtues, vetoed the new acquaintance and thenceforward the two met hurriedly and furtively in town. Had either of them any money they might have snatched their destinies from the hands of Fate and gone off together, but she has nothing and he has nothing and both, I suppose, are poor mortals when it comes to doing anything courageous and outright in this censorious world. So they drifted, drifting but not yet wholly wrecked."

"A formidable incentive for a weak and desperate man to secure a fortune by hook or crook, Max," said Carlyle dryly.

"That is the motive that I wish to make you a present of. But, as you will insist on your side, it is also a motive for a weak and foolish couple to steal every brief opportunity for a secret meeting. On Wednesday, the sixth, the lady was returning home from a visit to some friends in the Midlands. She saw in the occasion an opportunity, and on the morning of the sixth a message appeared in the personal columns of the *Daily Telegraph* – their usual channel of communication – making an assignation. That much can be established by the irrefutable evidence of the newspaper. Philip Loudham kept the appointment and for half an hour this miserable happy pair sat holding each other's hands in a dreary deserted waiting-room of Bishop's Road Station. That half-hour was from 4.15 to 4.45. Then Loudham saw Mrs Guestling into Praed Street Station for Victoria, returned to Euston and just caught the 5.07 St Abbots."

"Can this be corroborated – especially as regards the precise time they were together?"

"Not a word of it. They chose the waiting-room at Bishop's Road for seclusion, and apparently they got it. Not a soul even looked in while they were there.

"Then, by Jupiter, Max," exclaimed Mr Carlyle with some emotion, "you have hanged your client!"

Carrados could not restrain a smile at his friend's tragic note of triumph.

"Well, let us examine the rope," he said with his usual imperturbability.

"Here it is." It was a trivial enough shred of evidence that the inquiry agent took from his pocket-book and put into the expectant hand; in point of fact the salmon-coloured ticket of a "London General" omnibus.

"Royal Oak – the stage nearest Paddington – to Tottenham Court Road – the point nearest Trenion Street," he added significantly.

"Yes," acquiesced Carrados, taking it.

"The man who bought the bhurine dropped that ticket on the floor of the shop. He left the door open and Lightcraft followed him to close it. That is how he came to pick the ticket up, and he remembers that it was not there before. Then he threw it into a wastepaper basket underneath the counter, and that is where we found it when I called on him."

"Mr Lightcraft's memory fascinates me, Louis," was the blind man's unruffled comment. "Let us drop in and have a chat with him."

"Do you really think that there is anything more to be got in that quarter?" queried Carlyle dubiously. "I have turned him inside out, as you may be sure."

"True; but we approach Mr Lightcraft from different angles. You were looking for evidence to prove young Loudham guilty. I am looking for evidence to prove him innocent."

"Very well, Max," acquiesced his companion. "Only don't blame me if it turns out as deuced awkward for your man as Mrs G. has done. Shall I tell you what a counsel may be expected to put to the jury as the explanation of that lady's evidence?"

"No, thanks," said Carrados half sleepily from his corner. "Don't trouble; I know. I told her so."

Mr Lightcraft made no pretence of being glad to see his visitors. For some time he declined to open his mouth at all on the subject that had brought them there, repeating with parrot-like obstinacy to every remark on their part, "The matter is *sub judice*. I am unable to say anything further," until Mr Carlyle longed to box his ears and bring him to his senses. For the ears happened to be unduly prominent and at that moment glowing with sensitiveness, while the chemist was otherwise a lank and pallid man, whose transparent ivory skin and well-defined moustache gave him something of the appearance of a waxwork.

"At all events," interposed Carrados, when his friend turned from the maddening reiteration in despair, "you don't mind telling me a few things about bhurine – apart from this particular connection?"

"I am very busy," and Mr Lightcraft, with his back towards the shop, did something superfluous among the bottles on a shelf.

"I imagined that the time of Mr Max Carrados, of whom even you may possibly have heard, is as valuable as yours, my good sir," put in Mr Carlyle with scandalised dignity.

"Mr Carrados?" Lightcraft turned and regarded the blind man with interest. "I did not know. But you must recognise the unenviable position in which I am put by this gentleman's interference."

"It is his profession, you know," said Carrados mildly, "and in any case it would certainly have been someone. Why not help me to get you out of the position?"

"If the case against Philip Loudham breaks down and he is discharged at the next hearing you would not be called upon further."

"That would certainly be a mitigation. But why should it break down?"

"Suppose you let me try the taste of bhurine," suggested Carrados. "You have some left?"

"Max, Max!" cried Mr Carlyle's warning voice, "aren't you aware that the stuff is a deadly poison? One-fifth of a grain – "

"Mr Lightcraft will know how to administer it."

Apparently Mr Lightcraft did. He filled a graduated measure with cold water, dipped a slender glass rod into a bottle that was not kept on the shelves, and with it stirred the water. Then into another vessel of water he dropped a single drop of the dilution.

"One in a hundred and twenty-five thousand, Mr Carrados," he said, offering him the mixture.

Carrados just touched the liquid with his lips, considered the impression and then wiped his mouth.

"Now the smell."

The unstoppered bottle was handed to him and he took in its exhalation.

"Stewed mushrooms!" was his comment. "What is it used for, Mr Lightcraft?"

"Nothing that I know of."

"But your customer must have stated an application?"

The pallid chemist flushed a little at the recollection of that incident.

"Yes," he conceded. "There is a good deal about the whole business that is still a mystery to me. The man came in shortly after I had lit up and nodded familiarly as he said: 'Good evening, Mr Lightcraft.' I naturally assumed that he was someone whom I could not quite place. 'I want another half-pound of nitre,' he said and I served him. Had he bought nitre before, I have since tried to recall, but I cannot. It is a common enough article and I sell it, you might say, every day. I have a poor memory for faces I am willing to admit. It has hampered me in business many a time: people expect you to remember them. We chatted about nothing in particular as I did up the packet. After he had paid and turned to go he looked back again. 'By the way, do you happen to have any bhurine?' he inquired. Unfortunately I had a few ounces. 'Of course you know its nature?' I cautioned him. 'May I ask what you require it for?' He nodded and held up the parcel of nitre he had in his hand. 'The same thing,' he replied, 'taxidermy.' Then I supplied him with half-an-ounce."

"As a matter of fact, is it used in taxidermy?"

"It does not seem to be. I don't stuff birds but I have made inquiries and no one knows of it. Nitre is largely used, and some of the dangerous poisons – arsenic and mercuric chloride, for instance – but not this although it might quite reasonably have been. No, it was a subterfuge.'

"Now the poison book, if you please."

Mr Lightcraft produced it without demur and the blind man ran his finger along the indicated line.

"Yes; this is quite in form. Is it a fact, Mr Lightcraft, that not half a dozen chemists in London stock this particular substance? We are told that."

"I can quite believe it. I certainly don't know of another."

"Strangely enough, your customer of the sixth seems to have come straight here. Do you issue a price-list?"

"Only a localised one of certain photographic goods. Bhurine is not included."

"You can suggest no reason why Mr Philip Loudham should be inspired to presume that he might be able to get this unusual drug from you? You have never corresponded with him nor come across his name or address before?"

"No. As far as I can recollect, I know nothing whatever of him."

"Then as yet we must assume that it was pure chance. By the way, Mr Lightcraft, how does it come that *you* stock this rare poison, which has no commercial use and for which there is no demand?"

The chemist permitted himself to smile at the blunt terms of the inquiry.

"In the ordinary way I don't stock it," he replied. "This is a small quantity that I had over from my own use."

"Your own use? Oh, then it has a use after all?"

"No, scarcely that. Some time ago it leaked out in a corner of the photographic world that a great revolution in colour-photography was on the point of realisation by the use of bhurine in one of the processes. I, among others, at once took it up. Unfortunately it was only another instance of a discovery that is correct in theory breaking down in practice. Nothing came of it."

"Dear, dear me," said Carrados softly, with sympathetic understanding in his voice; "what a pity. You are interested in photography, Mr Lightcraft?"

"It is the hobby of my life, sir. Of course most chemists dabble in it as a part of their business, but I devote all my spare time to experimenting. Colour-photography in particular."

"Colour-photography. Yes, it has a great future. This bhurine process – I suppose it would have been of considerable financial value if it had worked?"

Mr Lightcraft laughed quietly and rubbed his hands together. For the moment he had forgotten Loudham and the annoying case and lived in his enthusiasm.

"I should rather say it would, Mr Carrados," he replied. "It would have been the most epoch-making thing since Gaudin produced the first dry plate in '54. Consider it – the elaborate processes of Dyndale, Eiloff and Jupp reduced to the simplicity of a single contact print giving the entire range of chromatic variation. Financially it – it will scarcely bear thinking about in these times."

"Was it widely taken up?" asked Carrados.

"The bhurine idea?"

"Yes. You spoke of the secret leaking out. Were many in the know?"

"Not at all. The group of initiates was only a small one and I should imagine that, on reflection, every man kept it to himself. It certainly never became public. Then when the theory was definitely exploded of course no one took any further interest in it."

"Were all who were working on the same lines known to you, Mr Lightcraft?"

"Well, yes; more or less I suppose they would be," said the chemist thoughtfully. "You see, the man who stumbled on the formula was a member of the Iris – a society of those interested in this subject, of which I am the secretary – and I don't think it ever got beyond the committee."

"How long ago was this?"

"A year – eighteen months. It led to unpleasantness and broke up the society."

"Suppose it happened to come to your knowledge that one of the original circle was quietly pursuing his experiments on the same lines with bhurine – what should you infer from it?"

Mr Lightcraft considered. Then he regarded Carrados with a sharp, almost startled, glance and then he fell to biting his nails in perplexed uncertainty.

"It would depend on who it was," he replied.

"Was there by any chance one who was unknown to you by sight but whose address you were familiar with?"

"Paulden!" exclaimed Mr Lightcraft. "Paulden by heaven! I do believe you're right. He was the ablest of the lot and he never came to the meetings – a corresponding member. Southem, the original man who struck the idea, knew Paulden and told him of it. Southem was an impractical genius who would never be able to make anything work. Paulden – yes, Paulden it was who finally persuaded Southem that there was nothing in it. He sent a report to the same effect to be read at one of the meetings. So Paulden is taking up bhurine again – "

"Where does he live?" inquired Carrados.

"Ivor House, Wilmington Lane, Enstead. As secretary I have written there a score of times."

"It is on the Great Western–Paddington," commented the

blind man. "Still, can you get out the addresses of the others, Mr Lightcraft?"

"Certainly, certainly. I have the book of membership. But I am convinced now that Paulden was the man. I believe that I did actually see him once some years ago, but he has grown a moustache since."

"If you had been convinced of that a few days ago it would have saved us some awkwardness," volunteered Mr Carlyle, with no little asperity.

"When you came before, Mr Carlyle, you were so convinced yourself of it being Mr Loudham that you wouldn't hear of me thinking of anyone else," retorted the chemist. "You will bear me out also that I never positively identified him as my customer. Now here is the book. Southem, Potter's Bar. Voynich, Islington. Crawford, Streatham Hill. Brown, Southampton Row. Vickers, Clapham Common. Tidey, Fulham. All those I knew quite well – associated with them week after week. Williams I didn't know so closely. He is dead. Bigwood has gone to Canada. I don't think anyone else was in the bhurine craze – as we called it afterwards."

"But now? What would you call it now?" queried Carrados.

"Now? Well I hope that you will get me out of having to turn up at court and that sort of thing, Mr Carrados. If Paulden is going on experimenting with bhurine again on the sly I shall want all my spare time to do the same myself!"

A few hours later the two investigators rang the bell of a substantial detached house in Enstead, the little country town twenty miles out in Berkshire, and asked to see Mr Paulden.

"It is no good taking Lightcraft to identify the man," Carrados had decided. "If Paulden denied it, our friend's obliging record in that line would put him out of court."

"I maintain an open mind on the subject," Carlyle had replied. "Lightcraft is admittedly a very bending reed, but there is no reason why he should not have been right before and wrong today."

They were shown into a ceremonial reception-room to wait. Mr Carlyle diagnosed snug circumstances and the tastes of an in-doors, comfort-loving man in the surroundings.

The door opened, but it was to admit a middle-aged, matronly lady with good humour and domestic capability proclaimed by every detail of her smiling face and easy manner.

"You wished to see my husband?" she asked with friendly courtesy.

"Mr Paulden? Yes, we should like to," replied Carlyle, with his most responsive urbanity. "It is a matter that need not occupy more than a few minutes."

"He is very busy just now. If it has anything to do with the election" – a local contest was at its height – "he is not interested in politics and scarcely ever votes." Her manner was not curious, but merely reflected a business-like desire to save trouble all round.

"Very sensible, too; ve-ry sensible indeed," almost warbled Mr Carlyle with instinctive cajolery. "After all," he continued, mendaciously appropriating as his own an aphorism at which he had laughed heartily a few days before in the theatre, "after all, what does an election do but change the colour of the necktie of the man who picks our pockets? No, no, Mrs Paulden, it is merely a – um – quite personal matter."

The lady looked from one to the other with smiling amiability.

"Some little mystery," her expression seemed to say. "All right; I don't mind, only perhaps I could help you if I knew."

"Mr Paulden is in his dark-room now," was what she actually did say. "I am afraid, I am really afraid that I shan't be able to persuade him to come out unless I can take a definite message."

"One understands the difficulty of tempting an enthusiast from his work," suggested Carrados, speaking for the first time. "Would it be permissible to take us to the door of the dark-room, Mrs Paulden, and let us speak to your husband through it?"

"We can try that way," she acquiesced readily, "if it is really so important."

"I think so," he replied.

The dark-room lay across the hall. Mrs Paulden conducted them to the door, waited a moment, and then knocked quietly.

"Yes?" sang out a voice, rather irritably one might judge, from inside.

"Two gentlemen have called to see you about something, Lance – "

"I cannot see anyone when I am in here," interrupted the voice with rising sharpness. "You know that, Clara – "

"Yes, dear," she said soothingly, "but listen. They are at the door here and if you can spare the time just to come and speak you will know without much trouble if their business is as important as they think."

"Wait a minute," came the reply after a moment's pause, and then they heard someone approach the door from the other side.

It was a little difficult to know exactly how it happened in the obscure light of that corner of the hall. Carrados had stepped nearer to the door to speak. Possibly he trod on Mr Carlyle's toe, for there was a confused movement; certainly he put out his hand hastily to recover himself. The next moment the door of the dark-room jerked open, the light was let in and the warm odours of a mixed and vitiated atmosphere rolled out. Secure in the well-ordered discipline of his excellent household, Mr Paulden had neglected the precaution of locking himself in.

"Confound it all!" shouted the incensed experimenter in a towering rage; "confound it all, you've spoiled the whole thing now!"

"Dear me," apologised Carrados penitently, "I am so sorry. I think it must have been my fault, do you know. Does it really matter?"

"Matter!" stormed Mr Paulden, recklessly flinging open the door fully now to come face to face with his disturbers – "matter letting a flood of light into a dark-room in the middle of a delicate experiment!"

"Surely it was very little," persisted Carrados.

"Pshaw," snarled the angry photographer, "it was enough. You know the difference between light and dark, I suppose?"

Mr Carlyle suddenly found himself holding his breath, won-

dering how on earth Max had conjured that opportune challenge
to the surface.

"No," was the mild and deprecating reply – the appeal *ad
misericordiam* that had never failed him yet – "no, unfortunately I
don't, for I am blind. That is why I am so awkward."

Out of the shocked silence Mrs Paulden gave a little croon of
pity. The moment before she had been speechless with indignation on her husband's behalf. Paulden felt as though he had struck
a suffering animal. He stammered an apology and turned away to
close the unfortunate door. Then he began to walk slowly down
the hall.

"You wished to see me about something?" he remarked, with
matter-of-fact civility. "Perhaps we had better go in here." He
indicated the reception-room where they had waited and followed them in. The admirable Mrs Paulden gave no indication of
wishing to join the party.

Carrados came to the point at once.

"Mr Carlyle," he said, indicating his friend, "has recently been
acting for the prosecution in a case of alleged poisoning that the
Public Prosecutor has now taken up. I am interested in the
defence. Both sides are thus before you, Mr Paulden."

"How does this concern me?" asked Paulden with obvious
surprise.

"You are experimenting with bhurine. The victim of this
alleged crime undoubtedly lost his life by bhurine poisoning. Do
you mind telling us when and where you acquired your stock of
this scarce substance?"

"I have had – "

"No – a moment, Mr Paulden, before you reply," struck in
Carrados with a warning gesture. "You must understand that
nothing so grotesque as to connect you with a crime is con-
templated. But a man is under arrest and the chief point against
him is the half-ounce of bhurine that Lightcraft of Trenion Street
sold to someone at half-past four last Wednesday fortnight.
Before you commit yourself to any statement that it may possibly
be difficult to recede from, you should realise that this inquiry
will be pushed to the very end."

"How do you know that I am using bhurine?"

"That," parried Carrados, "is a blind man's secret."

"Oh, well. And you say that someone has been arrested through this fact?"

"Yes. Possibly you have read something of the St Abbots mushroom poisoning case?"

"I have no interest in the sensational ephemera of the Press. Very well; it was I who bought the bhurine from Lightcraft that Wednesday afternoon. I gave a false name and address, I must admit. I had a sufficient private reason for so doing."

"This knocks what is vulgarly termed 'the stuffing' out of the case for the prosecution," observed Carlyle, who had been taking a note. "It may also involve you in some trouble yourself, Mr Paulden."

"I don't think that he need regard that very seriously in the circumstances," said Carrados reassuringly.

"They must find some scapegoat, you know," persisted Mr Carlyle. "Loudham will raise Cain over it."

"I don't think so. Loudham, as the prosecution will roundly tell him, has only himself to thank for not giving a satisfactory account of his movements. Loudham will be lectured, Lightcraft will be fined the minimum, and Mr Paulden will, I imagine, be virtuously told not to do it again."

The man before them laughed bitterly.

"There will be no occasion to do it again," he said. "Do you know anything of the circumstances?"

"Lightcraft told us something connected with colour-photography. You distrust Mr Lightcraft, I infer?"

Mr Paulden came down to the heart-easing medium of the street.

"I've had some once, thanks," was what he said with terse expression. "Let me tell you. About eighteen months ago I was on the edge of a great discovery in colour-photography. It was my discovery, whatever you may have heard. Bhurine was the medium, and not being then so cautious or so suspicious as I have reason to be now, and finding it difficult – really impossible – to procure this substance casually, I sent in an order to Lightcraft to procure me a stock. Unfortunately, in a moment of enthusiasm I had hinted at the anticipated results to a man who was then my friend – a weakling called Southem. Comparing notes with Lightcraft they put two and two together and in a trice most of the secret boiled over.

"If you have ever been within an ace of a monumental discovery you will understand the torment of anxiety and self-reproach that possessed me. For months the result must have trembled in the balance, but even as it evaded me so it evaded the others. And at last I was able to spread conviction that the bhurine process was a failure. I breathed again.

"You don't want to hear of the various things that conspired to baffle me. I proceeded with extreme caution and therefore slowly. About two weeks ago I had another foretaste of success and immediately on it a veritable disaster. By some diabolical mischance I contrived to upset my bottle of bhurine. It rolled down, smashed to atoms on a developing dish filled with another chemical, and the precious lot was irretrievably lost. To arrest the experiments at that stage even for a day was to waste a month. In one place and one alone could I hope to replenish the stock temporarily at such short notice and to do it openly after my last experience filled me with dismay . . . Well, you know what happened, and now, I suppose, it will all come out."

A week after his arrest Philip Loudham and his sister were sitting in the drawing-room at Hazlehurst, nervous and expectant. Loudham had been discharged scarcely six hours before, with such vindication of his character as the frigid intimation that there was no evidence against him afforded. On his arrival home he had found a letter from Max Carrados – a name with which he was now familiar – awaiting him. There had been other notes and telegrams – messages of sympathy and congratulation, but the man who had brought about his liberation did not include these conventionalities. He merely stated that he purposed calling upon Mr Loudham at nine o'clock that evening and that he hoped it would be convenient for him and all other members of the household to be at home.

"He can scarcely be coming to be thanked," speculated Loudham, breaking the silence that had fallen on them as the hour approached. "I should have called on him myself to-morrow."

Mrs Dupreen assented absent-mindedly. Both were dressed in black, and both at that moment had the same thought: that they were dreaming this.

"I suppose you won't go on living here, Irene?" continued the brother, speaking to make the minutes seem tolerable.

This at least had the effect of bringing Mrs Dupreen back into the present with a rush.

"Of course not," she replied almost sharply and looking at him direct. "Why should I, now?"

"Oh, all right," he agreed. "I didn't suppose you would." Then, as the front-door bell was heard to ring: "Thank heaven!"

"Won't you go to meet him in the hall and bring him in?" suggested Mrs Dupreen. "He is blind, you know."

Carrados was carrying a small leather case which he allowed Loudham to relieve him of, together with his hat and gloves. The introduction to Mrs Dupreen was made, the blind man put in touch with a chair, and then Philip Loudham began to rattle off the acknowledgment of gratitude for which he had been framing and rejecting openings for the last half-hour.

"I'm afraid it's no good attempting to thank you for the extra-ordinary service that you've rendered me, Mr Carrados," he began, "and, above all I appreciate the fact that, owing to you, it has been possible to keep Mrs Guestling's name entirely out of the case. Of course you know all about that, and my sister knows, so it isn't worth while beating about the bush. Well, now that I shall have something like a decent income of my own, I shall urge Kitty – Mrs Guestling – to apply for the divorce that she is richly entitled to, and when that is all settled we shall marry at once and try to forget the experience on both sides that has led up to it. I hope," he added tamely, "that you don't consider us really much to blame?"

Carrados shook his head in mild depreciation.

"That is an ethical point that has lain outside the scope of my inquiry," he replied. "You would hardly imagine that I should disturb you at such a time merely to claim your thanks. Has it occurred to you why I should have come?"

Brother and sister exchanged looks and by their silence gave reply.

"We have still to find who poisoned Charlie Winpole."

Loudham stared at their guest in frank bewilderment, Mrs Dupreen almost closed her eyes. When she spoke it was in a pained whisper.

"Is there anything more to be gained by pursuing that idea, Mr Carrados?" she asked pleadingly. "We have passed through a week of anguish, coming on a week of grief and great distress. Surely all has been done that can be done?"

"But you would have justice for your nephew if there has been foul play?"

Mrs Dupreen made a weary gesture of resignation. It was Loudham who took up the question.

'Do you really mean, Mr Carrados, that there is any doubt about the cause?"

"Will you give me my case please? Thank you." He opened it and produced a small paper bag. "Now a newspaper, if you will." He opened the bag and poured out the contents. "You remember stating at the inquest, Mrs Dupreen, that the mushrooms you bought looked rather dry? They were dry, there is no doubt, for they had been gathered four days. Here are some more under precisely the same conditions. They looked, in point of fact, like these?"

"Yes," admitted the lady, beginning to regard Carrados with a new and curious interest.

"Dr Slark further stated that the only fungus containing the poison bhurine – the *Amanita* called the Black Cap, and also by the country folk the Devil's Scent Bottle – did not assume its forbidding appearance until maturity. He was wrong in one sense there, for experiment proves that if the Black Cap is gathered in its young and deceptive stage and kept, it assumes precisely the same appearance as it withers as if it was ripening naturally. You observe." He opened a second bag and, shaking out the contents, displayed another little heap by the side of the first. "Gathered four days ago," he explained.

"Why, they are as black as ink," commented Loudham. "And the, phew! aroma!"

"One would hardly have got through without your seeing it, Mrs Dupreen?"

"I certainly hardly think so," she admitted.

"With due allowance for Lackington's biased opinion I also think that his claim might be allowed. Finally, it is incredible that whoever peeled the mushrooms should have passed one of these. Who was the cook on that occasion, Mrs Dupreen?"

"My maid Hilda. She does all the cooking."

"The one who admitted me?"

"Yes; she is the only servant I have, Mr Carrados."

"I should like to have her in, if you don't mind."

"Certainly, if you wish it. She is" – Mrs Dupreen felt that she must put in a favourable word before this inexorable man pronounced judgment – "she is a very good, straightforward girl."

"So much the better."

"I will – " Mrs Dupreen rose and began to cross the room.

"Ring for her? Thank you," and whatever her intention had been the lady rang the bell.

"Yes, ma'am?"

A neat, modest-mannered girl, simple and nervous, with a face as full, as clear and as honest as an English apple. "A pity," thought Mrs Dupreen, "that this confident, suspicious man cannot see her now."

"Come in, Hilda. This gentleman wants to ask you something."

"Yes, ma'am." The round, blue eyes went appealingly to Carrados, fell upon the fungi spread out before her, and then circled the room with an instinct of escape.

"You remember the night poor Charlie died, Hilda," said Carrados in his suavest tone, "you cooked some mushrooms for his supper, didn't you?"

"No, sir," came the glib reply.

" 'No,' Hilda!" exclaimed Mrs Dupreen in wonderment. "You mean 'yes' surely, child. Of course you cooked them. Don't you remember?"

"Yes, ma'am," dutifully replied Hilda.

"That is all right," said the blind man reassuringly. "Nervous witnesses very often answer at random at first. You have nothing to be afraid of, my good girl, if you will tell the truth. I suppose you know a mushroom when you see it?"

"Yes, sir," was the rather hesitating reply.

"There was nothing like this among them?" He held up one of the poisonous sort.

"No, sir; indeed there wasn't, sir. I should have known then.'

"You would have known *then*? You were not called at the inquest, Hilda?"

"No, sir."

"If you had been, what would you have told them about these mushrooms that you cooked?"

"I – I don't know, sir."

"Come, come, Hilda. What could you have told them – something that we do not know? The truth, girl, if you want to save yourself!" Then with a sudden, terrible directness the question cleft her trembling, guilt-stricken little brain: "Where did you get the other mushrooms from, that you put with those that your mistress brought?"

The eyes that had been mostly riveted to the floor leapt to Carrados for a single frightened glance, from Carrados to her mistress, to Philip Loudham, and to the floor again. In a moment her face changed and she was in a burst of sobbing.

"Oho, oho, oho!" she wailed. "I didn't know; I didn't know. I meant no harm. Indeed, I didn't, ma'am."

"Hilda! Hilda!" exclaimed Mrs Dupreen in bewilderment. "What is it you're saying? What have you done?"

"It was his own fault. Oho, oho, oho!" Every word was punctuated by a gasp. "He always was a little pig and making himself ill with food. You know he was, ma'am, although you were so fond of him. I'm sure I'm not to blame."

"But *what* was it? What *have* you done?" besought her mistress.

"It was after you went out that afternoon. He put on his things and slipped down into the kitchen without the master knowing. He said what you were getting for his dinner, ma'am, and that you never got enough of them. Then he asked me not to tell about his being down, because he'd seen some white things from his bedroom window growing by the hedge at the bottom of the garden and he was going to get them. He brought in four or five and said they were mushrooms all right and would I cook them with the others and not say anything because you'd only say too many weren't good for him if you knew. And I didn't know any difference. Indeed I'm telling you the truth, ma'am."

"Oh, Hilda, Hilda!" was torn reproachfully from Mrs Dupreen. "You know what we've gone through. Why didn't you tell us this before?"

"I was afraid. I was afraid of what they'd do. And no one ever guessed until I thought I was safe. Indeed I meant no harm to anyone, but I was afraid that they'd punish me instead."

Carrados had risen and was picking up his things.

"Yes," he said, half musing to himself, "I knew it must exist: the one explanation that accounts for everything and cannot be assailed. We have reached the bed-rock of truth at last."

The Speckled Band

A Sherlock Holmes Story

SIR ARTHUR CONAN DOYLE

In glancing over my notes of the seventy-odd cases in which I have during the last eight years studied the methods of my friend Sherlock Holmes, I find many tragic, some comic, a large number merely strange, but none commonplace; for, working as he did rather for the love of his art than for the acquirement of wealth, he refused to associate himself with any investigation which did not tend towards the unusual, and even the fantastic. Of all these varied cases, however, I cannot recall any which presented more singular features than that which was associated with the well-known Surrey family of the Roylotts of Stoke Moran. The events in question occurred in the early days of my association with Holmes, when we were sharing rooms as bachelors, in Baker Street. It is possible that I might have placed them upon record before, but a promise of secrecy was made at the time, from which I have only been freed during the last month by the untimely death of the lady to whom the pledge was given. It is perhaps as well that the facts should now come to light, for I have reasons to know there are widespread rumours as to the death of Dr Grimesby Roylott which tend to make the matter even more terrible than the truth.

It was early in April, in the year '83, that I woke one morning to find Sherlock Holmes standing, fully dressed, by the side of my bed. He was a late riser as a rule, and, as the clock on the mantelpiece showed me that it was only a quarter past seven, I blinked up at him in some surprise, and perhaps just a little resentment, for I was myself regular in my habits.

"Very sorry to knock you up, Watson," said he, "but it's the common lot this morning. Mrs Hudson has been knocked up, she retorted upon me, and I on you."

"What is it, then? A fire?"

"No, a client. It seems that a young lady has arrived in a considerable state of excitement, who insists upon seeing me. She is waiting now in the sitting-room. Now, when young ladies wander about the metropolis at this hour of the morning, and knock sleepy people up out of their beds, I presume that it is something very pressing which they have to communicate. Should it prove to be an interesting case, you would, I am sure, wish to follow it from the outset. I thought at any rate that I should call you, and give you the chance."

"My dear fellow, I would not miss it for anything."

I had no keener pleasure than in following Holmes in his professional investigations, and in admiring the rapid deductions, as swift as intuitions, and yet always founded on a logical basis, with which he unravelled the problems which were submitted to him. I rapidly threw on my clothes, and was ready in a few minutes to accompany my friend down to the sitting-room. A lady dressed in black and heavily veiled, who had been sitting in the window, rose as we entered.

"Good morning, madam," said Holmes cheerily. "My name is Sherlock Holmes. This is my intimate friend and associate, Dr Watson, before whom you can speak as freely as before myself. Ha, I am glad to see that Mrs Hudson has had the good sense to light the fire. Pray draw up to it, and I shall order you a cup of hot coffee, for I observe that you are shivering!"

"It is not cold which makes me shiver," said the woman in a low voice, changing her seat as requested.

"What then?"

"It is fear, Mr Holmes. It is terror." She raised her veil as she spoke, and we could see that she was indeed in a pitiable state of agitation, her face all drawn and grey, with restless frightened eyes, like those of some hunted animal. Her features and figure were those of a woman of thirty, but her hair was shot with premature grey, and her expression was weary and haggard.

Sherlock Holmes ran her over with one of his quick, all-comprehensive glances.

"You must not fear," said he soothingly, bending forward and patting her forearm. "We shall soon set matters right, I have no doubt. You have come in by train this morning, I see."

"You know me, then?"

"No, but I observe the second half of a return ticket in the palm of your left glove. You must have started early, and yet you had a good drive in a dog-cart, along heavy roads, before you reached the station."

The lady gave a violent start, and stared in bewilderment at my companion.

"There is no mystery, my dear madam," said he, smiling. "The left arm of your jacket is spattered with mud in no less than seven places. The marks are perfectly fresh. There is no vehicle save a dog-cart which throws up mud in that way, and then only when you sit on the left-hand side of the driver."

"Whatever your reasons may be, you are perfectly correct," said she. "I started from home before six, reached Leatherhead at twenty past, and came in by the first train to Waterloo. Sir, I can stand this strain no longer, I shall go mad if it continues. I have no one to turn to – none, save only one, who cares for me, and he, poor fellow, can be of little aid. I have heard of you, Mr Holmes; I have heard of you from Mrs Farintosh, whom you helped in the hour of her sore need. It was from her that I had your address. Oh, sir, do you not think you could help me too, and at least throw a little light through the dense darkness which surrounds me? At present it is out of my power to reward you your services, but in a month or two I shall be married, with the control of my own income and then at least you shall not find me ungrateful."

Holmes turned to his desk, and unlocking it, drew out a small case-book which he consulted.

"Farintosh," said he. "Ah, yes, I recall the case; it was concerned with an opal tiara. I think it was before your time, Watson. I can only say, madam, that I shall be happy to devote the same care to your case as I did to that of your friend. As to reward, my profession is its reward; but you are at liberty to defray whatever expenses I may be put to, at the time which suits you best. And now I beg that you will lay before us everything that may help us in forming an opinion upon the matter."

"Alas!" replied our visitor. "The very horror of my situation lies in the fact that my fears are so vague, and my suspicions depend so entirely upon small points, which might seem trivial to another, that even he to whom of all others I have a right to look for help and advice looks upon all that I tell him about it as the fancies of a nervous woman. He does not say so, but I can read it from his soothing answers and averted eyes. But I have heard, Mr Holmes, that you can see deeply into the manifold wickedness of the human heart. You may advise me how to walk amid the dangers which encompass me."

"I am all attention, madam."

"My name is Helen Stoner, and I am living with my stepfather, who is the last survivor of one of the oldest Saxon families in England, the Roylotts of Stoke Moran, on the western border of Surrey."

Holmes nodded his head. "The name is familiar to me," said he.

"The family was at one time among the richest in England, and the estate extended over the borders into Berkshire in the north and Hampshire in the west. In the last century, however, four successive heirs were of a dissolute and wasteful disposition, and the family ruin was eventually completed by a gambler, in the days of the Regency. Nothing was left save a few acres of ground and the two-hundred-year-old house, which is itself crushed under a heavy mortgage. The last squire dragged out his existence there, living the horrible life of an aristocratic pauper; but his only son, my step father, seeing that he must adapt himself to the new conditions, obtained an advance from a relative, which enabled him to take a medical degree, and went out to Calcutta, where, by his professional skill and his force of character, he established a large practice. In a fit of anger, however, caused by some robberies which had been perpetrated in the house, he beat his native butler to death, and narrowly escaped a capital sentence. As it was, he suffered a long term of imprisonment, and afterwards returned to England a morose and disappointed man.

"When Dr Roylott was in India he married my mother, Mrs Stoner, the young widow of Major-General Stoner, of the Bengal Artillery. My sister Julia and I were twins, and we were only two years old at the time of my mother's re-marriage. She had a considerable sum of money, not less than a thousand a year, and this she bequeathed to Dr Roylott entirely whilst we resided with him, with a provision that a certain annual sum should be allowed to each of us in the event of our marriage. Shortly after our return to England my mother died – she was killed eight years ago in a railway accident near Crewe. Dr Roylott then abandoned his attempts to establish himself in practice in London, and took us to live with him in the ancestral house at Stoke Moran. The money which my mother had left was enough for all our wants, and there seemed no obstacle to our happiness.

"But a terrible change came over our stepfather about this time. Instead of making friends and exchanging visits with our neighbours, who had at first been overjoyed to see a Roylott of Stoke Moran back in the old family seat, he shut himself up in his house, and seldom came out save to indulge in ferocious quarrels with whoever might cross his path. Violence of temper approaching to mania has been hereditary in the men of the family, and in my stepfather's case it had, I believe, been intensified by his long residence in the tropics. A series of disgraceful brawls took place, two of which ended in the police-court, until at last he became the terror of the village, and the folks would fly at his approach, for he is a man of immense strength, and absolutely uncontrollable in his anger.

"Last week he hurled the local blacksmith over a parapet into a stream and it was only by paying over all the money that I could gather together that I was able to avert another public exposure. He had no friends at all save the wandering gipsies, and he would give these vagabonds leave to encamp upon the few acres of bramble-covered land which represent the family estate, and would accept in return the hospitality of their tents, wandering away with them sometimes for weeks on end. He has a passion also for Indian animals, which are sent over to him by a correspondent, and he has at this moment a cheetah and a baboon, which wander freely over his grounds, and are feared by the villagers almost as much as their master.

"You can imagine from what I say that my poor sister Julia and I had no great pleasure in our lives. No servant would stay with us, and for a long time we did all the work of the house. She was but thirty at the time of her death, and yet her hair had already begun to whiten, even as mine has."

"Your sister is dead, then?"

"She died just two years ago, and it is of her death that I wish to speak to you. You can understand that, living the life which I have described, we were little likely to see anyone of our own age and position. We had, however, an aunt, my mother's maiden sister, Miss Honoria Westphail, who lives near Harrow, and we were occasionally allowed to pay short visits at this lady's house. Julia went there at Christmas two years ago, and met there a half-pay Major of Marines, to whom she became engaged. My stepfather learned of the engagement when my sister returned, and offered no objection to the marriage; but within a fortnight of the day which had been fixed for the wedding, the terrible event occurred which has deprived me of my only companion."

Sherlock Holmes had been leaning back in his chair with his eyes closed, and his head sunk in a cushion, but he half opened his lids now, and glanced across at his visitor.

"Pray be precise as to details," said he.

"It is easy for me to be so, for every event of that dreadful time is seared into my memory. The manor house is, as I have already said, very old, and only one wing is now inhabited. The bedrooms in this wing are on the ground floor, the sitting-rooms being in the central block of the buildings. Of these bedrooms, the first is Dr Roylott's, the second my sister's, and the third my own. There is no communication between them, but they all open out into the same corridor. Do I make myself plain?"

"Perfectly so."

"The windows of the three rooms open out upon the lawn.

That fatal night Dr Roylott had gone to his room early, though we knew that he had not retired to rest, for my sister was troubled by the smell of the strong Indian cigars which it was his custom to smoke. She left her room, therefore, and came into mine, where she sat for some time, chatting about her approaching wedding. At eleven o'clock she rose to leave me, but she paused at the door and looked back.

" 'Tell me, Helen,' said she, 'have you ever heard anyone whistle in the dead of the night?'

" 'Never,' said I.

" 'I suppose that you could not possibly whistle yourself in your sleep?'

" 'Certainly not. But why?'

" 'Because during the last few nights I have always, about three in the morning, heard a low clear whistle. I am a light sleeper, and it has awakened me. I cannot tell where it came from — perhaps from the next room, perhaps from the lawn. I thought that I would just ask you whether you had heard it.'

" 'No, I have not. It must be those wretched gipsies in the plantation.'

" 'Very likely. And yet if it were on the lawn I wonder that you did not hear it also.'

" 'Ah, but I sleep more heavily than you.'

" 'Well, it is of no great consequence, at any rate,' she smiled back at me, closed my door, and a few moments later I heard her key turn in her lock."

"Indeed," said Holmes. "Was it your custom always to lock yourselves in at night?"

"Always."

"And why?"

"I think that I mentioned to you that the doctor kept a cheetah and a baboon. We had no feeling of security unless our doors were locked."

"Quite so. Pray proceed with your statement."

"I could not sleep that night. A vague feeling of impending misfortune impressed me. My sister and I, you will recollect, were twins, and you know how subtle are the links which bind two souls which are so closely allied. It was a wild night. The wind was howling outside, and the rain was beating and splashing against the windows. Suddenly, amidst all the hubbub of the gale, there burst forth the wild scream of a terrified woman. I knew that it was my sister's voice. I sprang from my bed, wrapped a shawl round me, and rushed into the corridor. As I opened my door I seemed to hear a low whistle, such as my sister described, a few moments later a clanging sound, as if a mass of metal had fallen. As I ran down the passage my sister's door was unlocked, and revolved slowly upon its hinges. I stared at it horror-stricken, not knowing what was about to issue from it. By the light of the corridor lamp I saw my sister appear at the opening, her face blanched with terror, her hands groping for help, her whole figure swaying to and fro like that of a drunkard. I ran to her and threw my arms round her, but at that moment her knees seemed to give way and she fell to the ground. She writhed as one who is in terrible pain, and her limbs were dreadfully convulsed. At first I thought that she had not recognised me, but as I bent over her she suddenly shrieked out in a voice which I shall never forget, 'Oh, my God! Helen! It was the band! The speckled band!' There was something else which she would fain have said, and she stabbed with her finger into the air in the direction of the doctor's room, but a fresh convulsion seized her and choked her words. I rushed out, calling loudly for my stepfather, and I met him hastening from his room in his dressing-gown. When he reached my sister's side she was unconscious, and though he poured brandy down her throat, and sent for medical aid from the village, all efforts were in vain, for she slowly sank and died without having recovered her consciousness. Such was the dreadful end of my beloved sister."

"One moment," said Holmes; "are you sure about this whistle and metallic sound? Could you swear to it?"

"That was what the county coroner asked me at the inquiry. It is my strong impression that I heard it, and yet among the crash of the gale, and the creaking of an old house, I may possibly have been deceived."

"Was your sister dressed?"

"No, she was in her nightdress. In her right hand was found the charred stump of a match, and in her left a matchbox."

"Showing that she had struck a light and looked about her when the alarm took place. That is important. And what conclusions did the coroner come to?"

"He investigated the case with great care, for Dr Roylott's conduct had long been notorious in the county, but he was unable to find any satisfactory cause of death. My evidence showed that the door had been fastened upon the inner side, and the windows were blocked by old-fashioned shutters with broad iron bars, which were secured every night. The walls were carefully sounded, and were shown to be quite solid all round, and the flooring was also thoroughly examined, with the same result. The chimney is wide, but is barred up by four large staples. It is certain, therefore, that my sister was quite alone when she met her end. Besides, there were no marks of any violence upon her."

"How about poison?"

"The doctors examined her for it, but without success."

"What do you think that this unfortunate lady died of, then?"

"It is my belief that she died of pure fear and nervous shock, though what it was which frightened her I cannot imagine."

"Were there gipsies in the plantation at the time?"

"Yes, there are nearly always some there."

"Ah, and what did you gather from this allusion to a band – a speckled band?"

"Sometimes I have thought that it was merely the wild talk of delirium, sometimes that it may have referred to some band of people, perhaps to these very gipsies in the plantation. I do not know whether the spotted handkerchiefs which so many of them wear over their heads might have suggested the strange adjective which she used."

Holmes shook his head like a man who is far from being satisfied.

"These are very deep waters," said he; "pray go on with your narrative."

"Two years have passed since then, and my life has been until lately lonelier than ever. A month ago, however, a dear friend, whom I have known for many years, has done me the honour to ask my hand in marriage. His name is Armitage – Percy Armitage – the second son of Mr Armitage, of Crane Water, near Reading. My stepfather has offered no opposition to the match, and we are to be married in the course of the spring. Two days ago some repairs were started in the west wing of the building, and my bedroom wall has been pierced, so that I have had to move into the chamber in which my sister died, and to sleep in the very bed in which she slept. Imagine, then, my thrill of terror when last night, as I lay awake, thinking over her terrible fate, I suddenly heard in the silence of the night the low whistle which had been the herald of her own death. I sprang up and lit the lamp, but nothing was to be seen in the room. I was too shaken to go to bed again, however, so I dressed and as soon as it was daylight I slipped down, got a dog-cart at the Crown Inn, which is opposite, and drove to Leatherhead, from whence I have come on this morning, with the one object of seeing you and asking your advice."

"You have done wisely," said my friend. "But have you told me all?"

"Yes, all."

"Miss Stoner, you have not. You are screening your stepfather."

"Why, what do you mean?"

For answer Holmes pushed back the frill of black lace which fringed the hand that lay upon our visitor's knee. Five little livid spots, the marks of four fingers and a thumb, were printed upon the white wrist.

"You have been cruelly used," said Holmes.

The lady coloured deeply, and covered over her injured wrist. "He is a hard man," she said, "and perhaps he hardly knows his own strength."

There was a long silence, during which Holmes leaned his chin upon his hands and stared into the crackling fire.

"This is very deep business," he said at last. "There are a thousand details which I should desire to know before I decided upon our course of action. Yet we have not a moment to lose. If we were to come to Stoke Moran to-day, would it be possible for us to see over these rooms without the knowledge of your stepfather?"

"As it happens, he spoke of coming into town to-day upon some most important business. It is probable that he will be away all day, and that there would be nothing to disturb you. We have a housekeeper now, but she is old and foolish, and I could easily get her out of the way."

"Excellent. You are not averse to this trip, Watson?"

"By no means."

"Then we shall both come. What are you going to do yourself?"

"I have one or two things which I would wish to do now that I am in town. But I shall return by the twelve o'clock train, so as to be there in time for your coming."

"And you may expect us early in the afternoon. I have myself some small business matters to attend to. Will you not wait and breakfast?"

"No, I must go. My heart is lightened already since I have confided my trouble to you. I shall look forward to seeing you again this afternoon." She dropped her thick black veil over her face, and glided from the room.

"And what do you think of it all, Watson?" asked Sherlock Holmes, leaning back in his chair.

"It seems to me to be a most dark and sinister business."

"Dark enough and sinister enough."

"Yet if the lady is correct in saying that the flooring and walls are sound, and that the door, window, and chimney are impassable, then her sister must have been undoubtedly alone when she met her mysterious end."

"What becomes, then, of these nocturnal whistles, and what of the very peculiar words of the dying woman?"

"I cannot think."

"When you combine the ideas of whistles at night, the presence of a band of gipsies who are on intimate terms with this old doctor, the fact that we have every reason to believe that the doctor has an interest in preventing his stepdaughter's marriage, the dying allusion to a band, and finally, the fact that Miss Helen Stoner heard a metallic clang, which might have been caused by one of those metals bars which secure the shutters falling back into their place, I think there is good ground to think that the mystery may be cleared along those lines."

"But what, then, did the gipsies do?"

"I cannot imagine."

"I see many objections to any such a theory."

"And so do I. It is precisely for that reason that we are going to Stoke Moran this day. I want to see whether the objections are fatal, or if they may be explained away. But what, in the name of the devil!"

The ejaculation had been drawn from my companion by the fact that our door had been suddenly dashed open, and that a huge man framed himself in the aperture. His costume was a peculiar mixture of the professional and of the agricultural, having a black top-hat, a long frock-coat, and a pair of high gaiters, with a hunting-crop swinging in his hand. So tall was he that his hat actually brushed the cross-bar of the doorway, and his breadth seemed to span it across from side to side. A large face, seared with a thousand wrinkles, burned yellow with the sun, and marked with every evil passion, was turned from one to the other of us, while his deep-set, bile-shot eyes, and the high thin fleshless nose, gave him somewhat the resemblance to a fierce old bird of prey.

"Which of you is Holmes?" asked this apparition.

"My name, sir, but you have the advantage of me," said my companion quietly.

"I am Dr Grimesby Roylott, of Stoke Moran."

"Indeed, Doctor," said Holmes blandly. "Pray take a seat."

"I will do nothing of the kind. My stepdaughter has been here. I have traced her. What has she been saying to you?"

"It is a little cold for the time of the year," said Holmes.

"What has she been saying to you?" screamed the old man furiously.

"But I have heard that the crocuses promise well," continued my companion imperturbably.

"Ha! You put me off, do you?" said our new visitor, taking a step forward, and shaking his hunting-crop. "I know you, you scoundrel! I have heard of you before. You are Holmes the meddler."

My friend smiled.

"Holmes the busybody!"

His smile broadened.

"Holmes the Scotland Yard jack-in-office."

Holmes chuckled heartily. "Your conversation is most entertaining," said he. "When you go out close the door, for there is a decided draught."

"I will go when I have had my say. Don't you dare to meddle with my affairs. I know that Miss Stoner has been here – I traced her! I am a dangerous man to fall foul of! See here." He stepped swiftly forward, seized the poker, and bent it into a curve with his huge brown hands.

"See that you keep yourself out of my grip," he snarled, and hurling the twisted poker into the fire-place, he strode out of the room.

"He seems a very amiable person," said Holmes, laughing. "I am not quite so bulky, but if he had remained I might have shown him that my grip was not much more feeble than his own." As he spoke he picked up the steel poker, and with a sudden effort straightened it out again.

"Fancy his having the insolence to confound me with the official detective force! This incident gives zest to our investigation, however, and I only trust that our little friend will not suffer from her imprudence in allowing this brute to trace her. And now, Watson, we shall order breakfast, and afterwards I shall walk down to Doctors' Commons, where I hope to get some data which may help us in this matter."

It was nearly one o'clock when Sherlock Holmes returned from his excursion. He held in his hand a sheet of blue paper, scrawled over with notes and figures.

"I have seen the will of the deceased wife," said he. "To determine its exact meaning I have been obliged to work out the present prices of the investments with which it is concerned. The total income, which at the time of the wife's death was little short of £1,100, is now through the fall in agricultural prices not more than £750. Each daughter can claim an income of £250, in case of marriage. It is evident, therefore, that if both girls had married, this beauty would have had a mere pittance, while even one of them would cripple him to a serious extent. My morning's work has not been wasted, since it has proved that he has the very strongest motives for standing in the way of anything of the sort. And now, Watson, this is too serious for dawdling, especially as the old man is aware that we are interesting ourselves in his affairs, so if you are ready we shall call a cab and drive to Waterloo. I should be very much obliged if you would slip your revolver into your pocket. An Eley's No. 2 is an excellent argument with gentlemen who can twist steel pokers into knots. That and a tooth-brush are, I think, all that we need."

At Waterloo we were fortunate in catching a train for Leatherhead, where we hired a trap at the station inn, and drove for four or five miles through the lovely Surrey lanes. It was a perfect day, with a bright sun and a few fleecy clouds in the heavens. The trees and wayside hedges were just throwing out their first green shoots, and the air was full of the pleasant smell of the moist earth. To me at least there was a strange contrast between the sweet promise of the spring and this sinister quest upon which we were engaged. My companion sat in front of the trap, his arms folded, his hat pulled down over his eyes, and his chin sunk upon his breast, buried in the deepest thought. Suddenly, however, he started, tapped me on the shoulder, and pointed over the meadows.

"Look there!" said he.

A heavily timbered park stretched up in a gentle slope, thickening into a grove at the highest point. From amidst the branches there jutted out the grey gables and high roof-tree of a very old mansion.

"Stoke Moran?" said he.

"Yes, sir, that be the house of Dr Grimesby Roylott," remarked the driver.

"There is some building going on there," said Holmes; "that is where we are going."

"There's the village," said the driver, pointing to a cluster of roofs some distance to the left; "but if you want to get to the house, you'll find it shorter to go over this stile, and so by the footpath over the fields. There it is, where the lady is walking."

"And the lady, I fancy, is Miss Stoner," observed Holmes, shading his eyes. "Yes, I think we had better do as you suggest."

We got off, paid our fare, and the trap rattled back on its way to Leatherhead.

"I thought it as well," said Holmes, as we climbed the stile, "that this fellow should think we had come here as architects, or on some definite business. It may stop his gossip. Good afternoon, Miss Stoner. You see that we have been as good as our word."

Our client of the morning had hurried forward to meet us with a face which spoke her joy. "I have been waiting so eagerly for you," she cried, shaking hands with us warmly. "All has turned out splendidly. Dr Roylott has gone to town, and it is unlikely that he will be back before evening."

"We have had the pleasure of making the doctor's acquaintance," said Holmes, and in a few words he sketched out what had occurred. Miss Stoner turned white to the lips as she listened.

"Good heavens!" she cried. "He has followed me, then."

"So it appears."

"He is so cunning that I never know when I am safe from him. What will he say when he returns?"

"He must guard himself, for he may find that there is someone more cunning than himself upon his track. You must lock yourself from him to-night. If he is violent, we shall take you away to your aunt's at Harrow. Now, we must make the best use of our time, so kindly take us at once to the rooms which we are to examine."

The building was of grey, lichen-blotched stone, with a high

central portion, and two curving wings, like the claws of a crab, thrown out on each side. In one of these wings the windows were broken, and blocked with wooden boards, while the roof was partly caved in, a picture of ruin. The central portion was in little better repair, but the right-hand block was comparatively modern, and the blinds in the windows, with the blue smoke curling up from the chimneys, showed that this was where the family resided. Some scaffolding had been erected against the end wall, and the stonework had been broken into, but there were no signs of any workmen at the moment of our visit. Holmes walked slowly up and down the ill-trimmed lawn, and examined with deep attention the outsides of the windows.

"This, I take it, belongs to the room in which you used to sleep, the centre one to your sister's, and the one next to the main building to Dr Roylott's chamber?"

"Exactly so. But I am now sleeping in the middle one."

"Pending the alterations, as I understand. By the way, there does not seem to be any very pressing need for repairs at that end wall."

"There were none. I believe that it was an excuse to move me from my room."

"Ah! that is suggestive. Now, on the other side of this narrow wing runs the corridor from which these three rooms open. There are windows in it, of course?"

"Yes, but very small ones. Too narrow for anyone to pass through."

"As you both locked your doors at night, your rooms were unapproachable from that side. Now, would you have the kindness to go into your room, and to bar your shutters."

Miss Stoner did so, and Holmes, after a careful examination through the open window, endeavoured in every way to force the shutter open, but without success. There was no slit through which a knife could be passed to raise the bar. Then with his lens he tested the hinges, but they were of solid iron, built firmly into the massive masonry. "Hum!" said he, scratching his chin in some perplexity, "my theory certainly presents some difficulties. No one could pass these shutters if they were bolted. Well, we shall see if the inside throws any light upon the matter."

A small side door led into the whitewashed corridor from which the three bedrooms opened. Holmes refused to examine the third chamber, so we passed at once to the second, that in which Miss Stoner was now sleeping, and in which her sister had met her fate. It was a homely little room, with a low ceiling and a gaping fire-place, after the fashion of old country houses. A brown chest of drawers stood in one corner, a narrow white-counterpaned bed in another, and a dressing-table on the left-hand side of the window. These articles, with two small wicker-work chairs, made up all the furniture in the room, save for a square of Wilton carpet in the centre. The boards round and the panelling of the walls were brown, worm-eaten oak, so old and discoloured that it may have dated from the original building of the house. Holmes drew one of the chairs into a corner and sat silent, while his eyes travelled round and round and up and down, taking in every detail of the apartment.

"Where does that bell communicate with?" he asked at last, pointing to a thick bell-rope which hung down beside the bed, the tassel actually lying upon the pillow.

"It goes to the housekeeper's room."

"It looks newer than the other things?"

"Yes, it was only put there a couple of years ago."

"Your sister asked for it, I suppose?"

"No, I never heard of her using it. We used always to get what we wanted for ourselves."

"Indeed, it seemed unnecessary to put so nice a bell-pull there. You will excuse me for a few minutes while I satisfy myself as to this floor." He threw himself down upon his face with his lens in his hand, and crawled swiftly backwards and forwards, examining minutely the cracks between the boards. He did the same with the woodwork with which the chamber was panelled. Then he walked over to the bed and spent some time in staring at it, and in running his eye up and down the wall. Finally he took the bell-rope in his hand and gave it a brisk tug.

"Why, it's a dummy," said he.

"Won't it ring?"

"No, it is not even attached to a wire. This is very interesting. You can see now that it is fastened to a hook just above where the little opening of the ventilator is."

"How very absurd! I never noticed that before."

"Very strange!" muttered Holmes, pulling at the rope. "There are one or two very singular points about this room. For example, what a fool a builder must be to open a ventilator in another room, when, with the same trouble, he might have communicated with the outside air!"

"That is also quite modern," said the lady.

"Done about the same time as the bell-rope," remarked Holmes.

"Yes, there were several little changes carried out about that time."

"They seem to have been of a most interesting character –

dummy bell-ropes, and ventilators which do not ventilate. With your permission, Miss Stoner, we shall now carry our researches into the inner apartment."

Dr Grimesby Roylott's chamber was larger than that of his stepdaughter, but was plainly furnished. A camp bed, a small wooden shelf full of books, mostly of a technical character, an arm-chair beside the bed, a plain wooden chair against the wall, a round table, and a large iron safe were the principle things which met the eye. Holmes walked slowly round and examined each and all of them with the keenest interest.

"What's in here?" he asked, tapping the safe.

"My stepfather's business papers."

"Oh! you have seen inside, then?"

"Only once, some years ago. I remember that it was full of papers."

"There isn't a cat in it, for example?"

"No. What a strange idea!"

"Well, look at this!" He took up a small saucer of milk which stood on the top of it.

"No; we don't keep a cat. But there is a cheetah and a baboon."

"Ah, yes, of course! Well, a cheetah is just a big cat, and yet a saucer of milk does not go very far in satisfying its wants, I dare say. There is one point which I should wish to determine." He squatted down in front of the wooden chair, and examined the seat of it with the greatest attention.

"Thank you. That is quite settled," said he, rising and putting his lens in his pocket. "Hallo! here is something interesting!"

The object which had caught his eye was a small dog lash hung on one corner of the bed. The lash, however, was curled upon itself, and tied so as to make a loop of whipcord.

"What do you make of that, Watson?"

"It's a common enough lash. But I don't know why it should be tied."

"That is not quite so common, is it? Ah, me! it's a wicked world, and when a clever man turns his brain to crime it is the worst of all. I think that I have seen enough now, Miss Stoner, and, with your permission, we shall walk out upon the lawn."

I had never seen my friend's face so grim, or his brow so dark, as it was when we turned from the scene of this investigation. We had walked several times up and down the lawn, neither Miss Stoner nor myself liking to break in upon his thoughts before he roused himself from his reverie.

"It is very essential, Miss Stoner," said he, "that you should absolutely follow my advice in every respect."

"I shall most certainly do so."

"The matter is too serious for any hesitation. Your life may depend upon your compliance."

"I assure you that I am in your hands."

"In the first place, both my friend and I must spend the night in your room."

Both Miss Stoner and I gazed at him in astonishment.

"Yes, it must be so. Let me explain. I believe that that is the village inn over there?"

"Yes, that is the Crown."

"Very good. Your windows would be visible from there?"

"Certainly."

"You must confine yourself to your room, on pretence of a headache, when your stepfather comes back. Then when you hear him retire for the night, you must open the shutters of your window, undo the hasp, put your lamp there as a signal to us, and then withdraw with everything which you are likely to want into the room which you used to occupy. I have no doubt that, in spite of the repairs, you could manage there for one night."

"Oh, yes, easily."

"The rest you will leave in our hands."

"But what will you do?"

"We shall spend the night in your room, and we shall investigate the cause of this noise which has disturbed you."

"I believe, Mr Holmes, that you have already made up your mind," said Miss Stoner, laying her hand upon my companion's sleeve.

"Perhaps I have."

"Then for pity's sake tell me what was the cause of my sister's death."

"I should prefer to have clearer proofs before I speak."

"You can at least tell me whether my own thought is correct, and if she died from some sudden fright."

"No, I do not think so. I think that there was probably some more tangible cause. And now, Miss Stoner, we must leave you, for if Dr Roylott returned and saw us, our journey would be in vain. Good-bye, and be brave, for if you will do what I have told you, you may rest assured that we shall soon drive away the dangers that threaten you."

Sherlock Holmes and I had no difficulty in engaging a bedroom and sitting-room at the Crown Inn. They were on the upper floor, and from our window we could command a view of the avenue gate, and of the inhabited wing of Stoke Moran Manor House. At dusk we saw Dr Grimesby Roylott drive past, his huge form looming up beside the little figure of the lad who drove him. The boy had some slight difficulty in undoing the heavy iron gates, and we heard the hoarse roar of the doctor's voice, and saw the fury with which he shook his clenched fists at him. The trap drove on, and a few minutes later we saw a sudden light spring up among the trees as the lamp was lit in one of the sitting-rooms.

"Do you know, Watson," said Holmes, as we sat together in the gathering darkness, "I have really some scruples as to taking you to-night. There is a distinct element of danger."

"Can I be of assistance?"

"Your presence might be invaluable."

"Then I shall certainly come."

"It is very kind of you."

"You speak of danger. You have evidently seen more in these rooms than was visible to me."

"No, but I fancy that I may have deduced a little more. I imagine that you saw all that I did."

"I saw nothing remarkable save the bell-rope, and what purpose that could answer I confess is more than I can imagine."

"You saw the ventilator, too?"

"Yes, but I do not think that it is such a very unusual thing to have a small opening between two rooms. It was so small that a rat could hardly pass through."

"I knew that we should find a ventilator before ever we came to Stoke Moran."

"My dear Holmes!"

"Oh, yes, I did. You remember in her statement she said that her sister could smell Dr Roylott's cigar. Now, of course that suggests at once that there must be a communication between the two rooms. It could only be a small one, or it would have been remarked upon at the coroner's inquiry. I deduce a ventilator."

"But what harm can there be in that?"

"Well, there is at least a curious coincidence of dates. A ventilator is made, a cord is hung, and a lady who sleeps in the bed dies. Does not that strike you?"

"I cannot as yet see any connection."

"Did you observe anything very peculiar about that bed?"

"No."

"It was clamped to the floor. Did you ever see a bed fastened like that before?"

"I cannot say that I have."

"The lady could not move her bed. It must always be in the same relative position to the ventilator and to the rope – for so we may call it, since it was clearly never meant for a bell-pull."

"Holmes," I cried, "I seem to see dimly what you are hitting at. We are only just in time to prevent some subtle and horrible crime."

"Subtle enough and horrible enough. When a doctor does go wrong he is the first of criminals. He has nerve and he has knowledge. Palmer and Pritchard were among the heads of their profession. This man strikes even deeper, but I think, Watson, that we shall be able to strike deeper still. But we shall have horrors before the night is over: for goodness' sake let us have a quiet pipe, and turn our minds for a few hours to something more cheerful."

About nine o'clock the light among the trees was extinguished, and all was dark in the direction of the Manor House. Two hours passed slowly away, and then, suddenly, just at the stroke of eleven, a single bright light shone out right in front of us.

"That is our signal," said Holmes, springing to his feet; "it comes from the middle window."

As we passed out he exchanged a few words with the landlord, explaining that we were going on a late visit to an acquaintance, and that it was possible that we might spend the night there. A moment later we were out on the dark road, a chill wind blowing in our faces, and one yellow light twinkling in front of us through the gloom to guide us on our sombre errand.

There was little difficulty in entering the grounds, for un-repaired breaches gaped in the old park wall. Making our way among the trees, we reached the lawn, crossed it, and were about to enter through the window, when out from a clump of laurel bushes there darted what seemed to be a hideous and distorted child, who threw itself on the grass with writhing limbs, and then ran swiftly across the lawn into the darkness.

"My God!" I whispered, "did you see it?"

Holmes was for the moment as startled as I. His hand closed like a vice upon my wrist in his agitation. Then he broke into a low laugh, and put his lips to my ear.

"It is a nice household," he murmured, "that is the baboon."

I had forgotten the strange pets which the doctor affected. There was a cheetah, too; perhaps we might find it upon our shoulders at any moment. I confess that I felt easier in my mind when, after following Holmes's example and slipping off my shoes, I found myself inside the bedroom. My companion noiselessly closed the shutters, moved the lamp on to the table, and cast his eyes round the room. All was as we had seen it in the day-time, then creeping up to me and making a trumpet of his hand, he whispered into my ear again so gently that it was all that I could do to distinguish the words:

"The least sound would be fatal to our plans."

I nodded to show that I had heard.

"We must sit without a light. He would see it through the ventilator."

I nodded again.

"Do not go to sleep; your very life may depend upon it. Have your pistol ready in case we should need it. I will sit on the side of the bed, and you in that chair."

I took out my revolver and laid it on the corner of the table.

Holmes had brought up a long thin cane, and this he placed upon the bed beside him. By it he laid the box of matches and the stump of a candle. Then he turned down the lamp and we were left in darkness.

How shall I ever forget that dreadful vigil? I could not hear a sound, not even the drawing of a breath, and yet I knew that my companion sat open-eyed, within a few feet of me, in the same state of nervous tension in which I was myself. The shutters cut off the least ray of light, and we waited in absolute darkness. From outside came the occasional cry of a night-bird, and once at our very window a long drawn, cat-like whine, which told us that the cheetah was indeed at liberty. Far away we could hear the deep tones of the parish clock, which boomed out every quarter of an hour. How long they seemed, those quarters! Twelve o'clock, and one, and two, and three, and still we sat waiting silently for whatever might befall.

Suddenly there was the momentary gleam of a light up in the direction of the ventilator, which vanished immediately, but was succeeded by a strong smell of burning oil and heated metal. Someone in the next room had lit a dark lantern. I heard a gentle sound of movement, and then all was silent once more, though the smell grew stronger. For half an hour I sat with straining ears. Then suddenly another sound became audible – a very gentle, soothing sound, like that of a small jet of steam escaping continually from a kettle. The instant we heard it, Holmes sprang from the bed, struck a match, and lashed furiously with his cane at the bell-pull.

"You see it, Watson?" he yelled. "You see it?"

But I saw nothing. At the moment when Holmes struck the light I heard a low, clear whistle, but the sudden glare flashing into my weary eyes made it impossible for me to tell what it was at which my friend lashed so savagely. I could, however, see that his face was deadly pale, and filled with horror and loathing.

He had ceased to strike, and was gazing up at the ventilator, when suddenly there broke from the silence of the night the most horrible cry to which I have ever listened. It swelled up louder and louder, a hoarse yell of pain and fear and anger all mingled in the one dreadful shriek. They say that away down in the village, and even in the distant parsonage, that cry raised the sleepers from their beds. It struck cold to our hearts, and I stood gazing at Holmes, and he at me, until the last echoes of it had died away into the silence from which it rose.

"What can it mean?" I gasped.

"It means that it is all over," Holmes answered. "And perhaps, after all, it is for the best. Take your pistol, and we shall enter Dr Roylott's room."

With a grave face he lit the lamp, and led the way down the corridor. Twice he struck at the chamber door without any reply from within. Then he turned the handle and entered, I at his heels, with the cocked pistol in my hand.

It was a singular sight which met our eyes. On the table stood a dark lantern with the shutter half open, throwing a brilliant beam of light upon the iron safe, the door of which was ajar. Beside this table, on the wooden chair, sat Dr Grimesby Roylott, clad in a long grey dressing-gown, his bare ankles protruding beneath, and his feet thrust into red heel-less Turkish slippers. Across his lap lay the short stock with the long lash which we had noticed during the day. His chin was cocked upwards, and his eyes were fixed in a dreadful rigid stare at the corner of the ceiling. Round his brow he had a peculiar yellow band, with brownish speckles, which seemed to be bound tightly round his head. As we entered he made neither sound nor motion.

"The band! the speckled band!" whispered Holmes.

I took a step forward. In an instant his strange headgear began to move, and there reared itself from among his hair the squat diamond-shaped head and puffed neck of a loathsome serpent.

"It is a swamp adder!" cried Holmes – "the deadliest snake in India. He has died within ten seconds of being bitten. Violence does, in truth, recoil upon the violent, and the schemer falls into the pit which he digs for another. Let us thrust this creature back into its den, and we can then remove Miss Stoner to some place of shelter, and let the county police know what has happened."

As he spoke he drew the dog whip swiftly from the dead man's lap, and throwing the noose round the reptile's neck, he drew it from its horrid perch, and, carrying it at arm's length, threw it into the iron safe, which he closed upon it.

Such are the true facts of the death of Dr Grimesby Roylott, of Stoke Moran. It is not necessary that I should prolong a narrative, which has already run to too great a length, by telling how we broke the sad news to the terrified girl, how we conveyed her by the morning train to the care of her good aunt at Harrow, and how the slow process of official inquiry came to the conclusion that the Doctor met his fate while indiscreetly playing with a dangerous pet. The little which I had yet to learn of the case was told me by Sherlock Holmes as we travelled back next day.

"I had," said he, "come to an entirely erroneous conclusion, which shows, my dear Watson, how dangerous it always is to reason from insufficient data. The presence of the gipsies, and use of the word "band'" which was used by the poor girl, no doubt, to explain the appearance which she had caught a horrid glimpse of by the light of her match, were sufficient to put me upon an entirely wrong scent. I can only claim the merit that I instantly reconsidered my position when, however, it became clear to me that whatever danger threatened an occupant of the room could not come either from the window or the door. My attention was speedily drawn, as I have already remarked to you, to this ventilator, and to the bell-rope which hung down to the bed. The discovery that this was a dummy, and that the bed was clamped to the floor, instantly gave rise to the suspicion that the rope was there as a bridge for something passing through the hole, and coming to the bed. The idea of a snake instantly occurred to me, and when I coupled it with my knowledge that the doctor was furnished with a supply of creatures from India, I felt that I was probably on the right track. The idea of using a form of poison which could not possibly be discovered by any chemical test was just such a one as would occur to a clever and ruthless man who had had an Eastern training. The rapidity with which such a poison would take effect would also, from his point of view, be an advantage. It would be a sharp-eyed coroner indeed who could distinguish the two little dark punctures which would show where the poison fangs had done their work. Then I thought of the whistle. Of course, he must recall the snake before the morning light revealed it to the victim. He had trained it, probably by the use of the milk which we saw, to return to him when summoned. He would put it through the ventilator at the hour that he thought best, with the certainty that it would crawl down the rope, and land on the bed. It might or might not bite the occupant, perhaps she might escape every night for a week, but sooner or later she must fall a victim.

"I had come to these conclusions before ever I had entered his room. An inspection of his chair showed me that he had been in the habit of standing on it, which, of course, would be necessary in order that he should reach the ventilator. The sight of the safe, the saucer of milk, and the loop of whipcord were enough to finally dispel any doubts which may have remained. The metallic clang heard by Miss Stoner was obviously caused by her father hastily closing the door of his safe upon its terrible occupant. Having once made up my mind, you know the steps which I took in order to put the matter to the proof. I heard the creature hiss, as I have no doubt that you did also, and I instantly lit the light and attacked it."

"With the result of driving it through the ventilator."

"And also with the result of causing it to turn upon its master at the other side. Some of the blows of my cane came home, and roused its snakish temper, so that it flew upon the first person it saw. In this way I am no doubt indirectly responsible for Dr Grimesby Roylott's death, and I cannot say that it is likely to weigh very heavily upon my conscience."

The Tea-leaf

EDGAR JEPSON AND ROBERT EUSTACE

Arthur Kelstern and Hugh Willoughton met in the Turkish bath in Duke Street, St James's, and rather more than a year later in that Turkish bath they parted. Both of them were bad-tempered men, Kelstern cantankerous and Willoughton violent. It was, indeed, difficult to decide which was the worse tempered; and when I found that they had suddenly become friends, I gave that friendship three months. It lasted nearly a year.

When they did quarrel they quarrelled about Kelstern's daughter Ruth. Willoughton fell in love with her and she with him, and they became engaged to be married. Six months later, in spite of the fact that they were plainly very much in love with one another, the engagement was broken off. Neither of them gave any reason for breaking it off. My belief was that Willoughton had given Ruth a taste of his infernal temper and got as good as he gave.

Not that Ruth was at all a Kelstern to look at. Like the members of most of the old Lincolnshire families, descendants of the Vikings and the followers of Canute, one Kelstern is very like another Kelstern, fair-haired, clear-skinned, with light blue eyes and a good bridge to the nose. But Ruth had taken after her mother; she was dark, with a straight nose, dark-brown eyes of the kind often described as liquid, dark-brown hair, and as kissable lips as ever I saw. She was a proud, self-sufficing, high-spirited girl, with a temper of her own. She needed it to live with that cantankerous old brute Kelstern. Oddly enough, in spite of the fact that he always would try to bully her, she was fond of him; and I will say for him that he was very fond of her. Probably she was the only creature in the world of whom he was really fond. He was an expert in the application of scientific discoveries to industry; and she worked with him in his laboratory. He paid her five hundred a year, so that she must have been uncommonly good.

He took the breaking off of the engagement very hard indeed. He would have it that Willoughton had jilted her. Ruth took it hard, too; her warm colouring lost some of its warmth; her lips grew less kissable and set in a thinner line. Willoughton's temper grew worse than ever; he was like a bear with a perpetually sore head. I tried to feel my way with both him and Ruth with a view to help bring about a reconciliation. To put it mildly, I was rebuffed. Willoughton swore at me; Ruth flared up and told me not to meddle in matters that didn't concern me. Nevertheless, my strong impression was that they were missing one another badly and would have been glad enough to come together again if their stupid vanity could have let them.

Kelstern did his best to keep Ruth furious with Willoughton. One night I told him – it was no business of mine; but I never did give a tinker's curse for his temper – that he was a fool to meddle and had much better leave them alone. It made him furious, of course; he would have it that Willoughton was a dirty hound and a low blackguard – at least those were about the mildest things he said of him. Given his temper and the provocation, nothing less could be expected. Moreover, he was looking a very sick man and depressed.

He took immense trouble to injure Willoughton. At his clubs, the Athenaeum, the Devonshire, and the Savile, he would display considerable ingenuity in bringing the conversation round to him; then he would declare that he was a scoundrel of the meanest type. Of course, it did Willoughton harm, though not nearly as much as Kelstern desired, for Willoughton knew his job as few engineers knew it; and it is very hard indeed to do much harm to a man who really knows his job. People have to have him. But of course it did him some harm; and Willoughton knew that Kelstern was doing it. I came across two men who told me that they had given him a friendly hint. That did not improve *his* temper.

An expert in the construction of those ferro-concrete buildings which are arising all over London, he was as distinguished in his sphere as Kelstern in his. They were alike not only in the matters of brains and bad temper; but I think that their minds worked in very much the same way. At any rate, both of them seemed determined not to change their ordinary course of life because of the breaking off of that engagement.

It had been the habit of both of them to have a Turkish bath, at the baths in Duke Street, at four in the afternoon on the second and last Tuesday in every month. To that habit they stuck. The fact that they must meet on those Tuesdays did not cause either of them to change his hour of taking his Turkish bath by the twenty minutes which would have given them no more than a passing glimpse of one another. They continued to take it, as they always had, simultaneously. Thick-skinned? They were thick-skinned. Neither of them pretended that he did not see the other; he scowled at him; and he scowled at him most of the time. I know this, for sometimes I had a Turkish bath myself at that hour.

It was about three months after the breaking off of the engagement that they met for the last time at that Turkish bath, and there parted for good.

Kelstern had been looking ill for about six weeks; there was a greyness and a drawn look to his face; and he was losing weight. On the second Tuesday in October he arrived at the bath punctually at four, bringing with him, as was his habit, a Thermos flask full of a very delicate China tea. If he thought that he was not perspiring freely enough he would drink it in the hottest room; if he did perspire freely enough, he would drink it after his bath. Willoughton arrived about two minutes later. Kelstern finished undressing and went into the bath a couple of minutes before Willoughton. They stayed in the hot room about the same time; Kelstern went into the hottest room about a minute after Willoughton. Before he went into it he sent for his Thermos flask, which he had left in the dressing-room, and took it into the hottest room with him.

As it happened, they were the only two people in the hottest room; and they had not been in it two minutes before the four men in the hot room heard them quarrelling. They heard Kelstern call Willoughton a dirty hound and a low blackguard, among other things, and declare he would do him in yet. Willoughton told him to go to the devil twice. Kelstern went on abusing him, and presently Willoughton fairly shouted: "Oh, shut up, you old fool! Or I'll make you!"

Kelstern did not shut up. About two minutes later Willoughton came out of the hottest room, scowling, walked through the hot room into the shampooing room, and put himself into the hands of one of the shampooers. Two or three minutes after that a man of the name of Helston went into the hottest room and fairly yelled. Kelstern was lying back on a couch, with the blood still flowing from a wound over his heart.

There was a devil of a hullabaloo. The police were called in; Willoughton was arrested. Of course he lost his temper and, protesting furiously that he had nothing whatever to do with the crime, abused the police. That did not incline them to believe him.

After examining the room and the dead body the detective-inspector in charge of the case came to the conclusion that Kelstern had been stabbed as he was drinking his tea. The Thermos flask lay on the floor and some of the tea had evidently been spilt for some tea-leaves – the tea in the flask must have been carelessly strained off the leaves by the maid who filled it – lay on the floor about the mouth of the empty flask. It looked as if the murderer had taken advantage of Kelstern's drinking his tea to stab him while the flask rather blocked his vision and prevented him from seeing what he would be at.

The case would have been quite plain sailing but for the fact that they could not find the weapon. It had been easy enough for Willoughton to take it into the bath in the towel in which he was draped. But how had he got rid of it? Where had he hidden it? A Turkish bath is no place to hide anything in. It is as bare as

an empty barn – if anything barer; and Willoughton had been in
the barest part of it. The police searched every part of it – not
that there was much point in doing that, for Willoughton had
come out of the hottest room and gone through the hot room
into the shampooers' room. When Helston started shouting
"Murder!" he had rushed back with the shampooers to the
hottest room and there he had stayed. Since it was obvious that
he had committed the murder, the shampooers and the bathers
had kept their eyes on him. They were all of them certain that he
had not left them to go to the dressing-room; they would not
have allowed him to do so.

It was obvious that he must have carried the weapon into the
bath, hidden in the folds of the towel in which he was draped,
and brought it away in the folds of that towel. He had laid the
towel down beside the couch on which he was being shampooed;
and there it still lay when they came to look for it, untouched,
with no weapon in it, with no traces of blood on it. There was
not much in the fact that it was not stained with blood, since
Willoughton could have wiped the knife, or dagger, or whatever
weapon he used, on the couch on which Kelstern lay. There were
no marks of any such wiping on the couch; but the blood, flowing from the wound, might have covered them up. But why was
the weapon not in the towel?

There was no finding that weapon.

Then the doctors who made the autopsy came to the conclusion that the wound had been inflicted by a circular, pointed
weapon nearly three-quarters of an inch in diameter. It had
penetrated rather more than three inches, and, supposing that its
handle was only four inches long, it must have been a sizeable
weapon, quite impossible to overlook. The doctors also discovered a further proof of the theory that Kelstern had been
drinking tea when he was stabbed. Half-way down the wound
they found two halves of a tea-leaf, which had evidently fallen on
to Kelstern's body, been driven into the wound, and cut in half
by the weapon. Also they discovered that Kelstern was suffering
from cancer. This fact was not published in the papers; I heard it
at the Devonshire.

Willoughton was brought before the magistrates, and to most people's surprise did not reserve his defence. He went into the witness-box and swore that he had never touched Kelstern, that he had never had anything to touch him with, that he had never taken any weapon into the Turkish bath and so had had no weapon to hide, that he had never even seen any such weapon as the doctors described. He was committed for trial.

The papers were full of the crime; everyone was discussing it; and the question which occupied everyone's mind was: where had Willoughton hidden the weapon? People wrote to the papers to suggest that he had ingeniously put it in some place under everybody's eyes and that it had been overlooked because it was so obvious. Others suggested that, circular and pointed, it must be very like a thick lead-pencil, that it was a thick lead-pencil; and that was why the police had overlooked it in their search. The police had not overlooked any thick lead-pencil; there had been no thick lead-pencil to overlook. They hunted England through – Willoughton did a lot of motoring – to discover the man who had sold him this curious and uncommon weapon. They did not find the man who had sold it to him; they did not find a man who sold such weapons at all. They came to the conclusion that Kelstern had been murdered with a piece of steel or iron rod filed to a point like a pencil.

In spite of the fact that only Willoughton *could* have murdered Kelstern, I could not believe that he had done it. The fact that Kelstern was doing his best to injure him professionally and socially was by no means a strong enough motive. Willoughton was far too intelligent a man not to be very well aware that people do not take much notice of statements to the discredit of a man whom they need to do a job for them; and for the social injury he would care very little. Besides, he might very well injure, or even kill, a man in one of his tantrums; but his was not the kind of bad temper that plans a cold-blooded murder; and if ever a murder had been deliberately planned, Kelstern's had.

I was as close a friend as Willoughton had, and I went to visit him in prison. He seemed rather touched by my doing so, and grateful. I learnt that I was the only person who had done so. He was subdued and seemed much gentler. It might last. He discussed the murder readily enough, and naturally with a harassed air. He said quite frankly that he did not expect me, in the circumstances, to believe that he had not committed it; but he had not, and he could not for the life of him conceive who had. I did believe that he had not committed it; there was something in his way of discussing it that wholly convinced me. I told him that I was quite sure that he had not killed Kelstern; and he looked at me as if he did not believe the assurance. But again he looked grateful.

Ruth was grieving for her father; but Willoughton's very dangerous plight to some degree distracted her mind from her loss. A woman can quarrel with a man bitterly without desiring to see him hanged; and Willoughton's chance of escaping hanging was not at all a good one. But she would not believe for a moment that he had murdered her father.

"No; there's nothing in it – nothing whatever," she said, firmly. "If Dad had murdered Hugh I could have understood it. He had reasons – or at any rate he had persuaded himself that he had. But whatever reason had Hugh for murdering Dad? It's all nonsense to suppose that he'd mind Dad's trying all he knew to injure him as much as that. All kinds of people are going about trying to injure other people in that way, but they don't really injure them very much; and Hugh knows that quite well."

"Of course they don't; and Hugh wouldn't really believe that your father was injuring him much," I said. "But you're forgetting his infernal temper."

"No, I'm not," she protested. "He might kill a man in one of his rages on the spur of the moment. But this wasn't the spur of the moment. Whoever did it had worked the whole thing out and came along with the weapon ready."

I had to admit that that was reasonable enough. But who had done it? I pointed out to her that the police had made careful inquiries about everyone in the bath at the time, the shampooers and the people taking their baths, but they found no evidence whatever that any one of them had at any time had any relations, except that of a shampooer, with her father.

"Either it was one of them, or somebody else who just did it and got right away, or there's a catch somewhere," she said, frowning thoughtfully.

"I can't see how there can possibly have been anyone in the bath, except the people who are known to have been there," said I. "In fact, there can't have been."

Then the Crown subpoenaed her as a witness for the prosecution. It seemed rather unnecessary and even a bit queer, for it could have found plenty of evidence of bad blood between the two men without dragging her into it. Plainly it was bent on doing all it knew to prove motive enough. Ruth worked her brain so hard trying to get to the bottom of the business that there came a deep vertical wrinkle just above her right eyebrow that stayed there.

On the morning of the trial I called for her after breakfast to drive her down to the New Bailey. She was pale and looked as if she had had a poor night's rest, and, naturally enough, she seemed to be suffering from an excitement she found hard to control. It was not like her to show any excitement she might be feeling.

She said in an excited voice: "I think I've got it!" and would say no more.

We had, of course, been in close touch with Willoughton's solicitor, Hamley; and he had kept seats for us just behind him. He wished to have Ruth to hand to consult should some point turn up on which she could throw light, since she knew more than anyone about the relations between Willoughton and her father. I had timed our arrival very well; the jury had just been sworn in. Of course, the court was full of women, the wives of peers and bookmakers and politicians, most of them overdressed and overscented.

Then the judge came in; and with his coming the atmosphere of the court became charged with that sense of anxious strain peculiar to trials for murder. It was rather like the atmosphere of a sick room in a case of fatal illness, but worse.

Willoughton came into the dock looking under the weather

and very much subdued. But he was certainly looking dignified, and he said that he was not guilty in a steady enough voice.

Greatorex, the leading counsel for the Crown, opened the case for the prosecution. There was no suggestion in his speech that the police had discovered any new fact. He begged the jury not to lay too much stress on the fact that the weapon had not been found. He had to, of course.

Then Helston gave evidence of finding that Kelstern had been stabbed, and he and the other three men who had been with him in the hot room gave evidence of the quarrel they had overheard between Willoughton and the dead man, and that Willoughton came out of the hottest room scowling and obviously furious. One of them, a fussy old gentleman of the name of Underwood, declared that it was the bitterest quarrel he had ever heard. None of the four of them could throw any light on the matter of whether Willoughton was carrying the missing weapon in the folds of the towel in which he was draped; all of them were sure that he had nothing in his hands.

The medical evidence came next. In cross-examining the doctors who had made the autopsy, Hazeldean, Willoughton's counsel, established the fact quite definitely that the missing weapon was of a fair size; that its rounded blade must have been over half an inch in diameter and between three and four inches long. They were of the opinion that to drive a blade of that thickness into the heart a handle of at least four inches in length would be necessary to give a firm enough grip. They agreed that it might very well have been a piece of steel or iron rod, sharpened like a pencil. At any rate, it was certainly a sizeable weapon, not one to be hidden quickly or to disappear wholly in a Turkish bath. Hazeldean could not shake their evidence about the tea-leaf; they were confident that it had been driven into the wound and cut in half by the blade of the missing weapon, and that went to show that the wound had been inflicted while Kelstern was drinking his tea.

Detective-Inspector Brackett, who was in charge of the case, was cross-examined at great length about his search for the missing weapon. He made it quite clear that it was nowhere in that Turkish bath, neither in the hot rooms, nor the shampooing room, nor the dressing-rooms, nor the vestibule, nor the office. He had had the plunge bath emptied; he had searched the roofs, though it was practically certain that the skylight above the hot room, not the hottest, had been shut at the time of the crime. In re-examination he scouted the idea of Willoughton's having had an accomplice who had carried away the weapon for him. He had gone into that matter most carefully.

The shampooer stated that Willoughton came to him scowling so savagely that he wondered what had put him into such a bad temper. In cross-examining him, Arbuthnot, Hazeldean's junior, made it clearer than ever that, unless Willoughton had already hidden the weapon in the bare hottest room, it was hidden in the towel. Then he drew from the shampooer the definite statement that Willoughton had set down the towel beside the couch on which he was shampooed; that he had hurried back to the hot rooms in front of the shampooer; that the shampooer had come back from the hot rooms, leaving Willoughton still in them discussing the crime, to find the towel lying just as Willoughton had set it down, with no weapon in it and no trace of blood on it.

Since the inspector had disposed of the possibility that an accomplice had slipped in, taken the weapon from the towel, and slipped out of the bath with it, this evidence really made it clear that the weapon had never left the hottest room.

Then the prosecution called evidence of the bad terms on which Kelstern and Willoughton had been. Three well-known and influential men told the jury about Kelstern's efforts to prejudice Willoughton in their eyes and the damaging statements he had made about him. One of them had felt it to be his duty to tell Willoughton about this; and Willoughton had been very angry. Arbuthnot, in cross-examining, elicited the fact that any damaging statement that Kelstern made about anyone was considerably discounted by the fact that everyone knew him to be in the highest degree cantankerous.

I noticed that during the end of the cross-examination of the shampooer and during this evidence Ruth had been fidgeting and turning to look impatiently at the entrance to the court, as if she were expecting someone. Then, just as she was summoned to the witness-box, there came in a tall, stooping, grey-bearded man of about sixty, carrying a brown-paper parcel. His face was familiar to me, but I could not place him. He caught her eye and nodded to her. She breathed a sharp sigh of relief, and bent over and handed a letter she had in her hand to Willoughton's solicitor and pointed out the grey-bearded man to him. Then she went quietly to the witness-box.

Hamley read the letter and at once bent over and handed it to Hazeldean and spoke to him. I caught a note of excitement in his hushed voice. Hazeldean read the letter and appeared to grow excited too. Hamley slipped out of his seat and went to the grey-bearded man, who was still standing just inside the door of the porch, and began to talk to him earnestly.

Greatorex began to examine Ruth; and naturally I turned my attention to her. His examination was directed also to show on what bad terms Kelstern and Willoughton had been. Ruth was called on to tell the jury some of Kelstern's actual threats. Then he questioned Ruth about her own relations with Willoughton and the breaking off of the engagement and its infuriating effect on her father. She admitted that he had been very bitter about it, and had told her that he was resolved to do his best to do Willoughton in. I thought that she went out of her way to emphasise this resolve of Kelstern's. It seemed to me likely to prejudice the jury still more against Willoughton, making them sympathise with a father's righteous indignation, and making yet more obvious that he was a dangerous enemy. Yet she would not admit that her father was right in believing that Willoughton had jilted her.

Hazeldean rose to cross-examine Ruth with a wholly confident air. He drew from her the fact that her father had been on excellent terms with Willoughton until the breaking off of the engagement.

Then Hazeldean asked: "Is it a fact that since the breaking off of your engagement the prisoner has more than once begged you to forgive him and renew it?"

"Four times," said Ruth.

"And you refused?"

"Yes," said Ruth. She looked at Willoughton queerly and added: "He wanted a lesson."

The judge asked: "Did you intend, then, to forgive him ultimately?"

Ruth hesitated; then she rather evaded a direct answer; she scowled frankly at Willoughton, and said: "Oh, well, there was no hurry. He would always marry me if I changed my mind and wanted to."

"And did your father know this?" asked the judge.

"No. I didn't tell him. I was angry with Mr Willoughton," Ruth replied.

There was a pause. Then Hazeldean started on a fresh line.

In sympathetic accents he asked: "Is it a fact that your father was suffering from cancer in a painful form?"

"It was beginning to grow very painful," said Ruth, sadly.

"Did he make a will and put all his affairs in order a few days before he died?"

"Three days," said Ruth.

"Did he ever express an intention of committing suicide?"

"He said that he would stick it out for a little while and then end it all," said Ruth. She paused and added: "*And that is what he did do.*"

One might almost say that the court started. I think that everyone in it moved a little, so that there was a kind of rustling murmur.

"Will you tell the court your reasons for that statement?" said Hazeldean.

Ruth seemed to pull herself together – she was looking very tired – then she began in a quiet, even voice: "I never believed for a moment that Mr Willoughton murdered my father. If my father had murdered Mr Willoughton it would have been a different matter. Of course, like everybody else, I puzzled over the weapon; what it was and where it had got to. I did not believe that it was a pointed piece of a half-inch steel rod. If anybody had come to the Turkish bath meaning to murder my father and hide the weapon, they wouldn't have used one so big and difficult to hide, when a hat-pin would have done just as well and could be hidden much more easily. But what puzzled me most was the tea-leaf in the wound. All the other tea-leaves that came out of the flask were lying on the floor. Inspector Brackett told me they were. And I couldn't believe that one tea-leaf had fallen on to my father at the very place above his heart at which the point of the weapon had penetrated the skin and got driven in by it. It was too much of a coincidence for me to swallow. But I got no nearer understanding it than anyone else."

She paused to ask if she might have a glass of water, for she had been up all night and was very tired. It was brought to her.

Then she went on in the same quiet voice: "Of course, I remembered that Dad had talked of putting an end to it; but no one with a wound like that could get up and hide the weapon. So it was impossible that he had committed suicide. Then, the night before last, I dreamt that I went into the laboratory and saw a piece of steel rod, pointed, lying on the table at which my father used to work."

"Dreams!" murmured Greatorex, a trifle pettishly, as if he was not pleased with the way things were going.

"I didn't think much of the dream, of course," Ruth went on. "I had been puzzling about it all so hard for so long that it was only natural to dream about it. But after breakfast I had a sudden feeling that the secret was in the laboratory if I could only find it. I did not attach any importance to the feeling; but it went on growing stronger; and after lunch I went to the laboratory and began to hunt.

"I looked through all the drawers and could find nothing. Then I went round the room looking at everything and into everything, instruments and retorts and tubes and so on. Then I went into the middle of the floor and looked slowly round the room pretty hard. Against the wall, near the door, lying ready to be taken away, was a gas cylinder, I rolled it over to see what gas had been in it and found no label on it."

She paused to look round the court as if claiming its best attention; then she went on: "Now that was very queer, because every gas cylinder must have a label on it – so many gases are dangerous. I turned on the tap of the cylinder and nothing came

out of it. It was quite empty. Then I went to the book in which all the things which come in are entered, and found that ten days before Dad died he had had a cylinder of CO_2 and seven pounds of ice. Also he had had seven pounds of ice every day till the day of his death. It was the ice and the CO_2 together that gave me the idea. CO_2, carbon dioxide, has a very low freezing-point – minus eighty degrees centigrade – and as it comes out of the cylinder and mixes with the air it turns into very fine snow; and that snow, if you compress it, makes the hardest and toughest ice possible. It flashed on me that Dad could have collected this snow and forced it into a mould and made a weapon that would not only inflict that wound but would evaporate very quickly! Indeed, in that heat you'd have to see the wound inflicted to know what had done it."

She paused again to look round the court at about as rapt a

lot of faces as any narrator could desire. Then she went on: "I knew that that was what he had done. I knew it for certain. Carbon dioxide ice would make a hard, tough dagger, and it would evaporate quickly in the hottest room of a Turkish bath and leave no smell because it is scentless. So there wouldn't be any weapon. And it explained the tea-leaf, too. Dad had made a carbon dioxide dagger perhaps a week before he used it, perhaps only a day. And he had put it into the Thermos flask as soon as he had made it. The Thermos flask keeps out the heat as well as the cold, you know. But to make sure that it couldn't melt at all, he kept the flask in ice till he was ready to use the dagger. It's the only way you can explain that tea-leaf. It came out of the flask sticking to the point of the dagger and was driven into the wound!"

She paused again, and one might almost say that the court heaved a deep sigh of relief.

"But why didn't you go straight to the police with this theory?" asked the judge.

"But that wouldn't have been any good," she protested quickly. "It was no use my knowing it myself; I had to make other people believe it; I had to find evidence. I began to hunt for it. I felt in my bones that there was some. What I wanted was the mould in which Dad compressed the carbon dioxide snow and made the dagger. I found it!"

She uttered the words in a tone of triumph and smiled at Willoughton; then she went on: "At least, I found bits of it. In the box into which we used to throw odds and ends, scraps of material, damaged instruments, and broken test tubes, I found some pieces of vulcanite; and I saw at once that they were bits of a vulcanite container. I took some wax and rolled it into a rod about the right size, and then I pieced the container together on the outside of it – at least most of it – there are some small pieces missing. It took me nearly all night. But I found the most important bit – *the pointed end!*"

She dipped her hand into her handbag and drew out a black object about nine inches long and three-quarters of an inch thick, and held it up for everyone to see.

Someone, without thinking, began to clap; and there came a storm of applause that drowned the voice of the clerk calling for order.

When the applause died down, Hazeldean, who never misses the right moment, said: "I have no more questions to ask the witness, my Lord," and sat down.

That action seemed to clinch it in my eyes, and I have no doubt it clinched it in the eyes of the jury.

The Judge leant forward and said to Ruth in a rather shocked voice: "Do you expect the jury to believe that a well-known man like your father died in the act of deliberately setting a trap to hang the prisoner?"

Ruth looked at him, shrugged her shoulders, and said, with a calm acceptance of the facts of human nature one would expect to find only in a much older woman: "Oh, well, Daddy was like that. And he certainly believed he had very good reasons for killing Mr Willoughton."

There was that in her tone and manner which made it absolutely certain that Kelstern was not only like that, but that he had acted according to his nature.

Greatorex did not re-examine Ruth; he conferred with Hazeldean. Then Hazeldean rose to open the case for the defence. He said that he would not waste the time of the court, and that, in view of the fact that Miss Kelstern had solved the problem of her father's death, he would only call one witness, Professor Mozley.

The grey-headed, grey-bearded, stooping man, who had come to the court so late, went into the witness-box. Of course his face had been familiar to me; I had seen his portrait in the newspapers a dozen times. He still carried the brown-paper parcel.

In answer to Hazeldean's questions he stated that it was possible, not even difficult, to make a weapon of carbon dioxide hard enough and tough enough and sharp enough to inflict such a wound as that which had caused Kelstern's death. The method of making it was to fold a piece of chamois leather into a bag, hold that bag with the left hand, protected by a glove, over the nozzle of a cylinder containing liquid carbon dioxide, and open the valve with the right hand. Carbon dioxide evaporates so quickly that its freezing-point, minus eighty degrees centigrade, is soon reached; and it solidifies in the chamois-leather bag as a deposit of carbon dioxide snow. Then turn off the gas, spoon that snow into a vulcanite container of the required thickness, and ram it down with a vulcanite plunger into a rod of the required hardness. He added that it was advisable to pack the container in ice while filling it and ramming down the snow. Then put the rod into a Thermos flask, and keep it till it is needed.

"And you have made such a rod?" said Hazeldean.

"Yes," said the professor, cutting the string of the brown-paper parcel. "When Miss Kelstern hauled me out of bed at half-past seven this morning to tell me her discoveries, I perceived at once that she had found the solution of the problem of her father's death, which had puzzled me considerably. I had breakfast quickly and got to work to make such a weapon myself for the satisfaction of the court. Here it is."

He drew a Thermos flask from the brown-paper, unscrewed the top of it, and inverted it. There dropped into his gloved hand a white rod, with a faint sparkle to it, about eight inches long. He held it out for the jury to see, and said:

"This carbon dioxide ice is the hardest and toughest ice we know of; and I have no doubt that Mr Kelstern killed himself with a similar rod. The difference between the rod he used and this is that his rod was pointed. I had no pointed vulcanite container; but the container that Miss Kelstern pieced together is pointed. Doubtless Mr Kelstern had it specially made, probably by Messrs Hawkins and Spender."

He dropped the rod back into the Thermos flask and screwed on the top.

Hazeldean sat down. Greatorex rose.

"With regard to the point of the rod, Professor Mozley, would it remain sharp long enough to pierce the skin in that heat?" he asked.

"In my opinion it would," said the professor. "I have been considering that point, and bearing in mind the facts that Mr Kelstern would from his avocation be very deft with his hands, and being a scientific man would know exactly what to do, he would have the rod out of the flask and the point in position in very little more than a second – perhaps less. He would, I think, hold it in his left hand and drive it home by striking the butt of it hard with his right. The whole thing would not take him two seconds. Besides, if the point of the weapon had melted the tea-leaf would have fallen off it."

"Thank you," said Greatorex, and turned and conferred with the Crown solicitors.

Then he said: "We do not propose to proceed with the case, my Lord."

The foreman of the jury rose quickly and said: "And the jury doesn't want to hear anything more, my Lord. We're quite satisfied that the prisoner is not guilty."

"Very good," said the judge, and he put the question formally to the jury, who returned a verdict of "Not Guilty". He discharged Willoughton.

I came out of the court with Ruth and we waited for Willoughton.

Presently he came out of the door and stopped and shook himself. Then he saw Ruth and came to her. They did not greet one another. She just slipped her hand through his arm; and they walked out of the New Bailey together.

We made a good deal of noise, cheering them.

Death in the Kitchen

MILWARD KENNEDY

Rupert Morrison straightened himself, drawing a deep breath. He glanced round the little kitchen, deliberately looking at the figure which lay huddled on the floor; huddled, but yet in an attitude which Morrison hoped was as natural as its unnatural circumstances would permit. For the head was inside the oven of the rusty-looking gas-stove.

He wondered whether the cushion on which the head rested was a natural or an unnatural touch. He decided that if *he* were committing suicide, he would try to make even a gas-oven as comfortable as possible.

He walked silently (for he was in stockinged feet) into the passage, and so to the sitting-room. The curtains he had drawn so carefully that he had had no hesitation in leaving on the lights. Quickly but methodically he set to work. Nothing must be left which connected him in any way with George Manning. In any way? Well, how about that package addressed not to Manning but to himself from the local grocer? Probably it had been delivered in error. Still, he must take no chances. He put it aside for future attention.

Where did Manning keep his papers? He was a careless devil, not likely to hide them securely or ingeniously. No, here they were in the writing-table. Only six that concerned Rupert Morrison; was that really all? He untied the packet and read each of the six. His cheeks reddened as he read; they were certainly damning. What a fool he had been in those days; still, he had been wise enough to remember it when Manning turned up out of the blue (he could not have spent *all* the interval in gaol?) and started his blackmail. George Manning on the other hand had grown foolish, for he had not troubled to discover whether his victim had changed.

Morrison's clumsy gloved hands thrust the packet into his breast pocket. He considered. He had plenty of time. Manning, he knew, lived alone in the cottage, and had few friends, certainly none who were likely to call on him; his domestic staff was limited to an old woman from the distant village who came in for part of the day.

The important thing was to be thorough. He had no alibi, and knew that it would be folly to fake one. Provided that there was nothing to show that he had a motive for wanting Manning dead, he would not have to account for his own whereabouts; his tale of a country tramp across the fields and through the woods would not even be wanted. Outside the cottage there was, he knew, nothing to suggest any relationship between Manning and himself save such as might exist between two men, friends long ago in schooldays, who had drifted apart, and then by chance met again; the one respected and prosperous, the other – George Manning.

At last he was satisfied with the sitting-room, but there were still the two bedrooms. Bare, shabby rooms they were, and they did not keep him long. Down to the "parlour" once more. He was reluctant to leave it, for there, if anywhere, he would leave behind a key to the truth.

But he could think of nothing more, except the tumblers on the table and the grocer's package.

There must be only one glass, of course; one must be washed and put away in the kitchen. The other? It, too, must be washed, for when it was found there must be no trace of anything more deadly in it than whisky. Of course, he could wash it and provide fresh prints of Manning's fingers.

He had to make two journeys to the kitchen with the "properties" for the scene which he must set.

Soon one tumbler was back in the cupboard; and the other, on which after he had washed it, he had carefully pressed Manning's limp hand, stood on the table, a trace of neat whisky in it. Beside it the bottle, nearly empty; Manning certainly had been putting it away. That, no doubt, was why he had been so unnoticing when Morrison (none too neatly) had emptied his little flask into the tumbler. He gave a worried glance at the body; if the dose had been too strong the whole plan might go astray. But that was absurd – he had felt the pulse only a minute ago.

And now the last detail – to put that half-sheet of paper on the table. He placed it to look as if it had been folded to catch the eye; he dared not forge a superscription to the coroner.

He smiled; it was a bit of luck that those words had so exactly filled a half sheet in Manning's letter. Directly he had received it, months ago, he had seen its possible value.

"I am tired of it all. Who can blame me for taking the easiest way? So take it smiling – as I propose to do.
George Manning."

But it was cash that Manning had meant to take with a smile – not coal-gas.

There. And the window tight shut. Now to turn on the gas, leave the electric light burning, and be gone. Footprints? No, his stockinged feet had left none, he was sure. Boots on. Quietly out by the back door, with nothing to carry but a walking-stick and that grocer's packet . . .

Not a soul did Morrison meet on his way home, and when he had emptied the packet of sugar down the wash basin, and in the same way disposed of the ashes of its cover and of those six letters he took another deep breath – of relief this time . . .

Naturally the police would come to him, for he was a man of standing and he was known to be on terms of acquaintance with Manning. He would be able to tell them that the "poor chap" had seemed very neutroic . . . His "Good morning" smile as the sergeant was shown in was at these thoughts as well as a matter of policy.

"Yes, sergeant, I know him slightly." By Jove! As nearly as no matter he had said "knew"; he must watch his tongue.

"D'you recognise this, sir?"

Good God! What was the man holding up? A pocket-book,

dark blue, with a monogram. He put his hand to his breast pocket. No – could he – He had an appalling memory of pushing those papers into his pocket. His gloved fingers had felt so clumsy. *Could* he have pulled it out and left it lying on the carpet – there?

He put out his hand; his power of speech seemed to have vanished. He took the pocket-book, half surprised that the sergeant allowed him to do so, and turned it over and over, and stared at it. What use was a denial?

The sergeant was speaking. Was he warning him that anything he might say . . . ?

"That's the boy from Bayley's, the grocer, sir. Seems he delivered the wrong parcel – one for you, it was. Left it last evening at the cottage. Went first thing to get it back. Couldn't get a reply and the front door was locked, so he went round to the back. It seems the back door was open – of course, sir, he hadn't no right to go in, but . . ."

Why *would* the fool bother about that? Go on, man. My heart won't stand this.

"Light burning in the kitchen and this Manning lying with his head inside the oven. Gave the boy a shock, so *he* says, but if you ask me . . . Anyways, he came along on his bike to me – I found the pocket-book, sir, in the sitting-room. I thought I'd have a word with you. You see, this Mr Manning – well – sir – there's a police record."

Why must he pause? Did he expect an answer? Morrison could only stare, his lips trembling.

"Course, sir. You may have given it to him. Or it may just have been an accident . . ."

What was "it"? Even if he could have spoken, Morrison would have refused now.

"But apart from that, sir – his record and that, I mean – it struck me there was something queer about Manning. And I thought maybe you could help me. That gas-oven, sir, that looks like suicide, doesn't it, sir?"

"Yes – I suppose so."

Was that really his voice?

"There was a bottle of whisky on the table – that came from Bayley's yesterday afternoon, too, and it was empty all but a drain this morning. Maybe it was that that did it . . ."

What *had* gone wrong? How had this local bumpkin stumbled on the truth?

"At any rate, sir, whisky or lunacy, would you have thought anyone, drunk or sober, could put his head in a gas-oven and turn the tap – and forget the gas was cut off because he hadn't paid the bill? I can understand how it is he's forgotten every blamed thing about what happened last night, but – Hallo, sir, what's up?"

Rupert Morrison was lying at the sergeant's feet.

The Impossible Theft

JULIAN SYMONS

It was an impossible theft, as private detective Francis Quarles said when he told the story afterwards in the club, and like all impossible crimes it was really simple. The way the crime was committed, and the identity of the criminal, were obvious once you knew his occupation.

"And of course you guessed it," one of his listeners said nastily.

"Not guessed, deduced. That's the point of the story."

It began when Ossie Gregory – who was always called that for some reason, although he wasn't an Australian and his name was not Oswald but Dick – came to see him. Gregory also was a private detective, of a humble kind. After a couple of drinks he would tell you that he had been a boxer and a bodyguard, had worked in a casino and a circus, and had been a cowboy on the biggest ranch in Texas. Just now he was worried.

"It's Solly Rubens's daughter, she's getting engaged. You know Solly Rubens?" Quarles nodded. Solly was the flashiest bookmaker in London. "Solly likes to put on a show, you know that, he's bought her this rope of pearls as an engagement present, cost him I don't know how many thousand quid. Nothing'll do for him but the pearls are on show at her engagement party for everyone to see, then he'll take 'em out of the case, put 'em round her neck and everyone says hurrah for Solly, all right? So he's hired me to be there, keep an eye on 'em and on everything in general. Get it?"

"It sounds straightforward enough."

"Should be, but then yesterday he got this."

"This" was a sheet of paper, on which words cut from newspapers had been pasted. They read:

TEN O'CLOCK YOU'VE GOT YOUR PEARLS,
TEN FIFTEEN YOU HAVEN'T

Quarles raised his eyebrows. "Nice of him to tell us when he's going to take them."

"It's just about when Solly's going to put them round his daughter's neck. I don't like it, Mr Quarles. A straightforward job, taking care of toughs, that's okay, but something like this needs more in the upper story than I've got." He said wistfully: "I don't suppose you could come along? Two heads are better than one, especially when one of them is yours."

That was why Quarles attended Rebecca Rubens's engagement dance at London's newest hotel, the Lanchester.

There were two hundred guests, many of them looking uneasy in their dinner jackets. The pearls were in a showcase at one end of the room and Solly Rubens, with the biggest cigar Quarles had ever seen stuck in his red face, led guests up to them with pride. Ossie stayed near the showcase, his face set in a look of dogged suspicion. Quarles ate smoked salmon, turkey and strawberries, and reflected that although some of the guests might pick pockets, they did not look up to stealing pearls.

Solly came up to him. "Enjoying yourself, got all you want to eat? Seen what I'm giving to my little girl? And she deserves it, let me tell you." He put a large arm round the shoulders of his pert, pretty daughter. "Nothing's too good for her."

"Does that mean you think I'm not good enough?" That was Rebecca's young man, Julius Berry, dark and self-assured. He was wearing a conspicuous emerald-green double-breasted dinner jacket. Solly merely grunted, evidently not delighted by the prospect of having Julius Berry for a son-in-law, but now he turned to greet a small grey-haired man who had just arrived.

"Professor Burtenshaw, this is a real honour. You know my daughter – and Mr Quarles."

"We're old friends," Quarles said. Burtenshaw was one of the greatest British experts on precious stones, in particular diamonds and pearls.

"Hey, Gregory," Solly said. The detective nodded, obviously knowing what he had to do. He unlocked the showcase, carefully took out the rope of pearls and handed it to Solly, who passed it to the professor. Quarles looked at his watch. The time was one minute past ten.

"Beautiful," Burtenshaw said. "Perfectly matched. And such lustre. Quite beautiful."

"I'm not going to tell you how much they set me back." Solly looked as though he would have told very willingly if he had been pressed. The pearls went from hand to hand in the circle of a dozen people surrounding Solly. Julius Berry murmured something about them matching their wearer, and passed them on. Ossie watched their progress with unconcealed anxiety, sweat on his forehead, until they came back to him. He returned them to the showcase and locked it.

"Oh no, you don't," Berry cried out suddenly. He turned on a small foxy-looking waiter just behind him. "You had your hand on my wallet. Come on, turn out your pockets. What else have you got?"

The waiter protested innocence, and shook off Berry's hand. Everybody was looking at them.

"Please, darling," Rebecca said. "You've still got your wallet, after all. Don't spoil the evening."

Reluctantly, Berry gave way. Harmony was restored. Solly clapped his hands. "And now, ladies and gentlemen, your attention for a moment, please. Gregory."

Ossie unlocked the showcase, and then paused before touching the pearls. He looked frightened. The veins on his neck stood out like cords. He said in a strangled voice, "Mr Rubens, Professor, Mr Quarles. These don't look right."

Burtenshaw took out the rope in the showcase, looked at it

and said: "These are not the pearls, they're the crudest sort of paste."

Solly Rubens howled with anger. Rebecca began to cry. Quarles looked at his watch again. The time was ten fifteen.

At this point Quarles stopped, and beamed at his club audience. Somebody said: "Go on."

"That's all. The problem is: who stole the pearls and how did he do it?"

"The police searched everybody?"

"Everybody. And everyone who'd touched the pearls when they were passed round was searched and stripped, even Solly and Gregory. They searched the room, too. No good."

"That expert, what's his name, Burtenshaw," said an account-
ant named Sanders, who claimed to solve every detective story
he read. "He was a fake."

"No. I told you I knew Burtenshaw. Everything he said was
true."

Sanders was thinking hard. "That row Berry had with the
waiter was something to do with it. The waiter was an accomplice. Berry stole the pearls and slipped them to him."

"Berry had nothing to do with it. But you're right about the
waiter being an accomplice. His job was just to create a diversion,
so that the thief could hide the pearls."

"Solly Rubens stole them, for the insurance?"

"No."

Sanders's brow was wrinkled. "You're not going to tell us it
was Gregory."

"Yes. He wrote the warning letter, arranged the whole
thing."

"But he called you in himself."

"He wanted a respectable witness, and thought he could fool
me. That was his one mistake," Quarles said modestly.

"You told us he'd been searched, and there was nothing on
him."

"There wasn't."

"He hid them somewhere in the room. Under the showcase,
with chewing gum."

"He didn't hide them in the room."

"But that's impossible. Where were they?"

"When the real pearls were handed back to Gregory he
palmed them and put the paste ones back in the showcase. Then
he got rid of the real ones."

"But how?" Sanders cried. "How?"

"What was Gregory's occupation? I told you that was the
point of the story."

"Why, you told us he was a private detective."

"And what was he before that? I told you he'd worked in a
circus, and I told you he was called Ossie. I put two and two
together, and realised what Ossie might stand for."

There was silence. "Come on then," Sanders said. "What did it stand for?"

'The name of his act. He was a swallower. He used to swallow live frogs and rats, and bring them back alive. A string of pearls was nothing to him. They called him the Human Ostrich."

The White Line

JOHN FERGUSON

Before McNab had negotiated the pivoted chair at the dinner-table in the *Magnificent* – it was her first night out from Sandy Hook – he was greeted by a feminine welcome.

"So we meet again, Mr McNab."

Mrs Westmacott looked up at him with a smile on her clever face. She was a chance acquaintance made on the journey from Washington. McNab expressed his pleasure.

"You are in luck," said she with a nod.

"So I see," he returned with a ceremonious bow.

"Poof! It's not because they place you next *me*. You didn't think I meant *that*!"

McNab looked around as he picked up his spoon.

"Well, it's the luckiest thing I perceive at the moment. Quite enough to content me," he added.

"Why, man, they've given you a front seat for the comedy, and you don't know it. What a waste! There are people on board who'd give a thousand dollars, cash down, to change places with you."

"I wouldn't accept," said McNab, "unless you changed also."

"Ah! And in the train you denied you were Irish!"

To this McNab's only response was an enigmatic smile. People at the tables *were* a little hushed, subdued. But that was the usual state of affairs on the first night out. Later, when they got to know each other, the laughter and the chatter would flow. But the scene that met his eye was gay enough with the women's multi-coloured frocks and the shimmer of their jewels.

"Do you never ask questions, Mr McNab?"

As he turned to her Mrs Westmacott made a moue at him, evidently anxious to impart the information his roving glance had failed to discover. He laughed – internally – at the notion that he was an incurious person. His head ached yet with investigations which had kept his mind keyed up for weeks.

"I was looking for the comedy you spoke of," he said.

Mrs Westmacott turned to him, the morsel of fish poised on the end of her fork.

"And found it?"

He shook his head.

She leant towards him confidentially.

"To the right – opposite – the girl in black – between the two young men. You must recognise her."

"I am not up in types of American beauty – not feminine ones anyhow," he amended. "Still, I seem to – "

"I should think so, indeed. Her picture is in every paper. That is Sally Silver."

"Really? Sally Silver? Now where have I heard that name before?"

Mrs Westmacott laughed.

"How perfectly delicious you are. Oh, how I wish she could hear you!"

"I can be wonderfully dense," McNab admitted. "The times I've missed things under my very nose – you'd never believe. Tell me about her."

"She's Henry Silver's only child – and you won't say you haven't heard of *him*! She's just twenty, and the biggest catch that ever came out of a Chicago pig-pen. But no man's caught her yet."

McNab was regarding the girl with interest. He had wondered already why her presence there had drawn all eyes in her direction. The girl was undeniably pretty, but scarcely beautiful. There was not enough repose in her face for real beauty. The headlong pursuit of pleasure, the eager search for new sensations, were visibly marked on her restless and uneasy face. Her face, McNab thought, would miss the beauty designed for it, and become in a year or two the ruins of what it had *never* been! He felt a certain pity for her.

"The most envied girl we have just now," Mrs Westmacott remarked. "Her diamonds alone make the women hate her."

"She is wearing none."

"No. That is her pose for the moment. The little puss knows very well all the women on board are dying to see the famous Vernese necklace her doting father has just bought for her. That is why she has left it in her cabin."

"And they hate her still more for that?"

"Naturally."

McNab resumed his dinner.

"The men don't seem to miss the diamonds," he observed.

"No. She has a fine neck, and her shoulders are – well, brave."

McNab again looked over at the two men and the girl. With both elbows resting on the table, and with her chin on her clasped hands, she was still listening to the young man on her right, while the youth on her left, who had been getting her shoulder all through, sat crumbling his bread gloomily.

"The two favourites in the race," Mrs Westmacott explained *sotto voce*.

"Not much doubt which is making the running."

Mrs Westmacott looked at him almost in contempt.

"You men!" she said. "You think because at the moment she's showing a preference for Jefferson Melhuish she has turned down young Hilary Harben for good."

"Well, by the look on his face young Hilary Harben seems to share my view."

"Very likely he does, being a man. But any woman could tell him it doesn't follow. The minx knows the betting has lately been on Harben."

McNab was startled.

"What!" he cried. "You don't mean to say people are betting on it. I call that almost indecent."

"Indecent? I like that! You English who flog horses to make them run races for you to bet on – you call this indecent! Why, Sally Silver is proud to know America is betting on this, and both men must know it. Notoriety, Mr McNab, may not be so fine a thing as fame, but it is better than obscurity. As for Hilary's chances, I'm not sorry my money is on him."

"*You* have a bet on this?"

"I have. I stand to win what will pay my six months' trip to Europe twice over. You are surprised? You think I should have backed Melhuish, who is good-looking and wealthy, while Harben is almost poor, and still has the limp he got in the war?" She tapped McNab lightly on the arm and breathed into his ear: "That lameness is no handicap in a woman's eyes. You put something on him, too. You'll get long odds. No? Well, you'll see, in two days there won't be a soul on board from the ambassador to the stewardess who hasn't made a bet on it."

And Mrs Westmacott proved to be right. The daily sweepstake on the ship's progress was thin and tame compared with the zest and excitement aroused by the betting on Melhuish and Harben. McNab marvelled over it. They were all like children, he thought. There was nothing to show – so far as he could see – that Miss Silver must necessarily choose either of her suitors, much less choose one of them before they reached port. It was just a chance. He pointed out the absurdity of the thing one night in the smoking-room, and half a dozen voices promptly offered to bet him on that very chance. McNab went away puzzled. They could not really know. Of course, on board a liner the pace and rhythm of life quickened enormously. Minutes were as hours on land, and hours held as much in them as days. So many things happened quickly, things that would scarcely happen at all, to the same people anyway, ashore. That must be why they were all so confident something was bound to happen in the matter of Sally Silver.

Now, McNab was a keen student of human nature. Professionally his concern was with the darker side, but his connection with New Scotland Yard had not made him a narrow specialist; he remained interested in humanity, in all its infinite variety, which fact is probably the secret of his great professional success. Therefore, McNab turned an eye on Miss Silver, on her two suitors, and on the betting over their chances with all the interest he was wont to give to the study of innocent human foibles in his moments of leisure. The men, he found, all betted on Melhuish, who appeared to be well aware of the fact. He had a way of twirling up his moustache, a way of smiling till you caught just a glimpse of his gold-filled teeth that seemed to irritate the women. But the men backed him as confidently. And the women without exception backed Harben.

For three long days the good-looking, immaculate Melhuish basked in Miss Silver's honeyed smiles, while young Harben limped along the deck to his solitary chair, followed by the sympathetic glances of the ladies.

Then on the fourth day a change came. It came just at the moment when Melhuish's triumph seemed complete, when the men, convinced their bets were safe, were ceasing to chuckle among themselves, and the women almost began to doubt. That is to say, just when interest threatened to die down, Miss Sally Silver took it into her wayward head to readjust matters. Very early on the fourth morning one of Melhuish's backers, coming on deck, found her and Harben, their deck chairs side by side, holding each other's hands! The news circulated with mysterious quickness. At breakfast the men exchanged uneasy glances with each other. By lunch-time they were whispering together about it in odd corners. And all through the long afternoon there was a *hush* on the ship that reminded McNab of a Sunday afternoon he once had to pass in Tunbridge Wells. For all that afternoon Miss Silver and young Harben sat together, and Melhuish paced the deck alone, gnawing the end of his moustache. To the men who covertly watched the pair on the hurricane deck the afternoon seemed an eternity. What it seemed to Melhuish none but Melhuish knew, and he did not tell.

At tea Mrs Westmacott crossed to the corner in which McNab sat with Colonel Baylis.

"Well?" she said brightly.

The colonel almost scowled.

"It won't last!" he snapped.

The lady thrilled with triumph.

"I hear some of you men are already trying to hedge. Now *we* never did that!"

"Our man's not done yet."

She turned to McNab.

"Is that your view?"

"Well, I don't know. He's of the type that takes what he wants."

"It won't last, you'll see," the colonel repeated as Mrs Westmacott returned with the sugar basin. "That monkey is only taking Harben up to give the women a bigger drop. She knows that the cats don't love her much."

He stirred his tea angrily. Mrs Westmacott held out the sugar basin to him.

"An extra lump to-day?" she suggested sweetly.

But after dinner that night the affair took a new turn, one which brought McNab into the business in real earnest in his professional capacity.

It was a fine, still night, with the moon approaching the full, and McNab had gone up to the long hurricane deck to finish his cigar while taking a little gentle exercise. It was still early, but most of the men were down below in the smoking-rooms, while the ladies were in the music saloon. McNab therefore had the deck almost to himself as he paced up and down, first up one side and then down the other, with the long row of state rooms occupying the centre. So quiet was it that above the throb-throbbing of the vessel, as she cut her way across the smooth sea, McNab could distinguish the distant tinkling of a piano. But the deck, with its row of white, untenanted cabins, was like a deserted village, dominated by four great red incongruous chimney stacks. He was watching the silent rolling columns of black smoke from the funnels, following the smoke till it thinned out and the moonlight came through it, when his ear caught a sharp sound behind him. It was like the opening of a door which had been recently varnished when some of the varnish has adhered close to the hinges – a crack, short and abrupt. The unexpectedness of the sound on that quiet, deserted deck, the contrast it made to the continuous throbbing of the screw caught his attention. But after the little start it gave him, interrupting his thoughts, he resumed his silent promenade without giving any more heed to the occurrence. When he reached the aft termination of the deck, however, he found something that amused him – Miss Sally Silver was sitting there *alone*.

Several times that evening in the course of his promenade he had come close enough to see Harben seated by her side and hear the murmur of their voices. Not ten minutes earlier Harben had been there; but now his chair was vacant, a rug lying on the deck looked as if it had been tossed aside. The girl, her elbow on the arm of the chair, and her hand beneath her chin – a characteristic attitude – seemed to be gazing dejectedly into vacancy. If there had been a quarrel, and all the symptoms pointed to it, McNab smiled to think how, once known, it would stir the ship from end to end. Who would have dreamed that the affair would end, not with Sally Silver leaving Harben, but with Harben leaving Sally Silver!

Now McNab was by instinct and occupation an observer, not a talker. So he simply turned on his heel and continued his promenade. Turned on his heel, he distinctly remembered that afterwards. That is to say, instead of crossing over the deck and continuing down the other side as he had been doing for the best part of an hour, he for the first time went back the way he had come.

He had gone half the length of the deck when he saw a man step out of a state-room a little way ahead, close the door gently, and come quickly towards him. Then the man pulled up suddenly, as if at sight of McNab, hesitated an instant, and came on again. McNab, though the figure passed him with down-bent head and in the shadow of the deck houses, recognised him from his limp as young Harben. He was probably on his way to make it up with the girl, McNab thought with a smile, observing as he passed that the cabin bore the number 13. Looking back, he saw Harben now in the full moonlight awkwardly, painfully limping aft. McNab, tossing the butt of his cigar overboard, took out his watch. It was thirteen minutes to nine: his exercise was over. So he went to the lower deck.

He had been in the crowded smoking-room for nearly an hour,

indolently watching a group playing poker for rather high stakes, when a man entered so hurriedly and noisily as to attract immediate attention.

"Heard the latest?" he asked almost breathlessly.

There was so much significance in his tremulous tones that even those who had not cast a glance at his entrance looked up from their game. Indeed, everyone present looked up hopefully. Men reading put their magazines on their knees, even the man dealing out the cards arrested his arm in mid-air to regard the speaker. For it was obvious there was something new in the Silver-Melhuish-Harben affair – or, at least, they hoped so. McNab thought he knew what it was, and that he could have told them as much when he had entered an hour ago. He was slightly amused by this man's snatching at a piece of news which gave him a temporary importance.

"No!" came a chorus of impatient voices as the fellow hung on, enjoying the interest he had aroused.

"Sally's necklace has gone!"

"Gone?"

"Stolen from her cabin to-night."

"Is that all? Serve her jolly well right!" someone grunted in disgust. There came a chorus of approval.

The dealer continued with his cards and the old gentlemen lifted their magazines again.

"What else could she expect – canoodling up there with *that* fellow?"

The chorus of agreement seemed to McNab unfair. Had the thing happened when Melhuish was the girl's favourite the judgment would have been otherwise, and Melhuish would not have been "*that* fellow".

"She'll never get it back. The crooks on liners are smart."

"But on a ship – after all – they can't run away."

"You'll see. Depend on it they had a hiding place ready for the swag before it was lifted."

"This comes of her choosing cabin 13 out of pure bounce."

"I remember once – "

McNab heard no more. He left the saloon. He wanted to think.

Cabin 13! He was quite sure that was the one out of which he had seen Harben come. Harben, of course, might have been sent there for some purpose by Miss Silver herself. There was against that theory – it could easily be settled by Miss Silver – his hesitation on catching sight of someone approaching, and the furtive manner in which he had slunk past, in the shadow, close to the deck houses. But, again, Harben must have known that his limp would betray him. If he had no guilt, why had he been furtive?

Harben was no professional crook, of course, for the expert would not have been taken by surprise, and besides, he was, like his rival Melhuish, an old friend of the Silver family. But why had Harben been surprised to see him? It was to this question McNab recurred most. Harben must have been aware that he had been walking the deck all the time. Then whence came the surprise? He had hesitated and stopped a moment at sight of him. Why?

Suddenly the detective smote his fist on the taffrail as an explanation burst upon him. Of course!

"I'd been walking round and round the deck houses until I saw the girl and the empty chair," he muttered. "Just like a policeman on his beat. But that last time I *turned back*. And when he came out of the cabin he calculated that I'd be on the other side. But what a fool the man was not to put the thing back once he *knew* he had been seen."

McNab lighted another cigar reflectively. Perhaps, he mused, Harben had no chance to go back. Perhaps, as was not uncommon, he supposed his lameness less noticeable than it actually was, and believed he had avoided detection. The furtive slinking along in the shadows suggested he had that belief.

The detective, in his dark corner, grinned to himself. Harben would probably stick to the diamonds; he did not know with whom he had been playing that little game of "Here we go round the mulberry bush" up there in the moonlight! There was little danger of such an amateur in crime as Harben getting frightened and dropping the things overboard. He must need them badly indeed. Had he come away without sufficient funds for the trip? He could not take money from Miss Silver, and he would salve any qualms by telling himself it was for her sake, her ultimate happiness. Later he would tell her all, perhaps; own up, and she would cry out: "You poor boy! Why didn't you ask me for the money?" So the young fool would picture the happy ending!

McNab had no desire to thrust his professional services on those concerned – indeed, he did not suppose his services would be required – but being well aware of a witness's duties in such matters he went to see Miss Silver. Miss Silver, however, had retired, prostrated by her loss, so the maid informed him. Well, his knowledge of Harben's movements would keep till morning. McNab himself sought his berth.

Next morning he was much later at breakfast than usual. He had slept badly. He had not, somehow, been able to dismiss this

case from his mind so easily. He had lain awake, thinking it out.
He had traversed all the facts repeatedly, and some features of the
thing left him doubtful. He was, however, scarcely seated before
he sensed that something new had happened. People stood about
in little groups with their heads together. There were noddings
and whisperings. Mrs Westmacott, observing him, came across
and took a place beside him.

"Well," she said, "you've heard what they're saying?"

"No. What is it?"

"They say the thief is a man with a limp. He was seen coming
out of her state-room."

McNab almost bounded out of his chair.

"What?" he cried. "What's that you say?"

"Ah, you know what that means. There aren't many lame men
aboard, are there?"

"I've seen only one."

"Well, that seems to fasten the thing on him all right. Do *you*
think he did it?"

McNab regained his self-control. He looked at her fixedly.

"I did," he said, "till you told me others are saying he did it."

"What on earth do you mean by that?"

"It sounds odd, but the explanation is simple: *I* was the only
person who saw him come out of her state-room."

Her woman's wit took her at a bound to the vital point.

"And you have not mentioned it to anyone?"

McNab looked at her in admiration.

"Not unless I've been talking in my sleep."

"And do you?" she asked anxiously.

"No," he replied with a grin. "That is one of the things for-
bidden us at Scotland Yard."

Her face changed from anxiety to amazement.

"Scotland Yard! Are you – "

"Hush! Just tell me who you think did it?"

"Melhuish," she rejoined promptly. "He is your man."

McNab shook his head.

"It doesn't follow. The first question to ask in the presence of
a crime is, *cui bono – who benefits?*"

"Well, *he* does. Sally will certainly – "

He put a hand on her arm restrainingly.

"Yes, but this Vernese necklace in itself supplies a sufficient motive to a few hundreds of us, perhaps. Melhuish had *one* motive which no one else but Harben shared, that is Sally Silver herself. But the motive of Sally Silver's diamonds would be equally strong for a far larger number."

"Still, I feel *sure* it was Melhuish. Something tells me."

"Yes, your dislike of him. And if I were to put the case before any of these men, they would, for the same reason, be equally sure it was Harben."

"And you?" she asked.

"I suspect everyone but you. That is why I ask your help."

"Me!" she flushed with excitement. "Women are said to talk."

"They do. So do men. Look at them."

As he reached for the marmalade he nodded towards a group of men in eager converse.

"You mean to take up this case?"

"Yes. You see this infernal thief has brought me into it. He *used* me. That's what it amounts to. For it was someone who imitated Harben's limp and affected hesitation at the sight of me, he expects me to say I had seen Harben coming out of the cabin. He used *me*: that stings, you know. If it was Harben himself – "

McNab broke off pensively.

"You need my help because the thief knows you know and will be on the watch?" Mrs Westmacott asked.

"Especially when he finds I shall say nothing. You see," he went on, "we have not merely to detect the thief but to keep him, if he is startled, from dropping the necklace over the side."

Mrs Westmacott sighed with a half wry smile.

"To think I should find myself trying to save *her* necklace. I shouldn't *dream* of doing it if I wasn't *sure* Hilary Harben is innocent. You can't be sure that someone else wasn't hiding up there, watching both you and him."

"I don't deny it. Anything is possible. And if Harben is cleared, so much the better for your bet. Can I count on you?"

"What do you wish me to do?"

"Very little – and that little easy. I am not going to report what I saw to Miss Silver or to the captain. I am not going to make any inquiry. I am going to sit out on the promenade deck entirely absorbed in a book. All I want you to do is to stroll over, and give me news of what happens from hour to hour."

"It sounds just a man's idea of a woman's job. But what if nothing happens?"

"Then come and tell me."

At eleven she came to him with her first report. Harben had tried to see Miss Silver, but had been refused admission. A notice had been posted asking anyone who had been on the hurricane deck between the hours of eight and ten to see the purser in his office.

At half-past eleven she reported having seen Miss Silver and Melhuish together on the upper deck.

At noon she returned with the news that Harben's cabin was then being searched. There was a crowd outside the door. McNab sent her off to join the crowd, while he sat on apparently engrossed in his book.

She was back in half an hour. Nothing had been found, of course. She laughed:

"The amusing thing is that Harben finds that he himself has been robbed. Oh, it's nothing of consequence – just a leather collar-box missing."

"Ah!"

There was so much significance in the ejaculation that she was startled.

"Did Harben mention it?"

"No, the steward who does his cabin did."

"A leather collar-box? It would just do to hold the necklace, I suppose."

McNab lay back again in his chair and shut his eyes, while Mrs Westmacott waited.

She waited a long time, or so it seemed to her. She began to think McNab must have fallen asleep, so still was he. Then he startled her again.

"What is the colour of Harben's door, red or green?" he asked.

"Neither; it is white," she replied, wondering if he were mad.

"Good! Do you think you could get me a ball of wool?"

"A ball of wool?" she cried. "What for?"

"To snare the thief. If any lady friend can provide a ball of of wool, we have him."

"Heaven above us!" she murmured, aghast.

"Let me see," he went on, "there is to be some sort of entertainment tonight, isn't there?"

She welcomed what seemed a return to sanity.

"Yes – a concert. The Orpheus String Quartette have kindly – "

"Well," he cut in, "for the sake of variety we'll provide a conjuring trick also – if you can find me that ball of wool."

Mrs Westmacott was very nervous at the concert – thoroughly disquieted about McNab. Of course, the recent events had upset everyone; but the soothing effect of classical music is well known, and perhaps that is why practically every passenger in the ship was present. Even Miss Silver came in before the interval, looking very pale and tired, leaning on the arm of Melhuish. Melhuish, after finding her a seat, left the saloon, returning with a wrap for her just before the interval. McNab, Mrs Westmacott saw, was very fidgety. He kept looking at his watch, glancing keenly about him. When the interval came, most of the men seemed ready for a stimulant. She saw Colonel Baylis approach McNab with an invitation on his face; and she did not miss the curt refusal he received. The men began to filter towards the door. Captain York, who was acting as chairman, rose and tapped the table.

"Gentlemen," he said, addressing those who were moving towards the door, "I regret very much that for the moment it will be impossible for anyone to leave this saloon. You are aware that a necklace, a very valuable necklace, has disappeared from the cabin of one of our lady passengers. A general search for it, which I am sure no honourable or innocent person here will resent, is now in progress. There are, unfortunately, black sheep in most ships of – "

Mrs Westmacott saw McNab rise to his feet.

"Excuse me," he said in calm, determined tones. "There is no need to detain these gentlemen, nor to disarrange their baggage. The necklace is in a leather collar-box in Mr Hilary Harben's cabin."

A tense hush fell on the saloon – a moment's breathless silence, and then Harben, pushing aside the men in his way, came towards the platform with blanched face and clenched fists.

"That is a lie!" he called out. "I'll make you eat those words. How do you know what is, or what is not, in my cabin? Who are you?"

"I am the person who saw the man with the limp come out of Miss Silver's cabin last night."

An "Ah!" of astonishment ran round the saloon like a wave, and Mrs Westmacott sparing a glance for Miss Silver, saw the girl sink in her chair with both hands covering her face. Melhuish, standing beside the captain, was, like most, eagerly intent on McNab.

"I was not that man, I swear it!" Harben cried out helplessly, as if he did not expect them to believe him. And certainly nobody seemed to. Mrs Westmacott saw the gleam of gold as Melhuish smiled. In the tense, painful silence which ensued, the ship's purser entered and handed up to Captain York the little leather collar-case. As he opened the thing and took out the necklace, the man whispered something to him, and it was evident to all from the way in which he stared at McNab, who was still on his feet, that it had been found where McNab had said.

"I swear I had no hand in this – I never took it!" Harben cried passionately again.

"I know you didn't," said McNab.

Melhuish who had gone forward to receive the necklace from the captain, turned sharply.

"Since you know so much," said the captain, "perhaps you know who did?"

"I do," the reply came quietly, electrifying the whole saloon. "You see, at first I did think the thing had been done by this young gentleman. The man who passed me outside cabin 13 I took for Mr Harben. But in the morning, when I heard that a man with a limp was seen coming out of the cabin, I knew it was someone else. I knew it must be someone else because I was alone on that deck, and had not spoken *to anyone* of what I saw. Anyone might have imitated his walk. Later in the day, when I heard of the missing collar-box, it was clear that the guilty person, through fear of discovery or some other reason, meant to fix the guilt on Mr Harben. That little box which was missing in the forenoon would be found when the general search was made. The inference would be that it had been hidden till the earlier search was over, and when it was discovered later in his cabin with the necklace inside the conclusion would be irresistible."

McNab paused while everyone hung on his words.

"All that was easy. The real difficulty lay in detecting the guilty man. It was, of course, useless to watch Mr Harben's cabin all day. The real thief would not venture to go in so long as anyone was in sight. Well, the road was left open, and he did his trick exactly as I thought it would be done, about half an hour ago, and not a soul saw him do it."

Mrs Westmacott sighed miserably as she saw Melhuish's face brighten on hearing McNab's last words. Captain York himself voiced her fear:

"Then you cannot prove who this black sheep is? I suppose we must be content with – "

McNab held up his hand. "Pardon me, but that is exactly the task I set myself. I have *marked* the black sheep."

"How?"

Half a dozen cried out the question, and did not know they had spoken.

"The door of Mr Harben's cabin is white. I fastened a length of wool from one side to the other five feet five inches high, chalking it so that it was invisible against the door. The two broken ends will be found hanging there now, and the man who entered the cabin ought to have a chalk line across the lapels of his coat exactly five feet five inches from the floor."

Instinctively Melhuish had looked down. He saw what all saw, a thin white line across the collar of his faultless dress coat.

Pitiably the man wilted. The tense silence was broken suddenly by a girl's voice.

"Hilary, oh Hilary, I am so glad! *So glad!*"

The words in themselves might have committed her to nothing, but there was that in her tones which led every man who heard them to settle his bet without a murmur.

The Convict and the Clerics

J. S. FLETCHER

To a man who had just succeeded in escaping from prison, Brychester, in the still hours of an autumn morning presented possibilities and opportunities which Medhurst, who had been a shrewd citizen of the world before he became a criminal, was quick to perceive and to take advantage of. Brychester itself was unique in its arrangements. One of the smallest of English cathedral cities, it was packed into very little room; you could walk round its enclosing walls within half an hour. It only possessed two streets; one ran from north to south, the other from east to west; they met at the Cross in the middle of the city, and there split it up into four quarters. There were little lanes and alleys in those four quarters; there were also, at the backs of the old houses and mansions, large, roomy, leafy gardens. It was in one of these, a veritable wilderness that Medhurst hid himself about three o'clock in the morning, after breaking out of the city gaol, which stood a mile away beyond the walls.

There had been very little of actual breaking out to be done. Medhurst, recently sentenced to a considerable term of penal servitude, consigned to Brychester Gaol to await eventual delivery to Dartmoor or Portland, had kept his observant eyes wide open from the moment he exchanged his own smart apparel for the dingy, arrow-ornamented garb of the convict. He was naturally a man of resource and ingenuity, and he meant to escape the unpleasant consequences of his misdeeds. Brychester Gaol was old-fashioned; its warders were a little slack in attending to their duties. And Medhurst watched his opportunity, and, by means of a little interference with the lock of his cell, and a watchful observation of the movements of men on night duty, and a carefully acquired knowledge of the outer works of his prison-house, managed to get free with little difficulty. And here he was, in the earliest hours of an October day, shivering a little, but eager and ready, in the summer-house of a shady garden – wondering what to do next.

Medhurst's great immediate difficulty was that which confronts all convicts who break prison – his clothes. There was another in the lack of money, but the clothes problem was nearest and most important. If he only had clothes he could get away – he had no doubt he could get away even in a penniless condition. Of course, if he had money, he could get away all the more easily. But clothes were the prime necessity – and he reflected that they must be good. He was a man of exceptionally good presence – a tall, well set-up, rather distinguished-looking man, as many people had observed when he stood in the dock. He felt that he would be less conspicuous in really good attire – the use of which would be natural to him – than in, say, the garb of a navvy or of a labourer. One fact was certain, before daybreak he must find garments wherein to get out of Brychester. For reasons into which it is not necessary to enter, Medhurst believed that his escape would not be noticed until six o'clock in the morning. He had, therefore, three hours in which to do something. And, believing that if one has something to do, one should do it at once, he moved stealthily out of his hiding place and began to examine his surroundings. He was able to make out that the old-fashioned garden in which he stood was one of several lying at the rear of a number of quaint-roofed houses, situated between the high walls of Brychester Cathedral – houses, in fact, tenanted by the principal ecclesiastical dignitaries. Surely, he thought, there must be some means of penetrating into one of these quiet residences, of obtaining sober and befitting raiment? At any rate, seeing that much depended on the matter, he would have a try for it.

It was very quiet, almost painfully quiet, in these cloistered shades. Once or twice Medhurst heard an owl hoot from its retreat in some ruinous building on the outskirts of the city; now and then he caught the screech of a railway whistle far off across the land; every quarter of an hour the silvery chime of the cathedral clock rang above his head. But he heard nothing of the heavy tread of the patrolling policeman; in these quiet gardens there seemed to be small fear of interference. He climbed a wall or two, made his way through a paling or two, looked round the rearward premises of one or two houses, always careful, always watching. And suddenly, in one of the largest houses, he found an open window. It was not much open – only an inch or two – but it gave Medhurst the very chance he wanted. In another minute he had raised the sash, squeezed himself through the aperture, and dropped quietly into what appeared to be a softly carpeted passage.

Medhurst had lately spent so much time in the dark that he had learnt how to see in it. This is an accomplishment which may certainly be acquired by anyone who cares to acquire it; all you have got to do is to wait with patience until you perceive that darkness is not quite so impenetrable as you believed it to be. Objects begin to reveal themselves – especially against windows – besides, there are gradations of darkness. Medhurst, bringing his skill to work, quickly found that he was in a side passage which led into a hall; in the hall he had come to a broad staircase. The carpeting of passage, hall and staircase was particularly thick and soft; nevertheless, Medhurst sat down on the bottom steps of the staircase and took off his prison footgear. For he was going upstairs – which is where raiment is usually to be found.

Big man though he was, Medhurst went up the stairs with less noise than a cat would have made. He blessed the builder of the house; here was no inferior wood to creak at the slightest pressure. He blessed the taste of the owner of the house, who evidently loved velvet-pile carpets. And he was beginning to wish that he had a light when he saw one.

It was certainly not much of a light – a mere crack that shone from a slightly opened door. Medhurst tip-toed to it through a silence as deep as that which no doubt reigned in the aisles of the adjacent cathedral. Here, again, was matter for hearty self-congratulation; the people of the house were evidently all sound sleepers. He arrived at the door, and listened. He peered through the slight opening, and saw that the light came from an oil-stove, partially turned on. He had an idea that this might be a nursery, and he listened more carefully than before, trying to catch the sound of a child's faint breathing. But, as he heard no sound at all, he gently pushed open the door until he could introduce his head and shoulders. And he saw that this was a dressing-room. He hesitated, listened intently, and glided across the threshold.

Always an adept at sizing up a situation, Medhurst saw the splendid possibilities of this as soon as he had given it one quick, all-comprehending glance. He was in the palace of the Lord Bishop of Brychester! There, duly laid out on a dressing-bench, all ready against the morning's toilet duties, were the episcopal garments – the breeches, the apron, the gaiters, the straight-cut coat. There was spotless linen, the round collar, the episcopal stock – there was everything. It was evident that the bishop, having taken his tub of a morning, had nothing to do but walk into this comfortably warmed dressing-room and array himself in his clothes.

"Bishops, however," soliloquised Medhurst, "have doubtless several changes of raiment. At any rate, his Lordship of Brychester won't find these togs here when he next wants them."

For Medhurst saw his opportunity, his magnificent chance. He would go out of Brychester in episcopal attire; he would masquerade as the lawful bishop. He knew the bishop by sight – his lordship had visited the gaol during Medhurst's time. In build and appearance the convict and the ecclesiastic were not unlike. Both were tall, well-made, and athletic-looking men. This would do excellently – excellently! In the darkness of the autumn morning nobody would be able to tell the false from the true during the few minutes at the railway station which would be necessary. It was a veritable interposition of Providence.

Always keeping his ears cocked, Medhurst swiftly stripped off his convict garb, and got into the episcopal paraphernalia. He had a little trouble with the apron, and with the gaiters, and with the stock, but he was a handy man, quick of ideas and possessed of supple fingers, and in a very few minutes he found himself properly arrayed. There was a full-length mirror on one side of the room. He caught a glimpse of himself in the half light, and smiled complacently. But he smiled a great deal more when, turning to a dressing-table, he saw, lying upon its spotless cover, a sovereign, a half-sovereign, and a little silver. He gathered the coins together noiselessly, and deposited them in the episcopal breeches, feeling heartily thankful that their owner had emptied his pockets when he went to bed. Here, again, Providence certainly seemed to be favouring him.

Medhurst now wanted nothing but these very essential things: a muffler, an overcoat, and the Doctor of Divinity's hat which bishops always wear. These, he concluded, he would find in the hall, and he was about to set off in search of them when suddenly he caught sight of his convict's dress. It would never do to leave that about. Certainly it would come out in time – in a few hours really – that a convict had broken out of his gaol and into the palace, and had exchanged his clothes for the bishop's. But Medhurst desired that the knowledge should be restricted as long as possible. Here, again, he was favoured by an inspiration, and an opportunity. He saw a black handbag, inconspicuous and much worn, on the side of which was painted in faded white letters the words, 'The Bishop of Brychester". He lifted this on to a chair, and opened it. Inside it he found a complete Norfolk jacket-suit of dark grey cloth, together with a cap of the same material, and certain accompaniments in the way of shirts, stockings, and ties. This, in fact, was the outfit which the bishop kept in readiness for golfing expeditions. Whenever he took such jaunts there was nothing to do but pick it up, and march off with it. Medhurst saw splendid possibilities in this. Without further delay he crammed his convict garb into an empty space, closed the bag, and carried it quietly down to the hall.

Here Medhurst took a risk. After remaining for some time at the foot of the stairs he ventured on striking a match. One tiny gleam of its light showed him the coat, the hat, the muffler. He put all these things on in the darkness. No sound came from above, or from around; the house was as quiet as ever. And so, fully equipped for his journey, Medhurst sat down on a chair close to the hall door – to wait.

Medhurst knew Brychester. In his pre-criminal days he had often visited the city; in fact, he had spent a week there just before his arrest. And he knew that an express train to London left Brychester station at ten minutes past four every morning, arriving at Victoria a few minutes before six. By that train he proposed to travel – in the character of the Lord Bishop of the Diocese. According to his reckoning nobody would stir in the palace until six o'clock; it would be some time after that before the theft of the bishop's garments was discovered. Before any hue and cry could be roused he, Medhurst, would be safe in town. All that was necessary now was to wait until the cathedral clock chimed four; then he would let himself out, walk quietly through the close into the little station, take his ticket, and be whirled away.

Medhurst found no difficulty in putting his theory into practice. On the first stroke of four he quietly opened the front door picked up the handbag, and stole quietly away across the close and through the deserted streets to the station. And there everything turned out even better than he had dared to hope. He had pulled down the beribboned brim of his episcopal hat; he had swathed his face up to the tip of his nose in the episcopal muffler; he had turned the collar of the episcopal overcoat up to his ears. There were few people about in the half-lighted station, and the clerk in the booking-office, and the obsequious porter who possessed himself of the handbag, and opened the door of a first-class compartment, had not a doubt that the gentleman whom they sped on his journey was the Bishop of Brychester.

"And indeed I might almost begin to believe that I am he!" laughed Medhurst, when the train was sliding rapidly away over the dark country. "I am he, at any rate, for two hours. But what's going to happen then?"

As a preliminary to further operations, he searched the pockets of the appropriated garments. He found nothing in them, however, but a few cards in a well-worn case. He was not sorry to find these cards; he foresaw that they might come in useful later on. Then he searched the bag again. There was nothing in it but what he had already seen – and his own broad-arrowed attire. He thought once of throwing that out of the window, then of hiding it under the cushions of the carriage; on second considerations, he closed the bag on it and the bishop's mufti.

The possession of that mufti gave Medhurst a new idea. He wanted to reach the house of an old friend in Kent, a friend whom he could fully trust, and who would certainly manage to get him secretly away to the Continent. This friend lived in a small village near Sevenoaks, a village so small that its inhabitants would certainly be excited if a bishop's apron and gaiters were seen in it. But they would not take undue notice of a gentleman in an inconspicuous Norfolk jacket and knickerbockers. Obviously, then, the thing to do was to make yet another change of attire.

When the express ran into Victoria, Medhurst seized his bag and made for a taxicab which stood almost opposite the point where his compartment had come to a halt. The light was of the early morning order; the chauffeur was half asleep. He saw what he considered to be an ecclesiastical gent in leggings and a queer hat, and sprang down and opened the door.

"Go round to the hotel," said the supposed dignitary in muffled tones. The chauffeur drove round to the Grosvenor Hotel; his fare got out, took his bag, and spoke one word: "Wait!"

The chauffeur touched his cap, and Medhurst walked into the hall, to be welcomed by an obsequious official who knew a bishop when he saw one.

"I wish," said Medhurst, "for a room in which I can change my clothes. And perhaps you can send me some coffee up to it? I – the fact is, I am going into the country this morning to play golf, and I wish to put on more suitable attire. I shall leave my bag here, and call for it – and to change my garments again – towards evening. You will, of course, charge the room to me for the day."

Half an hour later Medhurst, much more comfortable in layman's garb, walked down to the hall, intending to re-enter his cab. But with his hand on the latch, he suddenly came to a dead halt. Through the glass panel of the door, he saw the taxicab moving off. And in it, just settling himself comfortably against the padded cushions was – a bishop.

Medhurst glanced cautiously around him. There was nobody about in the hall beyond a servant or two engaged in domestic occupations. On its stand near the window of the office reposed the register wherein guests signed their names. Medhurst went over to it, swung its heavy covers open, and found the recent entries. There, under date of the previous day, he read one line which, to him, stood out conspicuous from the rest.

"The Lord Bishop of Tuscaloosa and Mrs Sharpe-Benham."

Medhurst closed the heavy book, and turned away chuckling quietly. He understood the situation now. And he began to thank his stars that an unusually gloomy morning, a sleepy chauffeur, and the presence at the hotel of a Colonial prelate, who, no doubt, wished to get to some very early service, had made his own circumstances much easier. It was with a feeling of immense satisfaction that he walked out of the hotel, and strolled off into the unwonted liberty of the streets.

The chauffeur whom Medhurst had bidden to wait outside the hotel, had given no particular attention to his fare. He was not very well acquainted with the peculiarities of clerical attire; certainly he could not tell a dean from an archdeacon, nor an archdeacon from a bishop. All he knew was that there were clergymen who wore what he called leggings, and had the brims of their hats tied to the crowns with bits of ribbon, and that these were big pots in their walk of life.

He saw his fare go into the hotel, and he believed it was his fare who came hurriedly out of the hotel twenty minutes later, who jumped quickly into the cab, and who bade him make all haste to St Paul's Cathedral. He had not the ghost of a notion that this was not his original fare at all, but was in reality the Bishop of Tuscaloosa, a Colonial prelate, just then in England, who was due at St Paul's at five minutes to seven o'clock, who had slightly overslept himself, and who, rushing out of his hotel, had leapt into the first vehicle he saw.

And when he set this genuine prelate down at St Paul's, and had a better opportunity of looking at him, he still believed him to be the man he had taken up just an hour before, when the Brychester express steamed into Victoria. The Bishop of Tuscaloosa glanced up at the clock of St Paul's, and turned to the chauffeur.

"I think you had better wait for me," he said. "I shall not be here very long, and then I want to be driven elsewhere."

Even then nothing struck the chauffeur as being different. He merely glanced at the tall and athletic figure careering up the steps (Sharpe-Benham had been a noted man in the playing-fields in his ante-Colonial days), lighted his pipe, purchased a halfpenny morning paper from a passing itinerant, and settled himself down in his seat until the bishop had finished his business or his devotions. He was still reading the latest racing news when, forty minutes later, the bishop emerged from the cathedral in company with another clergyman. The other clergyman, as they came up to the cab, made some facetious remark about the wickedness of keeping taxicabs waiting while the meters ran on unchecked.

"I know – I know," said the bishop. "But the fact is, I am obliged to drive some distance into the East End, and this cab is so good and comfortable that I decided to keep it."

The other clergyman laughed, shook hands, and went off in the direction of the deanery, and the bishop turned to the chauffeur.

"I want you," he said, "to drive me to St Hedwige's Church at East Ham. That's a long way, isn't it?"

The chauffeur folded up his newspaper, and crammed it into his pocket.

"Pretty tidy way that, sir," he answered. "Whereabout is this church, sir?"

"That we must find out when we get to East Ham," said the bishop. "But – I think I must have some breakfast before I go so far." He paused, gazing wistfully around him at the tall buildings. "I suppose there is no restaurant or anything of that sort about here?" he asked.

"Cannon Street Station Hotel just round the corner, sir," suggested the chauffeur. "Get breakfast there, sir."

"That," replied the bishop, getting into the cab, "will do excellently. We will go there first, then."

The chauffeur drove along to Cannon Street Station, pointed out the hotel entrance to his fare, and prepared to do more waiting. The bishop, who was a man of kindly nature, looked at his driver thoughtfully.

"Perhaps you, too, would like to breakfast?" he said. "If so, pray do. I suppose I shall be three-quarters of an hour, at any rate."

"Thank you, sir," said the chauffeur. He glanced at the clock and saw that eight was about to strike. "I'll be back here at twenty-to-nine, sir," he went on. "Ain't had no breakfast meself yet!" he added, with a grin.

The bishop smiled, nodded, and walked into the hotel. He was shown into the coffee-room with the politeness due to his dignity. He ordered his food, he asked for *The Times*, he settled himself quietly and comfortably to his breakfast, he took his time over it. The waiter who attended to him had given him a seat near the fire; the bishop, satisfied with his own immediate affairs, did not pay any attention to the other people in the room. And he certainly did not observe a rather large, official-faced sort of person who came quietly in, and, under cover of a general look round, contrived to eye him, the bishop, with a searching inspection.

At a quarter to nine o'clock the bishop laid aside *The Times* on one hand, and his napkin on the other, and inserted his fingers in the pocket wherein he usually carried his ready cash. To his horror, he found that there was no cash there. He hastily felt for his pocket-book, in which he kept a banknote or two in readiness for possible emergencies. But his pocket was empty – all his pockets were empty. Then he suddenly remembered that, in the hurry incident upon his belated arising that morning, he had left his loose cash, his purse, his pocket-book, all his trifles, on his dressing-table. It was awkward, but it was no great matter after all. He summoned the head waiter, who came forward with a respectful presentation of the bill.

"I am sorry, but I have left my purse and all my belongings at the Grosvenor Hotel where I am staying," said the bishop. "I left there very hastily this morning to keep an appointment at St Paul's. But I have a taxicab waiting for me downstairs, and I will send the driver at once to fetch my purse."

The head waiter replied that that would be quite all right, and the bishop walked out of the room, a little vexed with himself for having slept ten minutes over his time. He went downstairs, and was about to step into the station, where he saw the taxicab awaiting him, when the official-faced person who had eyed him from the door of the coffee-room, and who had exchanged a word or two with the head waiter when the bishop walked out, came up from behind, and stopped him with a polite but frigid bow.

"May I have a word with you, sir?" he asked.

The bishop turned in surprise. There was a note of firmness in the man's voice which converted the request into something very like a command. The bishop, a man of spirit, felt his face flush a little.

"You wish to speak to me?" he said.

"If you please," replied the man. He indicated the door of a side room, and bowed the bishop within. "I am sorry," he continued, in the same firm and frigid tone; "I understand your bill is not paid?"

The bishop's first flush changed to something more vivid.

"Really!" he exclaimed. "This is – " But here he pulled himself up; after all, the fault was his own. "I have just explained to your head waiter that I am sending for my purse," he continued. "I left it on my dressing-table, being in a hurry this morning. I have a taxicab outside – the driver will fetch what I want."

The official-faced person still seemed very firm. He glanced at the episcopal apron.

"You are the Bishop of – " he began.

"I am the Bishop of Tuscaloosa," answered the captive, with some asperity.

"Where is that?" demanded the inquisitor, more firmly than ever.

"Really, really!" exclaimed the bishop. "This is – my good man, do you really suggest that – "

"I suggest nothing," replied the other. "I am merely asking for information. You come here, run up a bill, leave without paying it, and – to be plain – I may as well tell you that I am a police officer. The fact of the case is," he went on, as another formidable-looking person entered the room, "the fact of the case is, the palace of the Bishop of Brychester was broken into early this morning by an escaped convict, who is believed to have got away by the four o'clock train from Brychester in the bishop's clothes. Now you answer the description of that convict."

The bishop felt as if he were suddenly deprived of speech. Just as suddenly he laughed.

"My good sir!" he exclaimed. "This is ridiculous! Utterly ridiculous! I am the Bishop of Tuscaloosa, which is in Canada. I am at present staying at the Grosvenor Hotel; I have just come up from St Paul's Cathedral, where I am well known to many members of the Chapter. The chauffeur who is without will tell you that he has just driven me from the Grosvenor Hotel, and – "

The first man made a sign to the second, who left the room, and instantly returned with the driver of the taxicab. The first man directed the driver's attention to the bishop.

"Where did you drive this gentleman from?" he asked peremptorily.

The driver glanced at all three with signs of rising suspicion.

"Well, from St Paul's last," he answered, "and before that from the Grosvenor Hotel, and before that from Victoria Station!"

The bishop started.

"From Victoria Station!" he exclaimed. "My good fellow, you did not drive me from Victoria Station! You drove me – "

The driver became actively suspicious; so far he had not seen

the colour of the bishop's money. Besides, he had waited twenty minutes outside the Grosvenor.

"Ho, didn't I!" he exclaimed. "I suppose I didn't drive you round from Victoria 'rival platform to the Grosvenor, did I, where I waited twenty minutes for yer? Oh, no!" He made a derisive face, seeing how things were going, and turned to the two men.

"He come into Victoria by the Brychester express," he continued. "That what gets in just afore six – course he did!"

The detectives closed in upon the unhappy bishop. There was no doubt in their minds that they had effected a smart, if lucky capture. And it was only in accordance with the nature of things

that they convoyed their captive there and then to the nearest police station.

Medhurst strolled away from the hotel towards Victoria Street, thinking. His next move, he reflected, ought to be towards definite liberty. Already the discovery of his nocturnal doings at Brychester Palace would have been made. Well – it would take some little time for the local police to communicate with London. It would be found out – nothing more easy – that he had left Brychester by the four o'clock train; very good, but even then he reckoned that he still had an hour or two's start of everything. The first thing to do was to get to his trusty friend. And he suddenly remembered that the trusty friend had an office in London, close to the Mansion House. Why not go there instead of running the risk of a railway journey into Kent? The principal stations would be watched; he had better keep away from them until he had effected yet another change of clothes.

Medhurst accordingly made for the city. He turned into the Underground Railway, and took a ticket for the Mansion House. Amongst the early crowd of men going to shops and offices he would feel himself safe; however anxious to recapture him the police might be, they could not set patrols in every street of London. He would stroll about the city until nine o'clock or so, when his friend would be likely to put in an appearance – Medhurst remembered that the friend was an early bird, who came up by one of the first trains. He felt no fear now – it seemed to him that all was going very well indeed.

In the Underground train Medhurst made an interesting discovery. In the breast-pocket of the Norfolk jacket he found a cigar-case. There were four uncommonly fine cigars in it – he at once lighted one, with the keen zest and enjoyment of a man who had not tasted tobacco for long, weary weeks. But as he was examining the case, before resorting it to his pocket, he found something else. In a slip-pocket, obviously designed to carry stamps or similar small articles, he found a couple of blank cheques of the Brychester and County Bank. Their lawful owner, the bishop, was evidently a careful man, who provided for unforeseen contingencies; he carried a blank cheque in case he should want cash; anybody, of course, will cash a cheque for a bishop.

Medhurst laughed over this discovery. It was, however, of no particular interest to him just then, and he put the cheques back in their place, and the cigar-case in his pocket, and smoked in great contentment until he came to the Mansion House Station. There he got out and went up into the streets, which were already beginning to be busy.

It was immaterial to him where he went for the next hour or so; accordingly he loafed around anywhere, but took good care always to be moving, as if with a purpose. He went along by the Bank, and round by the Guildhall, and into Aldersgate, and through various small streets into Smithfield; there he turned south, and made his way into Ludgate Hill. And loafing about there he paused to gaze into the window of a bookseller's shop, and before he was aware of it he found himself staring at a book which stood with title-page and frontispiece exposed, on a shelf immediately in front of him. The title-page conveyed the information that this was a work on Athletics and Christianity, by the Lord Bishop of Brychester; the frontispiece was a photogravure of the right reverend author. And underneath it was a facsimile of the bishop's signature.

Medhurst was a man of rapid thought, and he was temperamentally quick at seizing opportunities. He saw a fine opportunity immediately before him. In his pocket reposed two of the Bishop of Brychester's blank cheques, there before him was a very good reproduction of the bishop's autograph. A rare opportunity, indeed; for Medhurst was an expert imitator of other people's handwriting. That, indeed, was why he had come into contact with the law. Those who had administered the law in his case had been so struck by his expertness, in fact, that they had judged it well to consign him for a good many years to regions where his ability would be stultified. And the judge who had announced his fate to him had been unkind enough to remark, in dry and laconic fashion, that within the memory of man forgers had made the acquaintance of the scaffold and the hangman.

Medhurst walked into the shop, fingering his loose change. His keen sense of humour made him smile as he bought the bishop's book with the bishop's own money. It was a small, thin, genteel book – merely a reprint of two or three lectures given to young men – and he slipped it into his outer pocket and went away. Pursuing his previous plan, he continued to stroll about the streets, up one, down another, always keeping within easy reach of the block of buildings near the Mansion House, in which his trusted friend had his office. But Medhurst had a task to perform, an adventure to undertake, before he went to his friend – he was going to make use of his criminal facility of imitating penmanship.

He turned into a teashop at last, and ordered a light breakfast. While it was being brought to him he carefully studied the facsimile of the Bishop of Brychester's signature. It was an easy signature to imitate, there were no marked peculiarities in it; it was not the writing of a literary man, nor of a scholar, but rather of a business-like, straightforward sort, without twirls, flourishes, or elongated downstrokes. By the time Medhurst had finished his simple breakfast he knew that handwriting so well, had so photographed it on his brain, that he had no fear of being able to write out a cheque in such accurate imitation of it that the bishop himself would be puzzled in detecting the forgery.

Medhurst went straight to business. He had already thought of a well-known jeweller's shop in Cheapside where he could do what he wanted; it had the great advantage of being practically next door to the block of buildings into which he meant to disappear as soon as his proposed transaction was safely over. He entered the jeweller's shop with all the assurance in the world and was politely greeted by a manager who, seeing a soberly attired gentleman in a clerical collar, set his customer down as a country parson who had come to town in his rustic garb. But Medhurst quickly disabused the manager of that impression. Drawing out the well-worn card-case, he laid one of the Bishop of Brychester's cards on the glass-topped counter. The manager bowed again, more politely than before, and gave his episcopal visitor a seat.

"I have frequently seen your watches advertised," said the supposed bishop, "and, as I have a little time to spare before going into the country to play golf, I thought I would call and inspect them. The fact is, I want to make a present to my domestic chaplain, who has just been preferred to a living, and I think a good watch – gold, of course – would be the best thing I could give him. As I say, I have noticed your advertisements in the newspapers. I believe you have a very good keyless hunter-watch at about – something under forty pounds?"

The manager hastened to lay before his customer a variety of gold watches of many prices. Medhurst examined them with interest and with care, talking pleasantly all the time. Eventually he selected an elegant and useful article which was priced at thirty-three guineas. And upon that he produced one of the blank cheques. "I will make out this cheque for fifty pounds," he remarked as the manager handed him writing materials. "Perhaps you can give me change?"

"With pleasure, my lord," responded the manager. He had no doubt of his visitor's identity. Had he not received the bishop's card? Was there not lying there beside the bishop's gloves a copy of a book, *Athletics and Christianity*, with the bishop's name upon it? He handed over fifteen pounds and seven shillings, and thanked his supposed lordship for his custom.

Medhurst made his most dignified bow, and put on his blandest smile. He glanced at a timepiece hanging behind the counter, and began to hurry.

"Dear me!" he exclaimed. "I have left myself little time to catch my train at Cannon Street. I must hasten."

The manager swept round the counter, and opened the door with a deep reverence.

"Just round the corner, my lord," he said. "Your lordship will do it in two minutes."

Medhurst smiled and nodded, and passed swiftly out. He certainly went round the corner which the manager indicated. Then he went round another corner, and round another. And then he plunged into a block of buildings contrived on the principle of a rabbit-warren. Within five minutes of leaving the jeweller's shop he was in the private office of the trusty friend, who had just admitted himself, and now made great haste to lock the door on both of them.

Meanwhile the jeweller's manager, having watched the supposed bishop round the corner, went back into the shop, rubbing his hands with satisfaction at having started the day so well.

Suddenly he caught sight of the book and the gloves – entirely forgotten by Medhurst – which still lay on the counter. He snatched them up, shouted a word to his assistants, and ran after the customer. He careered down Bucklersbury, he shot across

Queen Victoria Street, he raced along Walbrook, he made a perilous dash over Cannon Street and into the station. He was almost breathless when he ran up to the barrier of the departure platform, staring about him.

"Have you seen a bishop pass in?" he panted as he approached the ticket-puncher. "Tall gentleman – Bishop of Brychester!"

The ticket-puncher gave the jeweller's manager a glance.

"There was a party what called himself Bishop of Brychester arrested here this morning!" he growled. "Bilked the 'otel, he did. Stuffed himself, and had nothing to pay with – that's what 'e done! D'yer want im? 'Cause you'll find him round at the p'leece station."

The jeweller's manager suddenly felt very ill. His head swam. He walked away. Then he recovered just as suddenly. The bilker could not be the same man who had just visited him – impossible! Still, it would not be out of his way to visit the police station. He knew some of the officials there, and he went off to them and told his story. What he wanted to know was – how did this extraordinary coincidence come about?

The police official to whom the manager told his story listened in silence – in silence he remained for some minutes.

"Happened just now?" he suddenly asked.

"Within half an hour," answered the manager. He smiled bravely. "Of course," he said, "mine was the real bishop. But – who's your man – who's the impostor?"

The official crooked his finger.

"Come this way!" he said.

He led the manager to a certain stronghold, wherein the unhappy Bishop of Tuscaloosa was still expostulating with his incredulous guardians. But even as they entered it by one door, there was ushered in at another a very great ecclesiastical dignitary, as familiar in the city as St Paul's itself, at sight of whom everybody in the room became profoundly respectful.

He advanced upon the Colonial prelate with outstretched hands.

"My dear bishop!" he exclaimed. "What a lamentable – what a ridiculous mistake! What an unfortunate – "

The police official who had conducted the jeweller's manager into the room suddenly swept him out of it.

"Quick – quick!" he said. "Come and describe that fellow you've told me about! That's the real man! We must be on to him sharp! Come on! Where did you say he was off to? But, of course, he hasn't gone there – not he!"

In that the police official was quite right. At that moment Medhurst, who had already effected another change of clothes, was being quietly carried away to a reasonable prospect of ultimate liberty.

Portrait of Henry

ELISABETH BERESFORD

When Henry Masters died at the age of eighty-two the subsequent ripples of sorrow which passed through the family circle were also tinged with relief. As a second cousin put it after the funeral, Henry had not been really quite himself for the last two or three years. The nephew to whom this remark was addressed was of a younger generation than the cousin and rather more blunt.

"Off his chump," he said, "I don't know how Aunt Milly put up with him and that's a fact." They both glanced at the widow who was standing under a portrait of her late husband.

Millicent looked tired and drawn certainly, but there was an expression of gentle repose about her face which was somehow soothing and rather comforting. Life with Henry had been like a ride on a switchback. On the top of the ride they had been rich, but it had never lasted for long and down they would slide into debt as yet another of Henry's brilliant business schemes foundered. But Henry had loved her and she had loved him and that had been really all that mattered. Now ahead of her there stretched a plateau of tranquillity and she yearned for it desperately. The last years had been the hardest of all, for since his stroke Henry *had* been trying – there was no harm in admitting it to herself – and at the age of seventy-three she felt that she had earned a rest.

With a sigh of relief, carefully hidden naturally, Millicent saw the last of the funeral gathering out of the shabby little house, eased off her shoes and turned to Dorothy Carter. They had been friends since they were girls and they understood each other perfectly. Dorothy was a timid person and Henry had always frightened her, while he in his turn had treated her with only thinly disguised contempt. "Can't make out what you see in that fussy little hen," he'd said a thousand times, but Millicent only ever smiled and did not reply.

Now the fussy little hen, staring up at Henry's portrait, said, "It's funny, you know Milly, I never thought I'd miss him – but I do."

"It's the quietness," Millicent agreed. "Henry always managed to fill a house somehow. Dear Henry. Now then Dot, down to business. I've had a word with that man in the antique shop and he's given me the name of a Mr Mears who specialises in buying books. He's coming round on Saturday morning to have a look and, I hope, to make me an offer."

"You're so efficient," Dorothy said admiringly.

"I've always had to be," Millicent replied a little sadly. "Dear Henry was very, very clever in many ways, but he never quite understood about the little things in life which need to be arranged. He always said that he would leave me a small nest-egg for my old age, but somehow he never quite managed to get round to it."

Involuntarily both old women turned to study the portrait. It was not a good painting, but something of Henry's fierce vitality had been caught by the artist and there was a curiously knowing, even mischievous expression in the eyes. He was sitting in an arm-chair, one hand loosely holding a book, the other gripping the arm-rest. It had been painted shortly before his stroke and – even at seventy-eight – he appeared to be quite equal to making yet another fortune somewhere in the world.

"How much money do we still need?" asked Dorothy, dragging her eyes away from the picture. Even as a portrait Henry still had the power to make her feel uneasy.

"Five hundred pounds," Millicent replied promptly. "Only five hundred, Dot, and then we can buy that dear little bungalow and have quite enough to live on with our pensions."

"Only," said Dorothy, "it's still a great deal of money, Milly. I do hope Mr Mears is a nice sort of man."

At first glance he was not prepossessing. His face had a certain rat-like quality and when he smiled his eyes remained as hard and cold as grey pebbles. He had started life as a totter like his father before him, but it hadn't taken him long to learn that specialising was the only way to make real money and he had managed in a somewhat limited manner to become an expert on books. He was as sharp as a butcher's cleaver and he wouldn't give you the time of day unless there was something in it for him. He and the man at the antique shop had formed a somewhat uneasy alliance in which neither trusted the other. Their policy was that one good turn deserved another and that both of them kept the score. The report on Millicent Masters's situation had been short and pithy.

Old widow, down on her luck. Husband had been a fly old bird, but useless for the last four years. The furniture wasn't good enough for anything but a jumble sale, but there just might be something in the book line.

"Hardly seems worth wasting my time over," Mears grumbled. His informant shrugged.

"Take it or leave it. Anyway, if you do find anything, remember it was me tipped you off."

Now studying Millicent's gentle face Mears felt his spirits drop still further. She just didn't have the look of a collector.

"How good of you to come," said Millicent, "we've put all the books together in the living-room. My husband was always so fond of reading and somehow we seem to have acquired quite a library. In here Mr Mears."

It was no understatement. Between them Millicent and Dorothy had gathered up every book in the house and Dorothy was still busy writing out the list of titles.

"Nearly done," she said, rubbing her fingers. "Isn't it a splendid collection?"

The two elderly faces turned to him anxiously, but Mears didn't notice. He was too busy running his eyes over the bindings. It was just as he had feared, a right collection all right – of rubbish. Ancient bound volumes of the *Strand Magazine*, complete editions of H. G. Wells printed in a popular series, mounds and mounds of paper backs, Rider Haggards with bent bindings and even a heap of children's story books that were at least forty years old.

"The list," said Dorothy, finishing it with a flourish. "I hope you will be able to understand my writing. It's not in any kind of order I'm afraid, but there just wasn't time. However we thought it might help."

"Yes, thanks," Mears said.

There was a long silence during which Millicent saw in her mind's eye the dear little bungalow that she longed for with all her heart and soul. It was so peaceful, so orderly, so easy to manage. After fifty years of moving round the world with Henry from hotel to boarding house, from flat to rented house she had never once been able to put down roots. Now at last the dream was within her grasp. Surely so many books must be worth five hundred pounds?

"Henry was such a great reader," she said suddenly. "I expect you'd like some coffee, Mr Mears. Come along Dot."

Left to himself Mears scanned rapidly through the list. Even worse than he'd thought at first. *My Polo Pony Peter, Little Kiddies Annual* 1923, *The Businessman's Compendium, Happy Thoughts for Hard Days, Fairy Tales for Young and Old, Susan's Secret.*

"Hal-lo," said Mears flipping through this last, "not quite *all* kiddies stuff is it? Very daring this must have been in its day although nobody'd give it a second look now. Tut tut, Henry old boy."

Mears shook his finger at the portrait and yet whereas it always made Dot think of an impatient schoolteacher and Milly of a mischievous overgrown boy, to Mears, not usually an imaginative man, it suddenly conveyed something else.

"All right, all right," he said uneasily, "only my little joke, no need to take offence."

He turned his back on those hard all-seeing eyes and began to go through the pile with more concentration. Even so he nearly missed it and had put the book aside before the truth came to him. He stood stock still for a moment and then, his hand shaking a little, picked it up again. The book, like many of the others, had been given a brown paper dustcover. Slowly he turned the pages, his eyes devouring first the print and then the strange, almost serpentine illustrations. A princess bound to a tree by the tendrils of her long hair, entwining vine leaves and the tail of a truly terrible, even lecherous dragon. A knight in armour piercing the heart of a witch, with his lance dripping blood. An ogre so obese he seemed to weigh down the page.

Very gently Mears laid down the book and then carefully wiped his fingers and then his forehead, although new beads of sweat formed almost instantly. He took a deep breath and removed the paper cover. The blue and gold binding was intact and looked brand new although it was over a hundred years old. And there, final and absolute proof, was the inscription. "Humbly and respectfully dedicated to her Gracious Majesty, Queen of the British Empire, Empress of India and . . ." It flowed on and on, a sonorous, sly Victorian joke.

Mears sank down among the piles of books, the volume cradled in his lap. It had happened to him at last, under a mountain of junk he'd found the end of the rainbow. His photographic memory flicked back through the years to the last time a Beckwith *Original Fairy Stories* had been sold. It had reached over three thousand pounds he was sure of it and that had been in 1952 or 53, so the price might well have doubled since then. Professor Beckwith, that revered man of letters and brave explorer, had made a collection of the fairy stories in all the Eastern countries through which he had travelled. Had rewritten them and illustrated them himself and, because of the power of his name, had managed to get them published and dedicated to his Queen. The old lady, Mears recalled, had been anything but amused. She had been horrified. The stories were not at all nice and as for the drawings . . . The edition had been withdrawn hastily and the professor had left even more hastily for a protracted tour of South America. Overnight the *Fairy Tales* became a collector's item.

"And where did you find it, eh?" Mears asked the portrait. Henry looked back, his expression knowing, watchful. "You were a fly old chap all right," Mears acknowledged. He felt

distinctly respectful now, Henry Masters had been his kind of man and he found himself staring at Henry for inspiration.

"It's like this," Mears said, his hand caressing the book, "if I buy it off your old lady for well, quite a reasonable sort of price, and then resell, I might be in dead trouble. I mean it'll all come out that I might've been a bit on the close side, should she kick up a fuss. And the law's a funny business, they'd fall over themselves to help her, they'd never think of my point of view. And there's that bloodsucker at the antique shop, he'd be after his cut before I could turn round. But on the other hand if she *gave* it to me I'd be in the clear wouldn't I, old cock?"

There was hatred in the painted eyes, but Mears was too excited to see it. He put on the paper cover and carefully buried the book under a pile of bound *Punches* just as Milly came in with the coffee.

"Well?" she asked anxiously.

"It's a long job, a very long job," Mears said.

"Yes, you do look rather pale," Milly agreed.

"I'll have to come back this afternoon to finish it properly," Mears said. He drank the coffee in one gulp.

"Is there – is there anything?" Milly asked, her heart pounding.

"There might be one or two things," Mears replied vaguely, "hard to tell yet. I'll be here just after one if that suits?"

"Oh yes," Milly agreed, "yes of course. And thank you so much for all your trouble."

Mears was still trembling when he let himself into the block of flats where he lived. The plan was crystal clear in his mind now and he went straight to the caretaker's flat and knocked. The door was opened by the caretaker's daughter, a fat, unattractive child of twelve who disliked Mears as much as he disliked her. He smiled at her and she stared back dumbly.

"Hallo, Pammy dear," Mears said, "how'd you like to earn a little present, eh?"

"How much?" Pam asked.

"Ten bob."

"Make it a pound."

"You'll go far you will," Mears said, the smile vanishing. "All

The Cupid Mirror

NGAIO MARSH

"Bollinger '21," said Lord John Challis.

"Thank you, my lord," said the wine-waiter.

He retrieved the wine-list, bowed and moved away with soft assurance. Lord John let his eyeglass fall and gave his attention to his guest. She at once wrinkled her nose and parted her sealing-wax lips in an intimate smile. It was a pleasant and flattering grimace and Lord John responded to it. He touched his little beard with a thin hand.

"You look charming," he said, "and you dispel all unpleasant thoughts."

"Were they unpleasant?" asked his guest.

"They were uncomplimentary to myself. I was thinking that Benito – the wine-waiter you know – had grown old."

"But why – ?"

"I knew him when we were both young."

The head-waiter materialised, waved away his underlings, and himself delicately served the dressed crab. Benito returned with the champagne. He held the bottle before Lord John's eyeglass and received a nod.

"It is sufficiently iced, my lord," said Benito.

The champagne was opened, tasted, approved, poured out, and the bottle twisted down in the ice. Benito and the head-waiter withdrew.

"They know you very well here," remarked the guest.

"Yes."

"I dined here first in 1907. We drove from the station in a hansom cab."

"We?" murmured his guest.

"She, too, was charming. It is extraordinary how like the fashions of to-day are to those of my day. Those sleeves. And she wore a veil, too, and sat under the china cupid mirror as you do now."

"And Benito poured out the champagne?"

"And Benito poured out the champagne. He was a rather striking looking fellow in those days. Black eyes, brows that met over his nose. A temper, you'd have said."

"You seem to have looked carefully at him," said the guest lightly.

"I had reason to."

"Come," said the guest with a smile, "I know you have a story to tell and I am longing to hear it."

"Really?"

"Really."

"Very well, then."

Lord John leant forward a little in his chair.

"At the table where that solitary lady sits – yes – the table behind me – I am looking at it now in the cupid mirror – there sat in those days an elderly woman who was a devil. She had come for the cure and had brought with her a miserable niece whom she underpaid and bullied and humiliated after the manner of old devils all the world over. The girl might have been a pretty girl, but all the spirit was scared out of her. Or so it seemed to me. There were atrocious scenes. On the third evening – "

"The third?" murmured the guest, raising her thinned eyebrows.

"We stayed a week," explained Lord John. "At every meal that dreadful old woman, brandishing a repulsive ear-trumpet, would hector and storm. The girl's nerves had gone, and sometimes from sheer fright she was clumsy. Her mistakes were anathematised before the entire dining-room. She was reminded of her dependence and constantly of the circumstance of her being a benefactor under the aunt's will. It was disgusting – abominable.

They never sat through a meal without the aunt sending the
niece on some errand, so that people began to wait for the
moment when the girl, miserable and embarrassed, would rise
and walk through the tables, pursued by that voice. I don't
suppose that the other guests meant to be unkind but many of
them were ill-mannered enough to stare at her and wait for
her reappearance with shawl, or coat, or book, or bag, or
medicine. She used to come back through the tables with
increased gaucherie. Every step was an agony and then, when she
was seated, there would be merciless criticism of her walk, her
elbows, her colour, her pallor. I saw it all in the little cupid
mirror. Benito came in for his share too. That atrocious woman
would order her wine, change her mind, order again, say it was
corked, not the vintage she ordered, complain to the head-
waiter – I can't tell you what else. Benito was magnificent.
Never by a hairsbreadth did he vary his courtesy."

"I suppose it is all in their day's work," said the guest.

"I suppose so. Let us hope there are not many cases as advanced as that harridan's. Once I saw him glance with a sort of compassion at the niece. I mean, I saw his image in the cupid mirror."

Lord John filled his guest's glass and his own.

"There was also," he continued, "her doctor. I indulge my hobby of speaking ill of the dead and confess that I did not like him. He was the local fashionable doctor of those days; a *soi-disant* gentleman with a heavy moustache and clothes that were just a little too immaculate. I was, and still am, a snob. He managed to establish himself in the good graces of the aunt. She left him the greater part of her very considerable fortune. More than she left the girl. There was never any proof that he was aware of this circumstance but I can find no other explanation for his extraordinary forbearance. He prescribed for her, sympathised, visited, agreed, flattered. God knows what he didn't do. And he dined. He dined on the night she died."

"Oh," said the guest lifting her glass in both hands, and staring at her lacquered fingertips, "she died, did she?"

"Yes. She died in the chair occupied at this moment by the middle-aged lady with nervous hands."

"You are very observant," remarked his companion.

"Otherwise I should not be here again in such delightful circumstances. I can see the lady with nervous hands in the cupid mirror, just as I could see that hateful old woman. She had been at her worst all day, and at luncheon the niece had been sent on three errands. From the third she returned in tears with the aunt's sleeping tablets. She always took one before her afternoon nap. The wretched girl had forgotten them and on her return must needs spill them all over the carpet. She and Benito scrambled about under the table, retrieving the little tablets, while the old woman gibed at the girl's clumsiness. She then refused to take one at all and the girl was sent off lunchless and in disgrace."

Lord John touched his beard with his napkin, inspected his half bird, and smiled reminiscently.

"The auguries for dinner were inauspicious. It began badly. The doctor heard of the luncheon disaster. The first dish was sent away with the customary threat of complaint to the manager. However, the doctor succeeded in pouring oil, of which he commanded a great quantity, on the troubled waters. He told her that she must not tire herself, patted her claw with his large white hand, and bullied the waiters on her behalf. He had brought her some new medicine which she was to take after dinner, and he laid the little packet of powder by her plate. It was to replace the stuff she had been taking for some time."

"How did you know all this?"

"Have I forgotten to say she was deaf? Not the least of that unfortunate girl's ordeals was occasioned by the necessity to shout all her answers down an ear-trumpet. The aunt had the deaf person's trick of speaking in a toneless yell. One lost nothing of their conversation. That dinner was quite frightful. I still see and hear it. The little white packet lying on the right of the aunt's plate. The niece nervously crumbling her bread with trembling fingers and eating nothing. The medical feller talking, talking, talking. They drank red wine with their soup and then Benito brought champagne. Veuve Clicquot, it was. He said, as he did a moment ago, "It is sufficiently iced," and poured a little into the aunt's glass. She sipped it and said it was not cold enough. In a second there was another formidable scene. The aunt screamed abuse, the doctor supported and soothed her, another bottle was brought and put in the cooler. Finally Benito gave them their Clicquot. The girl scarcely touched hers, and was asked if she thought the aunt had ordered champagne at thirty shillings a bottle for the amusement of seeing her niece turn up her nose at it. The girl suddenly drank half a glass at one gulp. They all drank. The Clicquot seemed to work its magic even on that appalling woman. She became quieter. I no longer looked into the cupid mirror but rather into the eyes of my vis-a-vis."

Lord John's guest looked into his tired amused old face and smiled faintly.

"Is that all?" she asked.

"No. When I next watched the party at that table a waiter had brought their coffee. The doctor feller emptied the powder from the packet into the aunt's cup. She drank it and made a great fuss about the taste. It looked as though we were in for another scene when she fell sound asleep."

"What!" exclaimed the guest.

"She fell into a deep sleep," said Lord John. "And died."

The lady with the nervous hands rose from her table and walked slowly past them out of the dining-room.

"Not immediately," continued Lord John, "but about two hours later in her room upstairs. Three waiters carried her out of the dining-room. Her mouth was open, I remember, and her face was puffy and had reddish-violet spots on it."

"What killed her?"

"The medical gentleman explained at the inquest that her heart had always been weak."

"But – you didn't believe that? You think, don't you, that the doctor poisoned her coffee?"

"Oh, no. In his own interest he asked that the coffee and the remaining powder in the paper should be analysed. They were found to contain nothing more dangerous than a very mild bromide."

"Then – ? You suspected something I am sure. Was it the niece? The champagne – ?"

"The doctor was between them. No. I remembered, however, the luncheon incident. The sleeping tablets rolling under the table."

"And the girl picked them up?"

"Assisted by Benito. During the dispute at dinner over the champagne, Benito filled the glasses. His napkin hid the aunt's glass from her eyes. Not from mine, however. You see, I saw his hand reflected from above in the little cupid mirror."

There was a long silence.

"Exasperation," said Lord John, "may be the motive of many unsolved crimes. By the way I was reminded of this story by the lady with the nervous hands. She has changed a good deal of course, but she still has that trick of crumbling her bread with her fingers."

The guest stared at him.

"Have we finished?" asked Lord John. "Shall we go?" They rose. Benito, bowing, held open the dining-room door.

"Good evening, Benito," said Lord John.

"Good evening, my lord," said Benito.

The Drugged Cornet

JOHN VERNEY

Jeremy Fisher waited impatiently at the ticket barrier on No. 11 platform till all the passengers had left the train. His sister Jane was not among them.

"Typical. Absolutely typical. She's missed it," he uttered. "The next one gets to Waterloo at 7.13, assuming there's no delay at Woking. Say 7.20. Not much time for a snack, if we walk. Especially with this blasted leg . . ."

The electric train from Frimpton, where the Fishers lived, joined another train at Woking before continuing to London. Jeremy had come up earlier in the day to see a specialist. The plan was for his older sister to rush back from school, catch the 5.33 from Frimpton, and for them to go together to a Tony Crisp Jazz Session in the Festival Hall Recital Room at 8 o'clock. Jeremy often came to London by himself, but never before had he been allowed to stay up for the evening and return late. Parents being what they are, much depended on the present expedition passing off smoothly. Jane missing the train was a bad start.

Not that Mr Fisher objected to his son and daughter, aged 14 and 15 respectively, spending the evening in London. "Good Lord, at their age I was out in Saskatchewan on a – " "Yes dear, we know you led an adventurous boyhood," Mrs Fisher would reply. "But then, you weren't the dreamy type. Besides, you hadn't had polio." However, she had consented to this outing as an experiment and their father had bought them the train and concert tickets. Jeremy himself would have preferred a good mystery or horror film, but Jane had recently become a fan of

Tony Crisp, a star who had risen in the past few months. A photo of the young cornet-playing band leader hung, with the rest, above her bed, and their otherwise peaceful home echoed with the recorded sounds of Crisp's cornetmanship – if that's the word. Jeremy suspected that Crisp wasn't too hot as an instrumentalist. Certainly the great moment for fans appeared not to be the cornet, as such, but the deep gurgling sigh of anguish – like a punctured pig – with which the maestro interrupted his own playing at frequent intervals.

"Surely any fool could do that, if he had the jimjams in his belly?" Jeremy said to his sister, the first time he heard it.

"That just shows how much you don't understand," she answered. "Can't you see it's not the actual *noise* Tony makes? It's the rhythm, the *expression*, he puts into it."

Jeremy was too fond of her to criticise the Crisp genius any further. They were a devoted brother and sister. Jane, a tall, pretty, intelligent girl, had many friends, but perhaps her nicest side was that she never left her less attractive brother out of things. Nature had not been kind to Jeremy, at least in the matter of appearance, with his short dumpy figure, large head, untidy shock of black hair, glasses, withered leg . . . He walked with a stick, and to hide the boot and steel supports wore old-fashioned grey flannel trousers. No wonder that in his day-dreams – and they were many – Detective-Sergeant J. Fisher, terror of the English underworld, frequently leapt from high windows on to the roof of the crook's car, before socking all the crooks on the jaw . . .

"Typical," Jeremy said again, limping gloomily away from the ticket barrier. "Why don't women ever allow themselves enough time to catch a train?"

But perhaps Jane *hadn't* missed the train? His ever vivid imagination pictured the last-minute flap about clothes and make-up, the consequent rush (with Mrs Fisher driving the new and unfamiliar car) to the station, her attempt to nip across the changing traffic lights in front of the oncoming bus, the screech of brakes and tinkle of splintered glass, the urgent ambulance bell . . .

Jeremy decided to telephone home, to make sure. You could ring Frimpton on the automatic exchange for fourpence. He found he had two half-crowns and one penny. The question was how to get three more pennies. The sluttish woman with the mobile tea van said unpleasantly, "I don't do change, luv, unless you buy something." The woman on the paper stall said the same. A bright idea. "Can I have an evening paper then, please?" and he handed her a half-crown. Scowling, she gave him the paper and, as change, two shillings, a threepenny bit and a halfpenny. Defeated, Jeremy withdrew. Wasn't there some way of reversing a call, so that it was paid for the other end? He had never done this and loathed making a fool of himself, even with an unseen operator. Still, everything had to be attempted for the first time once . . .

Jeremy limped towards a row of telephone boxes, as usual trying to look as though he carried a stick for swagger rather than for support. He swung it round a couple of times by the curved handle, and nearly lost balance. All the telephone boxes were occupied, except one. Outside that two rather flashy youths lounged against the door, evidently waiting for a friend in the adjoining box. They wore jazzy pullovers, the tightest of black trousers, and the most pointed of shoes. Hardly less pointed was their stare when Jeremy asked, "Er, would you be needing this box?"

One said, sarcastically, "Take it beetle, it's all yours."

However, they moved aside to let him enter. Sweating a little, blushing much, Jeremy closed the door thankfully behind him and started to read the printed instructions above the telephone. He couldn't find any mention of how to reverse the charge of a call, but in any case his attention was more occupied by his neighbour in the next box. The third youth, wearing a duffle coat and a wide-brimmed sombrero-type hat, stared insolently at him through the glass partition while he talked on the phone. Jeremy could hear the voice quite clearly. He also thought he had seen the face before somewhere, but didn't like to stare back too obviously, for fear of giving offence. All three youths looked the sort who sliced you up with a razor on the smallest provocation . . .

"Well thanks, Sid," said the voice. "Last coach, next to last carriage. I'll get the stuff out O.K. S'long."

The youth – Jeremy reckoned he was probably the gang leader – banged down the phone and joined his pals. They strolled off, uttering rude and raucous noises directed – Jeremy felt sure – at himself. Somehow he seemed unable to concentrate on the problem of ringing home. He decided to wait, after all, till he had met the next train. If Jane still wasn't on it, then he really would try and reverse the charge, or perhaps ask someone else to change the threepenny bit . . .

There was a quarter of an hour to wait. Imagining that everyone on Waterloo station knew he had funked the call, he made for a bench and hid himself behind the evening paper.

POLICE HUNT DEADLY DRUGS. Glancing at the story Jeremy spotted the words *Sealham Research Centre*. He read the column carefully. Sealham was the next station to Frimpton. He had often passed the high wall which hid the government's hush-hush outfit from the prying vulgar gaze. No one knew what precisely went on behind the wall, though local rumour covered most possibilities, from bacteria to Bactrian camels. Those who lived near were well used to flaps about missing poisons. There had even been a couple of fires and a minor explosion. Now he learnt that on Sealham station, that same morning, a scientist had put down a small green suitcase containing bottled samples of some unspecified but highly dangerous powder, while he bought his ticket. When he turned to pick it up, the suitcase had vanished.

"Typical," Jeremy said aloud – his favourite word.

The thief carrying the bag, he reflected, could well have travelled to London on the same train as himself.

But no . . . The police, he read further, were convinced the suitcase was still in the Sealham area. The theory was that whoever pinched the bag was unaware of its contents and had probably dumped it when he found nothing of obvious value

inside. Anyone discovering a small green suitcase should take it immediately to the nearest police station. On no account must he open the eight tiny bottles which were wrapped up in the scientist's pyjamas.

Jeremy narrowed his eyes and sat back on the bench, lost deep in thought . . . The theory that the suitcase was still in the Sealham area was, of course, a blind. Obviously the thief knew perfectly well what it contained. The problem was how to get the suitcase to his confederates in London's underworld. Putting himself for a moment in the thief's skin, Jeremy considered various means of solving this problem. All hand luggage would, of course, be scrutinised along the line. A fast car? Well, you'd have to assume a road check. A helicopter would also be too risky. The first thing would be to transfer the bottles to another suitcase of a different colour. And then? So often, the most obvious course was the least suspicious. Why not simply put the different suitcase on the luggage rack of a later train and phone the confederates in London where to collect it.

But these speculations were interrupted by a Waterloo pigeon which swooped suddenly past Jeremy's face. He looked at the station clock; 7.12. Tucking the paper under his arm, he hastened back to No. 11 platform. The train was due in any minute.

He had intended to wait for Jane at the barrier; when he saw the three youths also standing there. The one who had called him "beetle" spotted him and nudged the others, so Jeremy quickly bought a platform ticket and joined the passengers passing through. Glancing over his shoulder he noticed the youth wearing the duffle following slowly behind. At that moment the train came rattling in.

Few passengers were travelling up at this hour. Jeremy limped past the first two half-empty coaches before, to his great relief, he saw Jane descending from the end coach. She spotted him too, and waved. But instead of walking forward she stood looking around and then disappeared back into the compartment. As he reached the coach she reappeared – carrying a small brown suitcase.

"Hullo Jerry, sorry about missing the 5.33."

Jane looked marvellous, like some gorgeous flower with her long fair hair flowing over her shoulders. But for once Jeremy wasn't interested in Jane's appearance.

"Why have you got that suitcase?" he asked sharply.

"Oh, some man popped it on to the rack at Woking. He asked me to keep an eye on it. He said a friend would pick it up at Waterloo . . . What on earth's the matter, Jerry . . ."

For he had snatched the case from her hand, saying "Come on, quick as you can. Tell you why later."

A voice beside them said, "That's *my* case you've got there, thanking you *very* much all the same."

The youth from the phone box barred their path. Stepping forward he took hold of the handle and tried to wrest it from Jeremy, who had no intention of letting go. "That's what *you* think. If you want this case you'd better come to the station master's office."

"Don't be a clot. I tell you it's my case. A friend put it on at Woking. He told me a smashing piece of goods would keep an eye on it, and smashing's the right word."

"Jerry. Jerry *please*." Jeremy gave his sister a quick glance and what he saw amazed him. She stood staring open-mouthed at the youth like a half-witted fish. He was disgusted to think that Jane, of all people, could fall for a corny compliment from a cheap spiv. But he was too busy hanging on to the case to have time for the complexities of female human nature.

"Here, beautiful, if this object is your baby brother, just call him off before he gets hurt, willya?"

Several passengers had gathered round, grinning. The guard had also come up. "What's the trouble?" he asked crossly.

"This suitcase," Jeremy gasped, hanging on to it with one hand while he waved both his stick and the evening paper with the other. "It's got the deadly drugs in it."

"The little blighter must be bats," gasped the youth in turn. "This is my suitcase. All it's got inside is my spare shirt and a cornet. And I need that cornet. I'm supposed to be playing on it in the flipping Festival Hall in about five minutes. My name is Tony Crisp."

But Jeremy's temper was up. "You may be Tony Crisp," he said. "But you won't play the cornet any more than you ever do. You'll just make yowling noises instead, full of rhythm and expression. And anyway how do we know the drugs aren't in here, whoever you may be?"

"Much more of your lip and I'll . . ." Crisp began, but the guard interrupted.

"The lad's quite right up to a point," he said. "There was a suitcase missing, but a green one. I heard it was found just before we started from Sealham."

"Were the drugs in it?" Jeremy asked sharply.

"As a matter of fact they weren't," the guard said. "Look, we can't stand arguing here. Come along, you three. We'll go to the station master's office. I'll take charge of the case."

The odd procession set off down the platform, with the guard in front, Tony Crisp beside him threatening to sue British

Railways if he arrived late at the Festival Hall, while Jane and Jeremy, the latter limping as fast as he could, brought up the rear. "I'll never *never* speak to you again," Jane hissed.

Passing through the barrier Jeremy noticed the other two youths. They looked furtive and made no effort to come forward and help their leader. A minute later the whole party was shut with the station master in his office. Jeremy's heart pounded so violently he had to sit on a chair near the door.

"Well, we can easily settle the argument can't we?" the station master said pleasantly, having heard the story from both sides. The suitcase lay on his desk and he opened it. As Tony Crisp stated, it contained merely a spare shirt and one cornet.

"You did a plucky thing all the same, young man," the station master added to Jeremy in a kind voice. "I don't mind telling you that the drugs are still missing. It is extremely important they should be found, as the papers said."

Jane looked at her brother sympathetically. She was still furious with him, but she knew what an utter fool he must feel. She was astounded when he replied with apparent calm. "Perhaps the drugs aren't missing, sir. Please ask Tony Crisp to blow a few notes on his cornet, to show he can."

The station master grinned and handed the instrument to the band leader. And then three things happened very quickly indeed.

The first was that the youth Crisp, instead of taking the cornet, made a sudden dash for the door. The second was that Jeremy's stick shot out and tripped him, so that he went sprawling. The third was the famous Tony Crisp gurgling noise, as Jeremy's dumpy body landed with its full weight on his head . . .

"Oh well, that's that," Jeremy said an hour or so later, when he and Jane sat in the train going home. "Sorry to mess up your concert, I really am. And of course after all this, we'll never be allowed another evening in London."

"Darling Jerry," Jane said laughing. "As if I cared about the concert, so long as they give the money back."

"Surely the Festival Hall will have to do that? I mean, it's their fault if they get taken in by a bunch of crooks."

"Oh, we all got taken in. You see, I admit you were right about Tony Crisp being no good on the cornet. I played the record again before leaving home – that's why I missed the train – and I suddenly saw through him, as you had."

"But you didn't mind when he called you a smashing piece of goods . . ."

"Of course not. Who would? What I still don't understand is why you were so *sure* the bottles were hidden inside the cornet?"

"I wasn't at all sure. But I'd heard him say on the phone 'I'll get the stuff out O.K.' I remembered that in the station master's office. By then I couldn't look a bigger fool so I took a last desperate chance. By the way, did you hear that detective tell the station master they'd already picked up the man you saw in Woking?"

"Yes. I wonder if they'll catch the other two, the ones you saw at the telephone box."

"I wonder," Jeremy sighed. "You know, I'm rather sorry about sitting on Tony Crisp's head. What I mean is, I do so wish it had been the head belonging to that other chap – the one who called me a beetle . . ."

What Sort of Person is this Amanda Jones Anyway?

JOAN AIKEN

The train was somewhere north of London when the rucksack fell on my head. My own fault, of course. It was insecurely perched and when we came to one of those sudden stops it bounced down and beaned me.

The only other person in the carriage was an elderly man, rather prissy-looking, folded into an evening paper. He put it down and came along and picked the rucksack off my feet, as I wasn't doing anything but sitting and looking at it vacantly.

"Are you all right?" he asked. He glanced towards the communication cord, but there didn't seem much sense in pulling it, as we were stationary anyway.

"Yes thanks," I answered automatically. I nodded to show how okay I was, and put up a tentative hand to the back of my neck, which felt as if I had been sandbagged. I certainly didn't intend to tell this fellow the embarrassing thing that had happened to me, and, after another doubtful survey, he went back to his corner and his paper.

I stared at my feet. Size three, or thereabouts, in suede shoes with laces. I didn't remember tying those laces. I didn't remember putting on the shoes. I had forgotten who I was.

We were still at a standstill, so I had time to take stock before flying into a panic. I'm female, I thought, he called me miss. I'm English. People in stories can always tackle this sort of situation, so I should be able to.

Furtively glancing at the man out of the corner of my eye, I began excavating my handbag, which must surely contain plenty of clues.

Evidently I had a sweet tooth – three packets of buttermints and half a bar of chocolate – I was over twenty-one, or, at any rate, owned a latchkey; I also had a chequebook and a return half from Edinburgh to King's Cross. Aha! Now I knew where to get out.

There were some postcards of Scottish lochs and a sprig of heather; it seemed fair to assume I'd been on holiday in Scotland.

Beneath these things was a letter addressed to Miss Amanda Jones, Flat F, Noble Crescent, N.6:

> Honey Darling,
>
> How wonderful that you've actually *sold a story*, and are rushing off to Scotland for ten days. Mind you take plenty of spare socks and sweaters – *it always rains in Scotland*.
>
> Father is well and sends love; he has just gone off with the parish magazines after telling me not on any account to weed the front border. *He doesn't trust me an inch*.
>
> Honey dear, don't forget, will you, that Aunt Leonie is coming to see you on the 20th and do please try, chickie, to make a good impression. I know she is an old Tartar but she is Father's only sister. And she's fond of you – – only the other day she was saying what a pity it was that you'd never married!
>
> Have a wonderful holiday. I'll send a cake and some eggs to greet you when you get back.
>
> Love and hugs from Mother

The letter made me chuckle, and gave me a vivid picture of Mother's face as she sat writing, a smudge of flour on her nose, a rose-cutting tangled in her cardigan sleeve, and a lock of untidy grey-fair hair falling over her eyes. Surreptitiously I peered into my compact mirror and confirmed that I was just like her – straight nose, same grey eyes, same untidy fair hair. And, dammit, what did Aunt Leonie mean by *never married*? – I couldn't be a day over twenty! I began to feel rather indignant towards the old trout.

But I still couldn't remember anything about myself – except for some dim childhood recollections of having tea on the rectory lawn and Father in his surplice going off for evensong. What kind of a person was this Amanda Jones?

The train had started again and now began to slow down, pulling in to King's Cross. The elderly man got out, giving me a last disapproving glance. He left his evening paper behind and I pounced on it as I followed him. Saturday September 20. That meant Aunt Leonie was coming this evening – I hadn't left myself much time for giving a good impression.

There were five ten-penny pieces in my purse and I decided this was definitely an occasion for a taxi. Sitting in it, I began to feel sorry for myself. Aunt Leonie had started it off. Here I am, I thought, going back to a lonely, empty flat, after a sad, solitary holiday walking about a Scottish moor. There won't be a soul to welcome me, and I don't know a thing about myself.

I paid off the cab outside a big house in a pleasant garden in a quiet road. There was a large entrance hall and in it, on a table with tenants' letters and packages, were two for me: a parcel addressed in mother's handwriting – the cake and eggs no doubt – and a letter. I fell on this. Perhaps it would yield another clue. But it was disappointingly brief:

Amanda dear,

It seems such a long time since I saw you though it is only a few days. Longing to have you back in London.

I'll be round in the evening to see you.   A.

Well, at least I've got a friend, and though he or she is pretty terse in his or her epistolary style, it's good to know that someone is pleased to have me back.

I was still chafing over that *never married*.

Picking up Mother's parcel I looked cautiously round till I found Flat F, which was on the ground floor. Luckily none of the other tenants was about; they would probably have thought I was mad.

Propped against my door were a bottle of milk and a packet of coffee, sitting on a bit of paper that said SEE YOU SOON, LOVE JENNIFER.

It was an odd feeling to turn the key in my own front door

without having the slightest notion what I should find inside. Habitat or period, Louis Quatorze or Swedish laminated? Did I play the violin? Watch telly? Make pots? Read Latin poetry?

The flat had a dusty, uncared-for smell, and my first thought was, I must get this place cleaned up before Aunt Leonie arrives.

From that I judged I was a housewifely sort of girl, but this optimistic notion was soon dashed. Intensive search failed to reveal any cleaning implements save an old dustpan and brush.

I began to have a very poor notion of Amanda Jones.

It wasn't a big flat – bathroom, kitchenette, bed-sitting-room, and a tiny spare room, six inches bigger than the bed. I made this up for Aunt Leonie and put out a clean towel.

The bathroom revealed another facet of me: two of its walls were papered solid with a montage of rejection slips, large, small, and medium, carefully pasted together and covered with poly-thene. There must have been hundreds of them – *Punch*, *Vogue*, *The New Yorker*, *Nova*, *Honey*, *Nineteen*, *Petticoat*, the *New States-man* – you name it, I had it. I must have been rejected by every magazine in the English-speaking world.

I had to admit that this Amanda Jones had staying-power; she didn't get discouraged. And, after all, I had in the end sold a story. More power to my elbow. Maybe my luck was turning. I wondered who I'd sold it to, and what they'd paid me.

There was a ring at the front door. Aunt Leonie! I dashed.

But it was a dark, pretty girl in a navy silk jersey Russian tunic and pants who hugged me warmly and said, "Honey dear! Super to have you back. Come in for breakfast tomorrow and have a good gossip. Darling, would you be an angel and look after William Walpole for me this evening – Don wants to go to *Ulysses*. William's missed you so, you can't think."

"Of course," I said automatically, and then I saw the carrycot on the floor beside her containing a brown-eyed baby who waved at me enthusiastically and exclaimed "Ba!"

"There, see! He's so pleased to have you back. Honey, I must rush. See you later."

I picked up William Walpole, took him inside, and put him, cot and all, on the divan. When I started sweeping with the brush and pan the dust got in his nose and made him sneeze. I moved him to the spare room but he didn't approve of that. His disapproval took the form of ninety-megaton screams and I had to move him back.

Affairs were in this condition of stalemate when the bell rang again.

Aunt Leonie! I dashed.

But it was a tall, military character with a fair moustache carrying a large carton. My heart leapt up. Could this be A? If so I took back some of the unkind thoughts I had been thinking about Amanda Jones.

"Miss Jones?" he said.

Not A, then.

"Yes," I said. He beamed.

"I've been trying to get you for the last ten days."

"I've been on a sudden, unplanned holiday."

"Come to demonstrate the new Whizzo Cleaner," he said, "in answer to your inquiry."

Good, sensible, Amanda!

"Come right in," I said. "You couldn't have arrived at a better moment. There's ten days' dust here that wants sucking up."

I will say for him he took it beautifully in his stride, though he was a bit shaken when he saw William Walpole sitting up in the carrycot brandishing his rattle.

"Not mine – a neighbour's," I said hurriedly. "Do you have any children, Mr – ?"

"Palliser, Charles Palliser," he said, rapidly taking the Whizzo from its carton and fitting it all together. "No, I'm a bachelor. Never had much to do with small kids."

He eyed William Walpole warily, but William was much intrigued by the ramifications of the Whizzo, and was quite happy to sit in his cot and watch while Charles cleaned up ten days' dust.

"I'd love to see how it works on the curtains," I kept saying and, "Does it polish too? Did you say there was an upholstery brush? Just show me how it cleans tiles, could you?" The Whizzo was a great success.

I made some coffee while Charles was cleaning the bathroom and had a cup ready with a chunk of Mother's cake. It seemed only civil. Now if Aunt Leonie turned up I was ready for her, *and* with a male in attendance.

"And how much does the Whizzo cost nowadays?" I asked, hoping to conceal my total ignorance of what it had ever cost.

"Twenty-nine, ninety-two, since the price went up," he said sadly.

"Oh dear," I said. "I wonder if I've got that much in my account." I wondered if there was a bank statement lurking in the flat somewhere.

Mr Palliser had put the Whizzo tidily back into its carton and was looking at my pictures. "Do you paint?" he said. "You've got some valuable originals here, did you know?"

"No, have I?"

He looked a little dashed, but my surprise was genuine.

Just at that moment the doorbell rang again. Aunt Leonie! I flew.

But it was a tall young character in gaberdine slacks, with a lovable transatlantic ugliness.

"Miss Amanda Jones?" he said. New York accent. This can't be A. either.

"Come in, come in," I said, a bit lightheaded from the way events were shaping. "We're just having coffee and cake."

"Oh, I'm sorry," said Charles. "I didn't know you were expecting company. I'd better be off."

"I'm not company," beamed the new arrival. "I'm Miss Jones's winnings."

"I beg your pardon?"

I poured him out a cup of coffee and another for Charles, while I thought over what he had said. It still made no sense.

"Could you explain that?"

"Remember the *Evening Dispatch* competition? 'Win Yourself a Man'? You won it, Miss Jones. I'm your man. Richard Brad-field Heppenstall."

This was the point at which I might have begun to think I was dreaming – but the coffee was good and strong and black. I hung on to the table edge and said, "How did I win it?" I had plainly misjudged Amanda Jones.

"You wrote a four-line verse. It must have been a humdinger, Miss Jones. Don't you remember how it went?"

"No, I can't," I said, not without relief.

"Darn it! That's too bad. Never mind, Miss Jones, here I am, so what would you like done? Painting, tile-laying, pig-sticking, escort to the opera? I'm in Europe on vacation for two months, completely at your disposal, and the *Evening Dispatch* pays for the outings. So what'll it be?"

"I'd love to go to Covent Garden next week," I said. "Right now – "

Stick about and impress Aunt Leonie, I was going to say, but he interrupted me gently.

"Right now I guess what you want is a baby-shusher."

It was true. William Walpole, on seeing the Whizzo go back into its box and stay there, had burst into a dismal howl.

"Hush, William Walpole," I said to him. "The flat's clean now, can't you see, it's clean? No more Whizzo." He didn't take a bit of notice, only howled the more. Richard scooped him out of the cot, shook all his nightwear into position, expertly patted his back, cocked him over one arm, and walked him into good temper in no time.

"You have children of your own?" I said respectfully.

"No, ma'am! I'm a bachelor. But I have plenty of nephews and nieces."

The doorbell rang. I dashed. This time there could be no doubt that it was Aunt Leonie, and I gave her a dutiful kiss. She marched straight past me into the sitting-room, which was beginning to look a bit cluttered. Her sharp black eyes took in Charles with his coffee-cup, Whizzo in its carton, and Richard Heppenstall with a piece of cake in one hand and William Walpole elevated over the other arm.

"That child is up far too late," she said formidably. "He should be taken home."

"No, Aunt," I explained hurriedly. "He lives here. That is – I mean – "

"Are you his father?" She fixed gimlet eyes on Richard.

"No, ma'am! Miss Jones won me in a competition."

She looked a little startled, but passed it over. "Are *you* his father then?"

Poor Charles was beginning to look out of his depth, and as if he didn't care whether he sold Whizzo or not.

"Neither of them is," I said hurriedly. "His *real* father's not here just now."

Aunt Leonie directed a bleak gaze at my left hand, unadorned by any ring. Her thoughts spoke louder than any number of decibels.

"No, no, he's not mine! I'm just looking after him for a friend. These gentlemen are helping me."

Put it how I might, it didn't sound the sort of occupation to create a favourable impression on Aunt Leonie.

"Mr Palliser has been selling me a Whizzo," I said, and told him, "Never mind the state of my bank balance. I'll buy it! Maybe I'll sell another story."

"In my young days," said Aunt Leonie, "gels did not entertain young men in their apartments without a chaperon."

"Well we are chaperoned now," said Richard Heppenstall comfortably, "so let's all sit down and relax." I threw him a grateful glance and poured Aunt Leonie a cup of coffee. The doorbell rang and Charles went to answer it.

Aunt Leonie had not finished her catechism. "This young man says you *won* him," she said, taking the coffee and giving me a piercing look. "Does he mean that you are engaged?"

"I'm not engaged – " I started crossly, but a deep voice behind my back made me spin round.

"Miss Amanda Jones," it said with dignity and a slight Scots accent, "is engaged to *me*."

Tall, dark, and grey-eyed. There could be little doubt about it: this was A.

The minute I saw him a whole lot of confused recollections which had been floundering about my mind for the last half-hour, clicked tidily into place.

I knew all about myself, the ten days I'd spent in Scotland, how I'd met Andrew McInnes while staying with my cousin Fiona, how we'd fallen in love – like being struck by lightning it was, which probably accounted for my unstable mental state, prone to fall into a state of amnesia the first time a rucksack fell on me – how Andrew had to come back to London three days before me.

I even remembered the four-line verse that, in an impulsive moment, I'd whizzed off on a postcard to the *Evening Dispatch*. I blushed.

Aunt Leonie looked Andrew up and down. She liked his looks. "The Ross McInneses or the Forfar McInneses?" she snapped. In five minutes she had his whole genealogy pegged out like a week's wash.

Charles and Richard melted tactfully away. "I'll call in tomorrow with the invoice," said Charles. "Covent Garden next week – I'll phone when I have the tickets," said Richard.

Jennifer and Don dropped in, radiant from *Ulysses*, hugged me, and collected the sleeping Walpole. Aunt Leonie declared that she was going to bed. Andrew said he must be off. I saw him to the door and he gave me a serious good night kiss, a very serious one. "You're different in London, Amanda," he said. "More forthright. In Scotland you seemed such a quiet, retiring kind of lass."

"To tell you the truth, Andrew darling," I said, "I still don't know *what* kind of a girl I am. Time will have to show." But whatever kind, I thought to myself, I know whom I love. Amanda Jones is a girl of sense.

"Amanda," Aunt Leonie called sternly from the spare room, "it's time you were in bed."

Andrew quietly closed the front door after him.

"Just going, Aunt," I called. "There's one thing I must do first."

I dumped the coffee cups in the kitchen, pulled out my portable typewriter from its hiding place under the bed, slid in a sheet of paper, and began to type rapidly:

"The train was somewhere north of London . . ."